I0692288

EAST LYNNE

A Fox Movietone Production.   East Lynne.

CAPTAIN LEVISON FINDS IT DIFFICULT TO REMAIN THE
RESPECTFUL ESCORT TO THE WIFE OF HIS FRIEND.

EAST LYNNE

By

ARLINE DE HAAS

Suggested by

MRS. HENRY WOOD'S
FAMOUS NOVEL

WITH SCENES FROM THE
FOX MOVIETONE
STARRING
ANN HARDING
AND
CLIVE BROOK

GROSSET & DUNLAP
PUBLISHERS   NEW YORK

COPYRIGHT, 1931, BY
GROSSET & DUNLAP, INC.

Made in the United States of America

EAST LYNNE

CHAPTER I

THE warm noon sun . . . June sun . . . laid
light, caressing fingers over the old city of London. It wandered through narrow passageways,
brightening for a brief moment the fog-stained
stones of walks and houses. It glazed with a
lacquer of its own gold the ancient, worm-eaten
wood of brown crossbeams and shutters; wood it
had already seared to the rich hues of tanned
leather. It lingered over Hyde Park and Turn-
ham Green, over Kensington Gardens and Pall
Mall, bringing to fullest glory the mellow greens
that are England's own. Even the murky, muddy
Thames seemed to catch something of the spirit
of the noon, June sun, and rocked in its walled
cradle, gurgling and sparkling. And above all
the ever-present dome of St. Paul's Cathedral
with its surmounting ball and cross sent back a
gilded answer.

Up tiny, winding streets that run like crooked
threads through London Town, glided the sun.
Up, and up, stopping here and there until it came
to Ludgate Hill. And then, as the chimes of Big
Ben stridently pealed the midday hour, it seemed
to stop and rest on the portico of St. Paul's as
though waiting for something. It crept around

1

and peered through rich, stained-glass windows, carpeting the pavement of black and white marble squares with the softly rosy hues of an after-sunset glow. It padded gently down the nave, slipped inside the chancel railing, and settled in a great, oblong shaft, upon two kneeling people.

The bishop in surplice and gown raised the book in his hands a trifle and peered over it, gazing upon the bowed heads before him.

"Whom God hath joined together," he said slowly and clearly, "let no man put asunder."

The subdued music of the great organ filtered through the solemn words like a tender refrain.

The thronged cathedral was a vast, silent sea of heads. Scarcely a ripple broke the intense silence. Here and there a dowager dabbed at her eyes with a little square of lace, her mind wandering back to her own wedding, or the weddings of her sons and daughters. Heavy, elderly men breathed a little more heavily; young men sat stolid or interested or bored by the whole proceedings.

And then the music of the organ swelled to a thundering, triumphant, glad pealing.

Robert Carlyle rose from the white, satin pillow upon which he had been kneeling before the bishop, drawing with him the girl who had knelt beside him. He kissed her upturned lips tenderly and then placed her hand within his arm. The Lady Isabel Vane, daughter of Lord Mount Severn, newly created the Lady Isabel Carlyle, glanced shyly at this man who was now her husband. And then they turned to face the long nave.

The maid of honor thrust the massive bouquet of white roses and lillies of the valley into the bride's hands.

As though with one concerted effort that vast sea of heads became a turbulent, rocking ocean. Great billowing ostrich plumes waved madly from tiny hats perched upon elaborate headdresses as necks turned, eyes strained to catch as many glimpses as possible of the couple pacing down the nave. Throaty whispers and little breaths of remarks filled the vast interior of the church. The "Ohs" and "Ahs," and "Isn't she a lovely bride" and "He's a very handsome man" ran from mouth to mouth.

And in the midst of it all, scarcely seeing, scarcely heeding, walked the Lady Isabel and Mr. Robert Carlyle . . . walked through the sifting sunlight, rosy hued . . . walked between the wide banks of white, white roses and maidenhair fern that tapestried walls and pillars . . . walked toward the noonday, toward life, and love and happiness.

Now they stood on the raised portico in the luminous sunshine. The bride's white satin crinolines glimmered softly, making little, swishy noises as the light air stirred them. The creamy white lace, old, old lace that had draped many a gown of a bride of the ancient Vane and Mount Severn families, clung yieldingly to the voluminous skirts, looped up with delicate clusters of rosebuds. A cloud of lace, caught with rosebuds woven into a halo, was flung back over fair, golden hair, and framed the exquisite oval of a fair, white face. Two clear, blue eyes, half veiled with long, dark lashes, still gazed shyly, yet steadily at the bridegroom.

Robert Carlyle smiled and patted the smooth, delicate hand that lay in the crook of his arm. Tall, he was, so that he looked down at the figure beside him when he smiled. And when he smiled, his face was pleasant, with an almost boyish pleasantness. It was when he didn't smile that he looked so severe . . . at least, that was what the Lady Isabel thought. Severe, and stern almost.

Horses and carriages were already lining up in front of the steps . . . prancing, stamping pairs drawing heavy, open carriages. Still in a dream-like ecstasy Lady Isabel moved forward on her husband's arm. Behind them the crowds of people were surging toward the daylight. The vibrant chords of the organ were dying . . . dying . . . being lost in the dimness of the Cathedral, in the hubbub of raised voices. The first carriage moved with a jerk, and then the clatter of horses' hoofs rang out on the cobbled pavements.

Not until they had arrived at her own home, and she was once more in the familiar surroundings of the charming old rooms of the Mount Severn town house in Mayfair did the Lady Isabel seem to rouse herself. Then the gay, laughing, chattering crowds brought back to her a sense of reality. Here were all her friends, the men she had laughed with and danced with; the girls who had been children with her, who had made their débuts with her, some married, some engaged, some still just laughing and dancing. And now,

here she was, the Lady Isabel . . . not the Lady
Isabel any longer. She was Lady Isabel Carlyle,
the wife of Robert Carlyle.

"May your father be the first to offer his blessing, my child?" The sound of the voice broke into
Isabel's thoughts. She turned to face the tall
man beside her, smiling.

Lord Mount Severn took his daughter's hands
and kissed her cheek.

"Everything went off smoothly," he nodded.
"Capital! Fine wedding . . . and a lovely
bride."

"The house looks beautiful, Father," Isabel
congratulated him.   "I'll hate to leave it,
but . . . " she hesitated, blushing.

"Never you mind," Mount Severn interposed
hastily. "You're in good hands. I'd trust
Carlyle. Fine man. He'll make a famous barrister one of these days. I'll . . . "

"Isabel, my dear! How lovely you look! It
was a perfectly beautiful wedding . . . Isabel, be
sure to throw me your bouquet . . . when are you
coming back . . ."

Crinolines swinging, curls bobbing, a group of
the bridesmaids, filmy and frothy in yards of pink
tulle and satin, swarmed about the bride.

Lord Mount Severn edged to the outskirts of
the crowd and pushed his way through to the
punch bowl and the buffet. Many eyes turned to
watch the progress of one of the most famous and
notorious of London's aristocrats . . . famous
because of the name he bore; notorious for the
manner in which he had dissipated the family for-

tune. Still in his early fifties, Mount Severn, on a good day, looked nearer sixty, and on a particularly bad day might have passed for seventy. His lean figure was still erect, but there were times when his hand shook, and the flabby flesh beneath his eyes and about his jowls took on a pasty, blue tinge.

"Did you hear that?" Sir Christopher Holmes, an elderly man with white hair and bushy side burns, propped himself against the elaborately carved mantelpiece in the drawing-room and turned to his companion.

"Hear what?" A jovial voice boomed in answer.

"Hear Mount Severn, there, giving Isabel his blessing!" Sir Chistopher sniffed. "Well, it's about the only thing he has left to give her."

The jovial-voiced one, Lord Denchester, puffed out red cheeks, took a long swallow of punch from the glass in his hand. "Hear he's in a pretty bad way," he volunteered.

"Pretty bad way! He's done for . . . not a ha' penny left, Miggsy." The white side burns shook dismally. "He had to rent this old home of his for this reception."

"What!" Red cheeks puffed and blew. "Not really! Not as bad as that!"

"Absolutely! This house was taken over by creditors a month ago. I don't think Isabel knows it. Mount Severn persuaded the hounds to hold off—for a consideration—until the wedding was over. And this was the last bit he had left. He'll be living off his friends for the rest of his life."

"Miggsy" considered the situation by having another go at the punch. "Well," he offered finally, "they won't have to support him for long if they take his brandy away from him. And if they give him enough, he may drink himself into an earlier grave. One way or the other, the brandy'll do for him."

"I doubt it," Sir Christopher negated. "He'll last for a long time yet."

"Rather a pity," Lord Denchester shook his head sadly.

"Well, he never was any good," Sir Christopher decided. "Fine family, splendid property ... but everything gone to rack and ruin. And what a legacy he's given her." He nodded in the general direction of the bride. "Seed ... breed ... and generation!"

"Miggsy" turned to stare at the figure in white holding sway in the midst of a crowd of men and women, all chattering, laughing, and gossiping. Isabel's cheeks were flushed, her color came and went, leaving trails of delicious pink across the whiteness. There was something so gay, so happy, so carefree about her every movement ... something almost childlike. She seemed scarcely old enough, sedate enough, to be the Lady Isabel Carlyle.

"Ah, well," Lord Denchester puffed and blew again. "But he did give her beauty ... no denying that!"

Sir Christopher turned and carefully appraised the lady in question. He nodded.

"Yes, she's beautiful. One of the most sought-after girls of the season. You know, it's a wonder to me how that chap Carlyle ever won her.''

"Miggsy" shrugged. "Why not? In the first place, he's got money. And he's certainly respectable.''

"You can say that of a chimney sweep. He has absolutely no social position . . . none whatsoever. By the way, there's none of his family here, is there? Strange, that! Heard he had a sister, or something of the sort.''

"Perhaps the sister doesn't fit into Mayfair.''

"Perhaps. After all, he's nothing but a country solicitor who's made money. He's probably got a future. But with a family like the Mount Severns . . .''

"Yet it wasn't a marriage for money?''

"Not at all. Purely a love match. They met at Lady Townsend's. Carlyle was doing some legal work for Townsend, and after that . . . well, it was love at first sight, I understand.''

"Then Carlyle is probably a very fascinating country solicitor. He's had a great deal of opposition, so I've noticed. Including that of one Mr. Francis Levison.''

Sir Christopher turned once more to follow "Miggsy's" nodding head toward the dining room where the buffet breakfast was being served.

"Levison," he said slowly, "Levison's all right —but not a penny. The diplomatic service was never renowned for liberality where money is concerned.''

"Nevertheless, the ladies, God bless 'em, seem to like him enough.'' Lord Denchester swallowed

his punch at a gulp and watched the group of
young, and not-so-young women who seemed to be
hovering about one main attraction.

In the center of the group, Francis Levison
stood and smiled and chattered about nothing,
about anything. He seemed to follow the conversation, to respond to it, with just the proper shade
of interest, the proper amount of respect, and yet
his eyes never lost sight of one person in the room.
He could have told exactly the number of people
who had spoken to Lady Isabel, almost repeated
what they had said. Once or twice he had caught
Isabel watching him, but he made not the slightest
sign, the slightest gesture.

Now, at last, however, he was bowing, offering
his excuses. He lingered over the hand of one
charming young matron.

"When I do return from the Continent, my dear
Lady Townsend," he smiled. "I shall run down
to Kent and visit you—whether you'll have me or
not. So, au revoir, for the present."

Bowing, Levison began to move slowly through
the maze of people in the general direction of the
bride. A number of heads turned to look after
him, curious to see what would happen, hear what
was said at his first meeting with Lady Isabel as
Lady Isabel Carlyle.

"He's brilliant, my dear, brilliant," whispered
an elderly dowager to Lady Townsend.

"Brilliant, but elusive," and Lady Townsend
sighed. "He's having an interesting career.
Lord Townsend thinks he'll become a very valuable man in the service." She watched the figure

disappear around the corner into the reception room.

"Carlyle's gain is our loss." A very young man with fresh, pink cheeks and yellow hair that crinkled, bowed over Lady Isabel's hand. "You know, London won't seem the same without you at all."

Isabel laughed. Her cheeks grew just a shade pinker. "Now, you're flattering me!" The laugh was for the very young man, but the deepened color rose at the sight of Levison.

She felt that she was blushing, and she didn't want to blush . . . there was no reason for it. She wasn't in love with Francis Levison; certainly not as she was with Robert Carlyle, Isabel assured herself. She liked Francis, liked to dance with him, had almost imagined herself in love with him, until Robert had appeared upon the scene. And after that . . . well, there was no one else who really mattered. She still liked Francis, probably always would. But it was Robert she had wanted to marry, not Francis.

But now Francis was bowing low over her hand, and holding it . . . just a little longer than necessary; and she was looking down at the sleek brown hair that waved back from the temples; at the gray eyes that seemed to rise to meet hers.

"May I . . ." Levison began.

"I was wondering if you were going to be the last," Isabel returned lightly, and was glad that her voice did sound so light.

Levison looked at her; kept looking at her.

Then, finally, "It's not an easy task, I can assure you, my dear Lady Isabel."

"Oh," Isabel's arched eyebrows raised.

"But I won't say that London won't be the same without you," he declared. "No, I'll change it. I'll say *life* won't be the same without you."

Isabel laughed, a low, singing laugh. "A very pretty speech, but not very original for a member of the diplomatic service."

"When one is sincere, one may forget to be diplomatic."

A little pause. Isabel felt her breath catch in her throat. "Oh, but how serious you've become!" she said at last.

"Yes," Levison returned quickly. "Seriously concerned for your happiness."

"That's sweet of you."

"I'm hoping that you won't find life in the country too quiet."

She felt Levison looking at her and her tumbled words came hurriedly. "Oh, no . . . no, I won't. You'll see! I'm going to move Mayfair down to East Lynne. We'll make it the most popular suburb of London. We'll have house parties every week. And then, I'll be running up to town . . . and, oh, there'll be all sorts of things . . ."

Levison nodded. "Well, that'll be splendid. Ah, how are you, Carlyle!" He held out his hand as Robert Carlyle joined the group.

"Well, Levison." Carlyle shook hands. "Are you offering Isabel congratulations or condolences?"

Levison laughed. "I'm wishing you both every happiness."

"Thank you," Carlyle bowed.

Isabel slipped her hand into her husband's arm. Now she was safe, secure. The funny little feeling . . . not exactly fear, but something very akin to it, left her. That warm, strong arm was crushing her hand tight. She was really, truly, in love with Robert. Francis couldn't mean to her what Robert meant. Francis was a person who fascinated one; one had to like him. He had never asked her to marry him. There had actually been nothing serious between them. He had shown her a great deal of attention; and she liked attention. But that was over, now . . . finished.

"It's understood," she heard Robert saying, "that when we return from our honeymoon we're expecting you to visit us at East Lynne."

Well, why shouldn't Francis come to visit them, Isabel asked herself. She wanted to bring her London friends to her new home . . . and Francis was one of her London friends. But before she had time to second the invitation, Levison had answered.

"That's kind of you, but I'm leaving for the Continent to-morrow. I'm off on a mission for Lord Townsend, and it may be months before I return. I can't tell."

"Months or years, you'll always be welcome," Carlyle answered heartily.

"Sorry to interrupt, you know." The fussy voice of Lord Mount Severn interjected itself into the conversation. "But I must remind you, my boy,'' he put his hand on Carlyle's arm, ''you've got to catch the boat train, and there's very little time left to change . . .''

''Oh, Father!'' Isabel caught her veil about her. ''Thanks! We must hurry. There'll be so many things at the last moment . . . I'll go right away.'' She turned and held out her hand to Levison. ''Good-by,'' she said demurely.

Levison took the outstretched hand. ''Good-by, Isabel.'' He released her and watched her hurry off toward the stairs, her maid of honor following in the wake of streaming tulle and lace.

''Good-by,'' he called again. ''And happiness, always!''

CHAPTER II

THE long, English twilight stretched luxuriously over wooded hill and lush meadowland. It dappled singing streams and flecked the golden ripples; cast long, unearthly shadows over pastures and tiny, winding lanes; carried the sweet scent of newly budding heather over the downs. An almost tangible thing, this twilight, so clear, so like velvet that it seemed as though one might reach out and gather it into open hands; yet so transparent, so ephemeral, that it fled through tightly closed fingers.

Sleepy birds stirred and twittered drowsily in their nests in the heavy old chestnut trees that lined the highways and byways of the countryside. Ewes bleated for their lambs; the tinkle of a lone cowbell sounded faintly from afar. The steady pad-pad-pad of horses' hoofs disturbed the reddish dust, sending up molten clouds that hung for a brief instant in the stillness and then settled to comfortable lethargy.

"Oh, it's all so lovely . . . so lovely!" Isabel sighed happily, leaned back against the cushions of the open carriage, and snuggled her hand more deeply into her husband's broad palm.

Carlyle smiled. "I'm sure you'll like it, dear. The country's a little dry, just at present, but it's beautiful in the spring. Primroses and cowslips

14

over the meadows, violets and bluebells in the woods . . .

"I love it just as it is now, Robert."

"I'm sorry we weren't able to stay in Italy longer. You did enjoy it there, didn't you? But I daren't neglect my business, now that I have you to look after, especially. But it was nice, wasn't it, dear?"

"Darling, I loved every minute of it!" Isabel looked up at Robert. Her lips curved in a smile, though her eyes were serious. "But I am glad we're home; truly, I am. And we are home . . . we're going home. That's the way it seems to me. Of course, I liked Italy; it was gorgeous. But there's something about England! Oh, it makes me feel so comfortable, so divinely restful. And then, I do want to see East Lynne."

"I'm glad you do, dear." Robert pressed the slender gloved fingers within his own, reached around and pulled the fitch collar about his wife's throat closer. "Mustn't have you taking cold. And it turns chilly in the evenings."

On and on they drove, every hoof beat, every turn of the carriage wheel bringing them nearer and nearer to East Lynne. She was going to be so happy there, Isabel decided; so very happy. She'd do everything in her power to keep that happiness for herself and for Robert. It wouldn't be a bit dull. She loved the country, loved the quiet solemnity of the long evenings before a wood fire. And then, there'd be people to entertain, friends constantly dropping in; little trips to London with Robert when he had to go up to argue a case.

Her father, by now, would be comfortably settled in a smaller place of his own. He had said he was giving up the town house, now that she was gone. Or he'd be visiting with friends; he was always going here or there for the shooting, the fishing, dinners, a house party. And there'd be . . . Isabel stopped. A panicky feeling swept over her but she checked it. There'd be Robert's sister, Cornelia. She did hope that Cornelia would like her. She had heard so many tales of relatives in law. And Cornelia hadn't come to the wedding. She had been ill.

But then, Robert had explained that Cornelia, much older than himself, had practically brought him up from the time of their mother's death. Cornelia was devoted to him; to his career. And Cornelia would love anyone he loved; would do anything to make him happy. Of course she would love Isabel.

"That's The Grove, Sir Richard Hare's estate," Robert was pointing to a lovely old house that stood far back from the road, half hidden by dense underbrush and great, old oaks. "The Hares are our nearest neighbors, so you'll probably see a lot of them. Old Sir Richard is quite a country squire, interested in cattle and his horses. A jovial, red-faced soul . . ."

"It's a beautiful house," Isabel exclaimed. "And Lady Hare? What's she like?"

"Lady Hare? Lady Hare was an invalid; she died a great many years ago. There's a daughter,

Barbara, who's about your age. We grew up together. You'll like Barbara . . .'' He broke off
suddenly to gesture toward a long avenue of oaks
that was opening wide before them. "We're here,
my dear! This is East Lynne!''

Isabel sat up erect and looked about, exclaim-
ing. The old, weather-beaten trees formed an
arch overhead. Hedges of hawthorn and black-
thorn bordered the pasture lands that ran back
from either side of the road. A tiny brook
babbled over stones, sounding louder and louder
as the carriage approached a rustic bridge. Here
the scenery took on a wilder, less cultivated air,
and tangles of bramble and wild roses sprang
from the craggy sides of a steep, narrow ravine.

"See, there's a fall of water on the left,''
Carlyle was pointing out. "It's quite deep, but
over here, on the right, there's a little flight of
steps cut into the stone so that you can walk down
to the brook where it's shallow. It's cool here,
even on the warmest days. And there . . . now,
now you can see the house!''

From the midst of sheltering trees set in a vast
park Isabel could glimpse the rising gables of the
old manor house. Tidy, trim lawns ran down as
far as the bridge. The broad avenue of oaks led
directly to the main entrance of the house that
was to be her home. Several rockeries with their
tiny, bright flowers made spots of color against
the gray stone of the building. The setting sun
turned to gold the casement windows with the
leaded diamonds of glass. The carriage stopped.
They were home.

In another moment the great oaken door had swung open on its heavy hinges, but only a butler appeared on the threshold. He came down the broad, stone steps. The groom jumped from his perch and ran to the horses' heads. The animals pawed the gravel, lowering their tired heads. They, too, knew that they were home. Behind them came the rumble of the wagon conveying the luggage.

"Oh! I never dreamed East Lynne was like this! It's beautiful . . . beautiful . . . beautiful!" Isabel's hands were clasped in ecstasy as she gazed up at the great pile of stones so softly gray in the fading, mellow light.

"I've always felt it needed one crowning touch of beauty," Carlyle smiled. "And you have contributed that." He jumped to the ground and held out his hand.

Isabel rose, stepped out of the carriage, still gazing about her as though she would impress every feature of the house and its surroundings on her mind.

"That's dear of you to say that," she whispered.

"Hello, Dodson!" Carlyle turned to the butler who waited, hands folded, on the steps. "My dear," he turned to Isabel, "this is Dodson."

Isabel nodded, smiling graciously. Dodson made a stiff, formal bow, but his eyes lighted at the sight of that warming smile.

"We are all very happy, milady," he said.

"Thank you . . . thank you, Dodson."

"You'll see to the luggage, Dodson," Carlyle

gestured toward the wagon and gave Isabel his
arm as they alighted from the carriage.

"Yes, sir. At once, sir."

Up the steps they went, Isabel on the arm of
her husband. A trim little maid curtsied as they
crossed the threshold. Then they were in the
great, paneled hall. And there, in the corner,
stood a middle-aged woman, a shawl gathered
about her shoulders, her features dim in the faint
light.

"Well, Cornelia!" Carlyle dropped his wife's
arm and went to greet his sister, kissing her.
"It's nice to be home. This is my wife, Isabel."
He took the girl's hand and led her with him.
"Isabel, this is my sister, Cornelia."

"How do you do?" Cornelia took Isabel's hand,
making a prim, formal gesture.

Isabel leaned forward as though to kiss her new
sister-in-law, but drew back, a little chilled, a little
frightened at the lack of response.

"I've been looking forward to meeting you,
Cornelia," she said, instead. "We were so disappointed that your illness prevented you from
attending our wedding. I do hope you're feeling
better. Robert tells me that you are . . . from
your letters, you know."

"Thank you, I am better." The voice was stiff
and unbending. "I hope you will like East Lynne.
We are plain people; we live very simply. I've
arranged your rooms as I thought you would like
them."

"That was very kind and thoughtful of you, I'm
sure," Isabel returned sweetly.

Outwardly she seemed composed enough . . .
at least, she hoped that she was giving that impression. But once more that panicky feeling was
surging over her. She mustn't allow Robert to
sense her panic, though. Undoubtedly, Cornelia
was a kindly soul. But a stranger, stepping into
your home, into the heart of one you loved . . . of
course, Cornelia must feel that to some extent,
and she, Isabel, must make allowances for it. It
would all work out in time. But if only the room
were a little brighter . . . if they'd light the
candles. It was so dark, so gloomy.

"If . . . if I may," she stammered, holding
Carlyle's arm tightly. "I . . . I'd like . . ."

"Of course, dear. Run along," Carlyle patted
her hand. "I know you're anxious to see your
room. Cornelia, would you mind taking Isabel
up and showing her what arrangements you've
made?"

"Certainly, Robert. I thought the suite next to
the library . . ." Cornelia turned to lead the
way upstairs.

"Yes, that's right," Carlyle nodded.

The swish of Cornelia's skirts as she slowly
ascended the beautifully carved oaken staircase
seemed to be the only live sound in the entire
house. There was no crackling of fire in grates,
no noise of servants moving about. It was dead
. . . dead. Isabel's fingers clutched at her throat
for a moment, and then the warming pressure of
Robert's hand on hers brought her to herself
again. They were standing on the stairway, and
Robert was saying something.

"You know," and now his voice was clearer, plainer. "It gives me the most exquisite pleasure, seeing you here on these stairs. The first recollection I have of my mother was watching her come down these stairs, radiantly beautiful, just as you are now. I shall always remember you standing here."

"Robert . . . Robert!" Isabel threw her arms about her husband's neck and kissed him. Now it was all right; everything was all right, and she was a silly goose to imagine all sorts of horrible things. She laughed. "And every time I come down this stairway, I shall remember how happy I am at this moment."

"You are beautiful, Isabel. My dear, I love you —love you!"

The golden glory of the waning sun streamed through the casement stairway window and outlined the girl's shining curls with a halo of light. The little velvet hat with its trailing plume made a soft frame for the lovely, delicate face. For that moment the two were lost in the dying beauty of the day. And then the swish of skirts recalled them. Laughing, a little abashed, they drew apart.

"Cornelia will show you our rooms, dear," Robert said gently, and then turned and went down the stairs.

With renewed courage Lady Isabel followed the sound of the swishing skirts. Down a long, dark corridor, and then a door was opened, and a round-faced, sweet-looking woman, with a little white cap on her head was bobbing up and down.

Cornelia swept past the maid and stood waiting in a huge, darkened room. Heavy, carved furniture was stiffly arranged, each piece in its proper place. Floor-length hangings of heavy plush velvet concealed the deep windows. The maid closed the door and stood inside, waiting.

"This is Joyce," Cornelia said flatly, gesturing toward the servant. "She will be your maid."

"Yes'm!" Joyce bobbed again and fell silent.

"Joyce has been instructed to unpack your trunks," Cornelia went on, "and to hang your frocks in the closets . . . if that meets with your approval."

"Thank you, Cornelia. I'd appreciate it very much, Joyce." Isabel noticed that Cornelia scarcely looked at her when she spoke to her, and yet she seemed to be observing her all the time. It gave her an uncanny sensation. "Oh! What lovely flowers!" Her eyes lighted on the one bright spot in the entire room. "And how thoughtful of you!" She turned impulsively to her sister-in-law, and then buried her face in the fragrant roses.

"I'm glad you like them," Cornelia returned stiffly. "This is the bedroom." She turned and led the way, throwing open a door to reveal another room, as large, as stuffy and as dismal as the sitting room.

Isabel glanced around quickly. Here, again, everything was in exactly the proper place. The dark, tapestried walls; the heavy curtains carefully arranged; the stiff chairs with their uncompromising pillows; the wide bed, bolstered and canopied. With a quick gesture she pulled off her hat and jacket and threw them onto a chair. Then she took a deep breath.

"You know," she smiled, "this is really the most marvelous place to give house parties? I had no idea that East Lynne was such a vast estate. My friends will be surprised when they see it!" She waited, but no answer came. "I've asked a number of people down for the week-end. Some very charming people . . . I'm sure you'll like them . . . and I do hope you don't mind. Robert said I might."

"Really!" Cornelia carefully picked up the hat and coat so carelessly flung aside, and just as carefully turned and handed them to Joyce, who went to the wardrobe and put them in place, and then disappeared.

Isabels hands felt cold, icy cold. She shouldn't have been so careless about her wraps. She should have tried to be a little more careful. This was quite a different atmosphere from any she had ever known. She must go carefully; it would take time, but she would work out a solution to the situation. If only there were something light and bright here; something youthful. All her own life she had spent in the midst of gay and bright and youthful things. People with the tiniest of homes contrived to give them an atmosphere of gayety and liveliness. But this monstrous, dark house! She shivered.

And now she was the mistress of this house. She must oversee its management, attend to servants, order things. But how? How was it to be done? She had never managed a household. Most of her life had been spent in the home of Lady Townsend, under the tutelage of a governess, or traveling on the Continent. The house in Mayfair . . . she had scarcely been there save for a few coming-out parties, and then Lady Townsend had taken her under her wing, chaperoned her, arranged everything for her. Now, the thought of the responsibility appalled her.

If only she had someone like Lady Townsend to turn to for assistance. It wouldn't take long to learn, but to try to look to Cornelia for comfort or sympathy! And then, perhaps, Cornelia would think that the management was being taken out of her hands. She had always superintended everything for Robert. Perhaps Cornelia would resent it. And Cornelia mustn't be made to feel that her place was being usurped. Oh, if Robert would only come and help her! She was twisting her handkerchief about nervously, scarcely knowing what to say, what to do.

"I . . . you know," she began at last, "I'm getting a little frightened. I . . . I've never managed a household And I'm afraid I shall muddle things terribly."

She looked at Cornelia for some encouragement, some little spark of graciousness. But the woman said nothing.

"You see," Isabel tried again, "My father didn't keep our home open after Mother died, so I spent part of my life with a governess on the Continent. When . . . when I returned to England, I lived with Lady Townsend."

Cornelia cleared her throat "I have always managed East Lynne for my brother," she declared tonelessly. "In fact, I practically brought him up, and I know how he likes things done."

"Oh . . . Oh, yes, of course!" Isabel faltered. "Won't you, I mean . . . you wouldn't mind, then, continuing in charge?"

"If you wish it."

"I do. I do, indeed!"

Isabel glanced about apprehensively. She couldn't stand this, couldn't endure it any longer. She must have some light, something alive. She ran to the window and threw open the draperies. Behind a thick woods a red sun flung out crimson daggers that set the diamond panes asparkle with color.

"Oh, what gorgeous windows!" Isabel leaned against the framework, staring out over the peaceful hills and meadows. "And what a lovely view. See, what a glow over everything! Everything bathed in light. Twilight, the lovliest hour of the day. It makes me sad . . . and yet, so happy. Something dying, yet out of it beauty is born. . . ." She stopped, suddenly conscious of the swish of Cornelia's skirts. Her dreams faded and she was again in the darkly tapestried room. She thought she detected a muffled sniff.

"If you'll excuse me," Cornelia was saying.

"Oh, yes, I'm so sorry," Isabel apologized. "But I do love the English twilight." She stepped away from the window.

Cornelia pulled the draperies into place and pressed them back in their accustomed folds with

the palm of her capable hand. She started toward
the door.

"I must see that Robert's luggage has been at-
tended to," she nodded briefly. "I'm sure that
Joyce will see that you have whatever you want."
And without more ado she was gone.

Isabel stared after the departed figure, a little
hurt, a little resentful, a little bewildered.

"Your trunks are here, milady." It was the
soft tones of Joyce's voice that brought Isabel to
attention.

"Oh, thank you, Joyce! And light the candles,
please!"

"Yes, milady." With a bob Joyce disappeared.

Would it always be like this, Isabel was wondering. No, it couldn't . . . it couldn't be! She
must change things, suit herself more to the ways
of East Lynne. It would take time . . . time,
that was all. And she mustn't be too hard on
Cornelia. Things would adjust themselves. She'd
have Robert. It was only this sensation of being
in a strange house, with strange people.

"There, milady." Joyce was back with a wax
taper, making the rounds of the candelabras in
the room. The little flames leaped up, sputtering,
and then steadied to an even glow.

"Your dresses, milady," Joyce was saying. "If
I may make so bold, they're beautiful. I've
started to unpack them."

Isabel turned, smiling. "Do you like them,
Joyce?"

"I've never seen any so beautiful in this house
before, milady, that I haven't."

"A little too gay for the country, perhaps,"
Isabel suggested.

Joyce wrinkled her nose. "No indeed, milady.
An' I should say they're just what East Lynne
needs. You'll excuse me, milady, but this old
house always seems to be full of twilight. If you
don't mind me sayin' so, we're all so glad the
master married someone like your ladyship . . .
young and happy."

"Oh, Joyce! You've touched my one weakness. I love to be flattered."

"Bless you, milady, that's no weakness."

"And I love to be happy more than anyone in
the world." Isabel prattled on. "Now, come,
I must hurry. Which dress shall I wear? I'll
tell you what, Joyce, I'll wear the one you like
best!"

"Oh, milady!" Joyce threw up her hands in delight. "Now there!" She turned to the bed
where she had laid out several gowns and lovingly
fingered a creation of heavy cream satin with
great bunches of pink brocade roses. "This one.
I'd like to see your ladyship in this!"

"Then that's the one it shall be. Come along!"
Isabel sped across the room, dropping clothes
right and left, the bad moments of the past forgotten, the future still before her.

CHAPTER III

Cornelia Carlyle walked slowly down the long corridor to Robert's old room, her skirts swishing. She drew her shawl about her shoulders with a determined pull. She must have a talk with Robert. That thought was uppermost in her mind. Her thin lips came together in a straight line. She meant to cause no trouble between a man and his wife, but there were limits to all things. Of course, Robert was within his rights to marry. Certainly, she had never said anything against that. She went over the opened luggage, saw that everything was in proper order, and then swished down the stairs to meet her brother in the hall.

"I've attended to your luggage for you, Robert," she announced stiffly. "It's being unpacked in your old room." She turned as though to go into the drawing-room.

Carlyle laid a restraining hand on her arm. "I say, Cornelia, aren't you going to . . . to say anything about my wife?"

Cornelia shook her head, raised her eyebrows. "What do you expect me to say?" she asked sharply. "You know my feeling regarding your marriage."

"You make it very difficult for me, you know. From the moment I wrote to you about Isabel you

28

objected to her. You made it impossible for me to bring her here before. And it was certainly very embarrassing when you refused to attend my wedding.''

''I couldn't do it honestly.''

''There was no reason whatsoever for your refusal. I made the usual excuses of illness, but it wasn't very pleasant. Frankly, Cornelia, I don't understand your attitude.''

Cornelia looked at her brother thoughtfully, rubbing her hands together beneath her shawl as though she were cold. Finally she spoke.

''Robert, I know you think I'm just prejudiced. But I'm not, and you'll find it out, all in good time. You've married a social butterfly . . . a girl who's been reared in luxury, without a sense of responsibility. Do you think she'll be satisfied living here as we do? Do you think that life in the country is going to keep her amused, after she's lived on the Continent, in London, traveling about——''

''I think you're exaggerating things.'' Carlyle looked at his sister as though trying to read her mind. But her face was an expressionless mask.

''I don't think so,'' Cornelia shook her head. ''If you could view the matter as an outsider, you would realize that there is a great deal of truth in what I say. Why, she's already planning to fill this house with her friends. She told me that this evening, as soon as she arrived. There'll be gay parties every week-end . . .''

''But surely, Cornelia, there's no reason to live like a hermit,'' Carlyle frowned. There was something a little deeper to his sister's objection than that. And, after all, why shouldn't Isabel have her friends about her. The house was large, comfortable, and needed a little livening.

"I don't believe we have ever lived like hermits, Robert," Cornelia interposed decisively. "We've always had our friends . . . people we've known all our lives. You and I, we belong here. But she doesn't. It's not that I don't like her, but I'm afraid of what may happen to you."

"Well, now, that's a bit odd. What do you think's going to happen to me?"

"If we do nothing but entertain, run back and forth to London, the whole routine of your life will be upset, and everything . . . everything I've planned for you . . ." Cornelia hesitated, then went on. "Your parliamentary career, nothing must happen to that, Robert."

"Is that what's worrying you, Corney!" Carlyle laughed, addressing his sister with the old, familiar nickname he had used for her in his childhood. "You think about me too much. My parliamentary career will go along swimmingly. Isabel will want that for me as much as I do myself."

"She may want it for you," Cornelia said grimly, "but she's not the sort of woman to help you to get it."

"I don't know why not." Carlyle's voice was sharp. "You may have had other ideas in your mind concerning my marriage . . ."

Cornelia stopped her brother with a gesture. "Please believe me, Robert, when I tell you that

I have never wanted to interfere in any way with whatever marriage you might make. I had no objection to your marrying, but I should liked to have seen you settled with someone a little more like ourselves; someone less frivolous, less spoiled.''

"Isabel is not spoiled. Because she was extremely popular in London is no reason why she shouldn't settle to East Lynne. It won't be quite so gay for her at first, but I've never felt that she wouldn't learn to adapt herself to our mode of living. We have been very quiet, but there's a happy medium to all things. I enjoy being in London myself, at times, but that doesn't mean that I don't like it here.''

"But her life, everything she has known, is in London, in towns,'' Cornelia protested. "You were brought up here.''

"Let's not go over all that again, Cornelia. I know that you're interested in my welfare. But Isabel is my wife, now. Won't you try to be kind to her . . . to make her feel at home? It will mean a great deal to her if you'll do that. And in time, I'm sure you'll grow to love her.''

"Very well, Robert. I shall do my best to like her.'' With a swish of her skirts Cornelia turned. Then, as though it were an afterthought, she looked back over her shoulder. "I have asked Barbara and Sir Richard for dinner this evening, so we shan't dine until seven.''

"Splendid,'' Carlyle smiled. "We're making a good beginning. A dinner party on our first evening at home.''

Cornelia raised her eyebrows, and then sailed off toward the regions of the pantry.

Slowly Carlyle walked across the hall and went upstairs to his room to change into dinner clothes.

The tall clock in the hall was chiming the half hour when Carlyle, freshened from the journey and smart in his black and white evening dress, came downstairs again. He wandered into the long, low, oak-beamed drawing-room, and walked over to the mantelpiece. On the hearth he paused, his forehead wrinkled in thought. Perhaps, he told himself, he was placing too much emphasis upon his sister's attitude. It was probably only natural that she should resent to some extent the intrusion into her domain.

After all, Cornelia had been both mother and father to him. Ever since he could remember she had taken care of him. It was only natural that she should feel interested, even responsible for him, as a parent feels responsible for a child. He could have wished that she might have accepted Isabel a little more gracefully, but she had always had a distrust, a chariness of anything connected with towns or with a life which she herself neither knew nor comprehended. If he had married . . . well, if he had married any one of the girls around East Lynne, Cornelia would probably have felt quite differently about it.

A slight noise, a rustling in the doorway, made him look up quickly. There stood Isabel, radiant in the candlelight, her soft golden hair with its clinging curls caressing her slender throat, her

cheeks flushed, her bare arms milk-white, her
fingers demurely entwined. The heavy satin
skirts with the great, pink roses billowed out from
her tiny waist, until she seemed to swim in a
frothy sea. Jewels gleamed on her neck and
wrists. It wasn't often, and certainly not recently,
that East Lynne had housed such a dazzling
creature.

Very, very serious, Robert Carlyle suddenly became. Very serious and dignified.

"Come here!" he commanded in his deepest
tone of voice.

For a moment Isabel's eyes widened in surprise,
and then, sensing his trick, walked primly forward until she stood before him. Her eyelashes
lowered, she folded her hands and waited.

"I suppose," Carlyle said with mock severity,
"that you realize that from now on I am your
lord and master!"

"Yes, milord!" The girl made a deep curtsy.

"And that you are to obey me in everything?"

She glanced at her husband quickly and then
nodded her head.

"Then kiss me," Carlyle ordered.

Very properly, Isabel raised herself on tiptoe
and very primly touched her lips to the lips of her
"lord and master." With a laugh Carlyle caught
her in his arms and held her, kissing the red
mouth, the closed eyelids, the smooth, cool forehead, the little hollow of her throat.

"Oh, my dear, my dear," he said at last, holding Isabel at arm's length and gazing at her ten-

derly. "It's a dream come true! Having you here, in my arms . . . you, the mistress of East Lynne."

"Robert, my darling!" Gently she smoothed the lapel of his dinner coat. "My . . . husband."

Again their lips met and clung in one, long kiss. At last Isabel looked up at her husband shyly. She was smiling, and her eyes were misty. Together they wandered about the drawing-room, arm in arm.

"Tell me," Carlyle questioned solicitously. "How do you like everything at East Lynne. Is your maid satisfactory? And our rooms? Is there anything you want changed?"

"Oh, Robert, there isn't a thing I'd change." And Isabel meant it, then.

Those brief moments with Cornelia when she had felt so miserable, so hurt, were forgotten. Isabel had faced very little sorrow in her life; every road had always opened ahead of her, wide and straight and strewn with roses. It seemed impossible that a dark future could loom before such charming loveliness. And here, beside her husband, she felt that nothing could harm her, nothing touch her.

"My maid's a dear," she rambled on. "You don't find maids like Joyce in London. She was so concerned with what I should wear, and so interested in my clothes. She even selected this gown for me to wear to-night. She wanted to see me in it." Isabel laughed.

"Well, then," and Carlyle laughed, too, "I'd suggest that you allow Joyce to select all your

gowns. I think you look more beautiful than ever
. . . if that were possible.''

"My darling! It's nice to have a husband who
can make such pretty speeches.''

"It's nice to have a wife who deserves them.''
Carlyle pressed her hand. He paused, and then
went on. "Oh, yes, Cornelia just told me that the
Hares would be over for dinner this evening.
You remember, Sir Richard and Barbara . . . I
pointed out their home to you this afternoon.''

"Oh that's delightful.'' Isabel said, but her
voice held a note of disappointment which she
tried to conceal.

"I didn't know they were coming myself,''
Carlyle added hastily. "Personally, I think I'd
rather have had our first dinner at East Lynne
alone. I hope you're not feeling the same way.''

"No . . . no! Of course not, Robert. It'll be
lovely meeting the Hares. And you said they
were our neighbors, so I suppose I really should
meet them right away. I think it'll be charming.''

"I'm glad of that, my dear,'' and Carlyle sighed
as though relieved. "Perhaps it is better to have
some company. It won't make you feel so isolated
. . . so out of things entirely. Of course, this
isn't London society, but these people are very,
very dear friends. And Cornelia seems to think
that you may be lonely here, at first. That's
probably why she asked them over.''

"Oh, I'm sure it is,'' Isabel nodded. She was
feeling happy enough now to believe that Cornelia,
with all her severity and hardness, had honestly
tried to do something for the comfort of the new-

comer. Her heart went out to her sister-in-law
and she determined more than ever that she would
make Cornelia like her.

"What a lovely old piano!" Isabel exclaimed,
her attention caught by the gleaming rosewood
of a grand piano. "I want to try it!"

She ran to the instrument and seated herself
before it, running her fingers over the keys. The
music broke into a light waltz, making rippling,
trilling sounds that reverberated through the
long room. Carlyle listened for a moment and
then went to the piano and leaned against the top.
He put his hands over the running fingers.

"Please!" he pleaded. "You know what I want
to hear."

Isabel's head came up sidewise like a canary's
and she looked at her husband with twinkling
eyes. Then, more somberly she broke into the
strains of "Then You'll Remember Me," from the
opera "The Bohemian Girl."

"When other lips, and other hearts . . .
Their tales of love shall tell . . ."

Her low voice, delicate yet rich with nuances
and shadings, sounded clear and vibrant in the
stillness. Carlyle stared fascinated at the smooth,
white throat that fluttered as the notes rolled
forth; at the red, arched lips as they formed the
words. Sight and sound lulled his senses like a
sedative. He saw nothing save the beautiful face
beside him; heard nothing but the mellow war-
bling. He was carried back, in memory, to his first

ANN HARDING

CLIVE BROOK

FLORA SHEFFIELD

BERYL MERCER

CONRAD NAGEL

DAVID TORRENCE

CECILIA LOFTUS

meeting with Isabel at a dinner given by the Townsends. He rememebered how he had sat, enthralled, as Isabel sang that song. And he had loved it ever since, for it was then that he had realized that he loved the girl who sang it.

"Well, well! The bride and groom! Hullo—hullo!"

A deep bass voice blasted the intervening space between the door and the piano, and a bulky form came striding toward the engrossed pair.

"Well, my boy, this is an occasion! Welcome home!"

"Why, Sir Richard!" Carlyle straightened to attention, holding out his hand.

The big man, with a round face reddened by wind and rain, port wines and solid provender, grasped the outstretched hand and shook it hard.

"Isabel, may I present Sir Richard Hare? Sir Richard, my wife, Lady Isabel," Carlyle was saying.

Isabel rose from the piano and found her hand seized in a hearty grasp.

"May you indeed!" Sir Richard boomed. "My dear," he turned to Isabel, "we are tremendously pleased . . . and oh! yes!" He looked behind him at the girl who had come quietly in his wake. "This is my daughter, Barbara."

"I'm delighted to meet you, Lady Isabel." Barbara shook hands smilingly.

"Thank you. I've heard so much about you," Isabel returned the smile. "We're neighbors, so I'm hoping that we'll see you often."

At first meeting she rather liked this Barbara.

She seemed a quiet, shy girl, especially in contrast to her blustering father. A pretty girl, too, with soft brown hair and clear, hazel eyes. Her costume, Isabel noted, was of yellow satin, quite plain; indeed, almost severe by comparison to her own dazzling toilet. But she looked fresh and charming in it.

Before Barbara had time to answer, Sir Richard's deep voice rang out. "You'll see a lot of us, my dear," he assured Isabel. "We live so near that we run in and out without so much as 'by your leave'! Don't we, m' boy?" And without giving his host time to speak he rumbled on. "Do you know how long I've known him?" He nudged Carlyle playfully. "Ever since he was that much!" Sir Richard measured off the space of two inches with his great, pudgy hands.

Carlyle laughed. "Isabel, my dear, you'll be getting bits of my biography for months."

"I'll love it," the girl declared stanchly. "I shan't mind a bit how much you talk to me about Robert, Sir Richard."

"We do hope you'll like East Lynne," Barbara interposed in her soft, sweet voice.

"Well, East Lynne likes you already," Sir Richard assured Isabel.

"Thank you; that's very kind."

"Come along to the library, Sir Richard," Carlyle suggested. "We'll leave Barbara and Isabel to discuss us."

"Right, m' boy, right!" Sir Richard seized Carlyle's arm and bustled toward the door. "I want you to come over as soon as you've time.

I want you to see my new Hereford bull. He's a beauty! He just took the blue ribbon . . ."
The voice trailed off as the two men disappeared.

And so through dinner, through the long, long evening that seemed to have no ending . . . at least, to Isabel. She tried to take part, tried to be entertaining. But this was not the sort of dinner she had ever known. Where before she had been fêted, lionized, deferred to, she now found herself being, so she felt, smiled at and patronized. Her contributions to the conversation semed to consist of an occasional "Oh, yes?" and a "Really," and an "How interesting!" And it wasn't . . . it wasn't interesting in the least!

There was talk of stock shows and fairs, church bazaars and poor Mrs. Cullin's rheumatism, and should chickens with the pip be fed on warm milk? Now, really, should they? And Mrs. This, and Mr. That, and Lady So-and-so, and the new vicar at West Lynne. A round of names, controversies over people, none of whom Isabel knew. She tried to console herself with the thought that after a little time she would know all these people, and they might assume a tremendous importance in her life. But she didn't think she'd ever know what to do about a chicken with the pip or a horse with a spavin.

In and out Sir Richard's voice still boomed and bellowed; Barbara's soft tones fluttered; Cornelia's hard and fast decisions stood defiantly awaiting contradiction; Carlyle's tempered, even remarks were listened to with respectful deference. Then Carlyle and Sir Richard lingered over their port, while Cornelia, with the two girls, withdrew to the drawing-room. Cornelia and Barbara showed Isabel all the daguerreotypes, photographs of Robert . . . Robert at the tender age of two years; Robert in the guise of a choir boy with brown curls; Robert and his rugby team; Robert . . . Robert . . . Robert!

It was amusing for a while, looking at these funny, old pictures of Robert; listening to little anecdotes of his life. Barbara semed to know as many as Cornelia; seemed to have followed Robert faithfully through his career. A pang of jealousy seized Isabel. Perhaps Robert was in love with Barbara. But how silly, she told herself. If Robert had been in love with Barbara, he would have married her. And he hadn't. She put the thought away from her and tried to listen to what Cornelia and Barbara were saying.

The two were discussing a forthcoming meeting of the Ladies Guild. And now Isabel was entirely at sea. If only Robert would come in. She waited, her eyes half closed, dreaming . . . dreaming of Robert, and London, and dinners, and her friends. And then Robert and his guest joined them at last, and Sir Richard decided that, it being ten o'clock, it was high time for everybody to be in bed. And the evening was over.

As she stood in the hall with Cornelia, while Robert saw the Hares to their carriage, Isabel reviewed the dinner in her mind. Finally she turned to her sister-in-law, speaking more for the sake of hearing her voice once again than anything else.

"Miss Hare seems to be a very charming girl,"
she said.

Cornelia nodded. "My brother was very fond
of her," she announced dispiritedly. "They've
known one another since childhood."

Isabel sighed. That fact had certainly been
made obvious this evening. "How interesting!"

"Yes!" And Cornelia's voice seemed to carry
a little warmth. "Barbara seems to understand
my brother as I do. You see, he's rather set in
his mode of living . . . has certain ideals. I have
always felt that his wife should be in absolute
sympathy with him. Here's Robert now. Good
night." Abruptly she turned and left.

"Tired?" Carlyle questioned brightly, taking
Isabel's arm.

Together they went up the stairs.

"No." Isabel shook her head and fell silent.

So that was it. Cornelia had wanted Robert to
marry Barbara. Barbara, who knew and understood him. He needed a wife who'd be in sympathy with him. Well, Robert hadn't married
Barbara. And she, Isabel, would do everything in
her power to show Cornelia that she was the
proper wife for Robert. If she could only throw
herself into her husband's arms and sob out the
whole story. But she couldn't . . . she mustn't.
That would upset everyone, and Robert might
think that she was jealous, or else that something
had happened between herself and Cornelia. And
he might be hurt.

No, there was nothing for it but to fight the
battle alone.

CHAPTER IV

SUMMER passed. And autumn came. A flare of color and then gray drabness like licking tongues of flame soon extinguished. Fog and mist rolled over the valleys, blanketed the downs, chilled the desolate moors. London was lost in a greenish haze through which flickering lamps shone sickly yellow. The dome of St. Paul's was blotted out as though it had never been. Damp streets grew rain soaked, froze, lay buried beneath layers of ice and snow. And winter was in power.

Then winter passed. Mud oozed through country roads hub high. But deep in the bare woods a yellow carpet of primroses was spread. The purple violets clustered in their leaf-green beds. The smell of fresh earth and burgeoning things was wafted on the cold, rain-soaked air. The sun burst through the clouds and brought the light spring greens to fullest beauty. The flower girls of Piccadilly Circus stoically thrust great trays of vivid flowers under the eyes of passers-by.

Once again summer came and the hills about East Lynne were sweet with the scent of budding white and purple heather . . . heather that spread like one vast velvet blanket over the countryside. Pastures were green once more; the lowing cows wandered over the meadows, their calves scampering and kicking up their heels. Carmine,

pink and white, the rhododendrons massed in
parks and gardens. Winding lanes were splotched
with shifting shadows of sunlight that danced like
live things as the light breezes shook the leafy
trees.

Within the old manor house there arose a sudden bustle, hustle, and strange activity. People
moved on tiptoe up and down the stairway. A
nurse in stiffly starched clothes bustled in and out
with a determined air. A doctor came and went
with a regular frequency. And then there em-
anated through the ancient halls an odor of warm
milk and medicines and antiseptics. From behind one closed door came the sound of a thin
little voice that rose and fell in wailing; then
silence again.

And the seasons came and went. Again it was
June, with all the soft and lovely fragrance of
June in the English countryside. Isabel set before the mirror in her bedroom and stared at the
person who looked back at her with clear, blue
eyes. It was three years now, she reflected . . .
three years since she had come as a bride to East
Lynne. Was she changed? How had she
changed? She tried to visualize the happy, laughing girl who had been, three years ago, the Lady
Isabel Vane.

That Lady Isabel had been a thing of golden
curls and laughter, of dancing feet and frou-frou
gowns. Now this Isabel, who was the wife of
Robert Carlyle, wore a prim little dress of English eyelet muslin. Her hair was smoothed back
from the high, white brow and caught in a tidy

knot at the nape of her neck. A simple cameo brooch held the collar of lace tight about her throat. No jewels shone on the white hands, save a wedding and an engagement ring.

What had happened? Isabel frowned as she stared at her reflection. Where were all the house parties she had visualized; all the little trips to London with Robert, seeing her friends again? Why, she suddenly realized with a start, she hadn't seen any of her London friends for . . . how long was it? Two years . . . no, almost three. Of course, there had been the baby, and she had stayed very much at home before its advent, and afterwards she seemed to be caught up in the routine of innumerable, tiny things. Could it actually be three years ago that she walked up the nave of St. Paul's Cathedral on Robert's arm?

Yes, it was three years, there was no getting away from that. Then how, why? Why had this change taken place? She looked back now over those three years and remembered her half-hearted attempts at livening East Lynne. Cornelia was always having an attack of headache when anything was suggested. And then Robert was forever busy. He really couldn't take her to London with him. He had so much to attend to, and was too anxious to cut his stay in town short and hurry back to East Lynne.

Friends . . . yes, once or twice friends had been invited to East Lynne. They came, were delighted to see Isabel again, but somehow they never came a second time. Of course there were

the neighbors who paid friendly calls and talked of
horse shows, cattle, rheumatism, and the new
vicar at West Lynne. He was still the "new
vicar," though he had been new three years ago.

Cornelia still retained her rights to manage
affairs for her brother. The servants deferred to
her; came to her for their orders. It was "Miss
Conelia says this," or "Miss Cornelia wouldn't
approve of that." And through it all Robert had
said nothing. He didn't seem to notice. But
then, why should he, Isabel asked herself sharply.
He was entangled deeply in his legal affairs. He
was forging ahead in his career as a barrister, going by leaps and bounds. And things, so far as he
could see, ran smoothly and evenly. He was comfortable.

She never once mentioned her feelings to him,
Isabel reflected. At first she had tried to hint
delicately. But Robert never seemed to understand what she meant. And it had been so im-
pressed upon her by Cornelia, by everybody, that
Robert was the really important person in the
household that she had a wholesome fear of doing
anything that would disturb him or his routine.
He still loved her, that she didn't doubt. But he
was no longer the lover she had married. He was
the formal barrister at law who provided his wife
with a good living, everything, so he thought, that
her heart desired. She should be happy in her
home and her child.

Wearily, Isabel rose and walked about the room.
It was no good making herself miserable sitting
here and going over and over these problems.

What to do about them, she confessed to herself that she didn't know. Her little boy, William, was her sole comfort. In him she found a kindred spirit . . . something of the life and laughter that had been in herself . . . something of her own child-like spirit. She started toward the stairway, thinking to find the baby and romp with him for a bit.

As she went downstairs the sound of voices coming from the drawing-room caught her ears. She pressed her hand to her mouth. She had forgotten! The vicar of East Lynne, his wife, and several members of the Ladies Guild had been invited for tea and a conference concerning the forthcoming Charity Bazaar. She must make an appearance. Although why she should, she didn't know, she told herself bitterly. Cornelia could do quite well without her. But if she didn't appear, there would be a little comment dropped, a little suggestion made.

Patting her hair and smoothing the lace collar at her neck, Isabel pushed open the door of the big, long room. A group of elderly women were gathered about the tea table, Cornelia in their midst. They all looked like counterparts of Cornelia, only some were thinner, some stouter. But they all had prim mouths, superior noses and eyebrows that could lift at least half an inch on any given occasion.

"It was imperative for my brother to go to London," Isabel heard Cornelia addressing the aged, white-haired vicar, who leaned against the

mantelpiece, a cup of tea balanced in his hand.
"He regretted very much that he could not be
here."

"In view of the fact that Mr. Carlyle has taken
such a keen interest in the welfare of the church,"
the vicar returned ponderously, "I should like to
suggest that we postpone making any definite
plans until his return from London."

"My brother always approves of any decisions
made by me." Cornelia's answer was flat and
decisive.

How like her . . . how like everything in this
house, Isabel thought.

"Of course . . . of course!" the vicar interposed hastily. "Showing his usual good judgment . . . if I may say so."

And how like him! Oh, well, Robert had the
living of the church at East Lynne to give, Isabel
told herself. And everybody knew Cornelia's
power. So why shouldn't the vicar say just that?
She went steadily into the room. The vicar was
the first to note her arrival.

"Ah!" he murmured, "good afternoon, Lady
Isabel."

The women about the tea table looked up, nodding their greetings. But there was no one of
them who made a really friendly gesture. They
spoke, and were ready to return to the business at
hand.

"Good afternoon," Isabel addressed the group
in general and then found a chair near the vicar's
wife and seated herself.

"Good afternoon, my dear," the woman said gently. "And how is that beautiful baby of yours?"

"Quite well, thank you." Isabel settled quietly to listen.

"Tea, Isabel?" Cornelia asked shortly.

"If you please." Isabel took the cup handed to her and sipped at the hot liquid.

"We were just discussing the forthcoming bazaar," the vicar explained politely. "The details are as yet more or less chaotic. It is our intention to make this function a greater success than last year's, and, if possible, achieve a more substantial financial return. Now, if I may," he made a slight bow which included the entire group about him. "Suggestions are in order."

There was a short silence as though each and everyone seemed to be pondering the question. But no one spoke. For all of them knew who should speak first, who should make whatever suggstions were to be made.

"The bazaar last year was dignified and decorus," Cornelia began at last. She looked about as though awaiting any contradiction. But none was forthcoming. "I think we could not do better," she went on, then, "than to follow the same general line."

There was a nodding of heads, a unanimous agreement.

"Have you any ideas on the subject, Lady Isabel?" the vicar asked, glancing first at Cornelia as though not quite certain of himself.

There was a pause. Isabel could feel all eyes

turning toward her, watching her. A swift vision
of the last year's bazaar rose before her. There
were the little booths full of hand-embroidered
tea cozies, grim shopping bags that cried "I am
a useful object"; knitted shawls of frightful hues,
knitted baby jackets and bootees, crocheted ties,
yards of tatting, carpet slippers. Isabel shuddered.

A little hesitant, conscious of her own position
as a rank outsider among these people of East
Lynne, Isabel finally spoke.

"I'd like to suggest," she began timidly, "that
we make the bazaar a little more attractive for the
young people. They might enjoy a little gayety
. . . a dance . . . a masquerade . . ."

If she had thrown a bomb into their midst,
Isabel could have caused no more confusion.
There was a stirring of crinolines, a pulling of
shawls, glances exchanged. And then, stony
silence. The vicar coughed apologetically.

"My dear lady," he frowned, embarrassed,
"anything of that sort would violate custom and
tradition. I'm certain Mr. Carlyle would
never . . ." He stopped lamely, not knowing
quite how to continue.

I might have known it . . . I might have known
it, Isabel reminded herself. Why did I ever
speak? It's no good . . . I've tried it before.
Why can't I learn? Her eyes felt misty with tears
and she was afraid that she was going to cry. It
seemed so terrible, so dreadful, after all this time,
to be a stranger still in one's own home. Sur-
reptitiously she dabbed at the corners of her eyes

with her handkerchief. She wouldn't allow them to see that they had hurt her, that they made her feel as though she were ostracized.

"If it is the wish of the members present," Cornelia broke the silence in a cold, hard tone of voice, "that I take charge this year as I have done in the past, I shall be glad to do so."

Now the little movements, the little murmurs were pleasant, warm things. A chorus of voices came in answer.

"Why, of course. . . . Everything went so nicely last year. . . . We couldn't do better. . . . I'm certain, Cornelia, you'll make a success. . . . Most decidedly. . . . That will be best. . . ."

"I think that plan will be most practicable," the vicar made himself heard above the light babble.

"Yes, indeed," agreed his wife. "No one could do better, I'm sure."

In the midst of it all, Isabel rose and placed her cup on the tea table. "You will excuse me, please." She turned and fled across the room, out of the door, and into the quiet, enveloping safety of the gloomy hall.

"I think the tickets should be priced the same as last year." As though nothing had happened, Cornelia continued the discussion.

"Let me see, what were they last year?" the vicar questioned.

"One and six," Cornelia informed him.

"Oh, yes, yes . . . one and six. Quite so . . . quite so. Yes, I agree with you. That's quite right and proper. Not too much . . . not too little.''

Isabel sighed. Well, she had tried . . . tried as she had so many times before. And nothing had ever come of her trying. Matters went along in their usual routine as though she had never existed. She sighed again. She'd go and find William. At the thought of the baby, she smiled. Then she ran along a corridor until she came to a side door which opened onto a great stretch of lawn dotted here and there with fine oak trees.

Across the lawn she sped until she saw the white cap and apron of Joyce and a big fur robe spread on the grass. She stopped and held out her arms.

''William!'' she called. ''William!''

The bulky little form of a two-year-old made wriggling movements and then the child gained his feet. His sturdy, chubby legs propelled him forward. His face was one wide, beaming smile, Isabel caught him up in her arms and he emitted chortling, gurgling noises that might have been interpreted to mean anything.

Carrying him back to the fur rug, Isabel sat there, holding the baby.

''Has he been a good boy, Joyce?'' she asked.

''Oh, very good, milady.'' Joyce jumped to her feet, bobbing. ''We've been here all afternoon.''

The baby pulled at Isabel's ear and tousled her hair and gurgled something that sounded like ''bear.''

"O-o-o-o! So you want to play bear, do you?"
Isabel laughed. "All right. Mummy will be the
big mamma bear, and you'll be the little baby
bear, and we'll go and eat up all the people with
long faces who talk about charity bazaars."

Joyce made a little sound in her throat. "Beggin' your pardon, milady," she bobbed, "but Miss
Cornelia's forbidden Master William to play
bear."

Isabel frowned, biting her lip. Then: "Why,
Joyce?"

"Well, milady, you see his clothes were torn
yesterday. . . ."

"Oh, that doesn't matter, Joyce," Isabel
laughed. "I ordered some new ones for him from
London last week."

"I—I'm sorry, milady." Joyce hesitated painfully as though she hated to say what she had to
say. "But Miss Cornelia's countermanded that
order."

Isabel stared uncomprehendingly at the maid.
Slowly the meaning of the words penetrated her
mind. Cornelia had countermanded an order she
had given . . . had told her nothing of it. Yet
she had told the servants. Even the servants
knew that she had no power in her own home.
Joyce was faithful, loved her and the baby. But
Joyce did not dare to brave Cornelia's frozen
wrath. And she, the Lady Isabel Carlyle, could
not even order a suit of clothes for her own child.
It was monstrous! Monstrous! She felt shamed
and humiliated.

"We won't need you for a little while, Joyce,"
was all she said.

"Very good, milady." Joyce bobbed and
started for the house.

So that was what things were coming to. Perhaps, after all, she had better go straight to
Robert and tell him of the occurrence. But what
good would it do? There would be Cornelia's
version of the story. And Robert had grown accustomed to listening to his sister, to taking her
advice in all matters. But things couldn't go on
this way. Perhaps if she had spoken that very
first night they had come to East Lynne? But
she hadn't, and whether it would have made any
difference was still open to doubt.

But what should she do? The question went
racing around and around in her mind. She loved
Robert, she loved her home. And there was
William. She crushed the child to her. All the
pent-up love and affection she would have so
freely lavished on her husband was given to the
child. William came first . . . above everything
else. For he was the only one who seemed to return her love.

Robert was kind to her. But it was stern, cold
kindness. And she had been accustomed to such
warmth of feeling. She had been ready to do anything, go to any lengths to make East Lynne a
happy place for Robert. Time after time she had
subjugated her own will to that of Cornelia for
the sake of peace. She, herself, gave out love
without stint. But she seemed to face a blank

wall . . . a wall that chilled her, frightened her.
If she should leave her home . . . leave her husband. No! No! No! She put the thought from
her as though it were a poisoned thing.

The baby's soft, warm hands caught at her
cheek, at her neck, trying to draw her attention
to himself. He felt that he was being rudely deserted and he wasn't accustomed to that sort of
treatment from his mother. Again he gurgled
and lisped "bears."

"You darling!" Isabel rumpled the golden
curls that were like soft fuzz on the baby's head.
"And who said we mustn't play bear?" She set
the child on his feet, got down on all fours, and
pulled the fur rug over herself.

"Now you run and hide! Quick!"

With a shout of glee the child scrambled for a
tree trunk. The big, furry form came after him,
growling and making all sorts of absurd noises.
So many noises, indeed, that the ears beneath the
fur rug did not catch the sound of carriage wheels
scrunching on the graveled road near by.

CHAPTER V

CARLYLE flecked the whip over the black flanks of the two small trotters and set them to stepping high. The dogcart sped smoothly over the well cared for roads. The groom in the back seat plopped up and down with the rhythm of the beating hoofs. Francis Levison, seated beside Carlyle, surveyed the country with an intentness that was born partially of curiosity, partially of real interest.

"I was quite pleasantly surprised to find that you were in England," Carlyle was saying. "Although I'm sorry that your return was necessitated by your uncle's death. But it would have been impossible for me to settle the estate without your presence."

"I don't mind telling you that I rather enjoy being in England again," Levison replied. "It's been quite a time."

"How long have you been away?" Carlyle asked.

"Well, three years, now," Levison returned thoughtfully. "Unless you'd count one day . . . I had to come back from Paris and spend a day in London on business and then hurry off again. But that's all. I've been on the Continent from Paris to Berlin to Budapesth and back again. I shan't mind a little rest. And then, it's good to see old friends.''

"It's good to see you," Carlyle said heartily.

Silence fell, and Levison studied his companion's face. Carlyle had changed little in the three years since his marriage, he thought. He wondered if he were as little changed himself. It seemed as though he had been gone for years and years. And then, again, as though he had never been away from England. Carlyle had evidently been quite a success, he mused. At least from all he'd heard.

As he looked more closely he noted that the puckered lines between his companion's eyes were just a little deeper. Yes, and he could see that the line of the jaw was firmer. There was a hardness about the face that had not been there before. Nothing actually tangible, and yet one could feel it. There was less of youthfulness and boyishness when he smiled. That seemed to be the main difference. Arguing cases probably left that mark of firmness, of hardness.

And Isabel? He wondered whether she, too, had changed. What had East Lynne done to her? Was she still the same light, bright, happy girl whose hand he had held there in the Townsend's conservatory, whose cheek his lips had brushed that one memorable evening? Or had she, too, matured, became older? No, not Isabel. She wasn't that sort. All curls and ruffles and furbelows, all sunshine and laughter. He started at the sound of Carlyle's voice.

"By the way, Isabel will be surprised, won't she?" Robert was saying.

It was almost as though he had read his thoughts, Levison told himself. For a moment it frightened him, and then very quietly he asked: "How is she?"

"She's in splendid health, thank you," Carlyle informed him. "The country seemed to agree with her from the very first. She thoroughly enjoys it, I believe."

"She must," Levison agreed. "I understand she hasn't been seen in London for the last two seasons."

"Oh, she hasn't time for that sort of thing any more," Carlyle laughed. "There's the child, you know. And the estate . . . the affairs of the parish. In fact, she's kept quite busy."

Levison sent a sharp glance toward his companion's face. But Carlyle was paying attention to the horses and the road. Isabel, busy with a child, an estate, and the affairs of the parish! It sounded almost incredible. And yet, he knew for a fact that no one in London had seen anything of the girl, for, as he had said, the last two seasons.

When he had first been called to London to attend to the affairs of an estate left by an elderly uncle who had seen fit to turn over his money to his nephew on his demise Levison had asked for news of Isabel from friends. But there was little or no news that anyone could tell him. While in Berlin someone had written him that there had been a child born to the Carlyles, and subsequent English newspapers which found their way to the Continent had carried an announcement to that effect.

He had watched the papers, expecting to find an item from time to time stating that Isabel had been visiting some person, here or there. But no such items ever appeared. And he didn't know exactly whether he had been surprised or not. Now and again he recalled that wedding day when Isabel had laughingly told him that she was going to take Mayfair to East Lynne, and make East Lynne "the most popular suburb of London." He even recalled her exact words, the tone of her voice.

He had wondered then whether any such thing would ever come to pass, even though Isabel should do all in her power to bring it about. Mayfair ran around and around in its own little circles, with its own little cliques. The inhabitants of Mayfair went north at times for the shooting or to some very brilliant house party. But Mayfair didn't spend week-ends at the home of an obscure country lawyer, even though its mistress was the Lady Isabel Carlyle.

Levison had been rather surprised when he had found that it was Carlyle who was settling up his uncle's estate. Surprised, and a little pleased. And he had very quickly accepted the invitation to spend a few days at East Lynne. That, at least, meant a sight of Isabel. And although he tried not to admit it, he realized that he had not forgotten her; that there were times when he grew terribly conscious of a great longing to see her, if only for a moment, to talk to her again.

"How old is the baby?" he asked abruptly.

"Not quite two years old. He'll be two the twenty-fifth of this month," Carlyle answered with a young father's proud air. "He's quite a good-sized boy. I think he looks exactly like his mother, but my sister, Cornelia, says he has the Carlyle nose and chin. He talks very plainly for a child of his age."

Levison smiled. "You are the doting parent, aren't you?"

"Well," Carlyle laughed, "I suppose I am. But then, William's an extraordinarily interesting child. Never you mind, you'll feel the same way when you have one of you own. You haven't, by any chance, married, have you?"

"No, oh, no!" Levison shook his head decisively. "I suppose I haven't been settled long enough in one place to consider the matter seriously. One becomes so accustomed to bachelor's quarters, moving about the way I do."

"Yes, I suppose so," Carlyle agreed. "And then, you don't meet very many English girls on the Continent, and of course you wouldn't want to marry a foreigner."

Levison shot a quick glance out of the corners of his eyes at the man beside him. How typical, he thought, how absolutely typical. The snug, self-righteous way in which Carlyle had said the word "foreigner" made him wish that he could present a wife who knew not one syllable of the English language. Perhaps, he told himself, he

was beginning to understand why it was that
Isabel hadn't been seen in London for the last
two seasons.

"Well, here we are, Levison," Carlyle exclaimed. "This is East Lynne."

They were crossing the bridge beneath which
the little brook in the ravine tinkled melodiously.
It was just another such day three years before
that Isabel had had her first glimpse of the estate.
Levison looked about, seeing the avenue of oak
trees with the great park and a glimpse of the
house beyond. It was a beautiful situation, without doubt. But Isabel, buried here! Now he no
longer wondered whether she had changed, but
rather, how great that change had been.

The trees and hedges sheltered from sight the
furry figure that growled and romped and played
with the child on the lawn. Only peaceful serenity
met the eye. No carriages passed the dogcart on
the road. Gradually the gray stone building took
shape and form and in a few moments the dogcart
paused in front of the steps. The groom jumped
down from behind and ran to the horses' heads.

Carlyle stepped out of the cart, throwing the
reins over the dashboard. Levison noticed that
he looked around as though seeking someone. But
the entrance was deserted.

"Come right along," Carlyle invited. "Dodson will see to your luggage."

"Thanks." Levison dismounted and went up
the steps with his host.

The big door swung open and Dodson stood
waiting.

"Hullo, Dodson," Carlyle greeted. "Will you attend to Mr. Levison's luggage please? It's in the dogcart."

"Yes, sir," Dodson bowed. "Miss Cornelia's in the drawing-room, sir, with the committee for the Charity Bazaar."

"Thanks." Carlyle led the way. "I had forgotten," he explained, "that the committee was coming here this afternoon. Isabel's probably in there with them. You've never met my sister, Cornelia, have you?"

"No, I'm sorry I've never had the pleasure," Levison murmured.

And all the while he was trying to picture Isabel in the midst of these surroundings . . . the big lonely estate, the gloomy, cavernous hall where he now walked; the committee for the Charity Bazaar. But Carlyle was throwing open a door, and from the room beyond came a murmur of voices which died abruptly as the master of the house entered with his guest.

"Cornelia, my dear, how are you?" Carlyle went to his sister and kissed her. "May I present Mr. Francis Levison; Mr. Levison, my sister, Miss Carlyle."

"How do you do, Miss Carlyle." Gravely Levison bowed. "I am most happy to make your acquaintance at last."

"Thank you." Cornelia nodded stiffly.

"And this is our vicar, the Reverend James Hartledge, and Mrs. Hartledge," Carlyle made the necessary gestures while Levison greeted the assembled group. "And this is Mrs. Hume . . .

Mrs. Worthington . . . Mrs. Gibbons, and Miss Sethridge.''

"Delighted, I'm sure," Levison was murmuring.

And all the while his eyes wandered in search of one face, one figure. But certainly Isabel was not of this group. He noted the somber, dark clothes; the elderly visages, the pursed, straight-line mouths. In his wildest imaginings he could not place Isabel in the midst of this.

"Where is Isabel?" he heard Carlyle questioning his sister.

"I believe she's in the garden," Cornelia answered austerely. And then, quickly, as if to divert attention, she asked: "Will you take tea, Mr. Levison?"

"If you please."

"Robert? You must want a dish of tea after that dusty trip."

"If you don't mind." Carlyle excused himself, "I'll see if I can find Isabel. Pardon me, for a moment."

"Won't you sit here, Mr. Levison?" Cornelia pushed forward a straight-backed chair near her own.

"Thank you." And Levison saw his host vanish.

Carlyle hurried along the corridor and went out by the side door. He started across the lawn and then stopped suddenly, his eyes riveted to a white blotch on the lawn. He looked over his shoulder to make certain that this portion of the park could not be seen from the drawing-room windows, and then with tight-set lips he strode toward the big woolly bear.

Beneath the fur rug Isabel could see nothing save the ground and the feet of William, running this way and that to elude her grasping hands. The child was shrieking and shouting in the excitement of the chase. Suddenly his legs were caught by the white bear and he was smothered amidst fur and went rolling on the ground. Isabel threw back the rug and straightened to her knees, righting the baby.

"Isabel!" There was consternation, horror, and dreadful severity all concentrated in that one word.

With a little gasp Isabel scrambled to her feet and ran to meet her husband, her arms outstretched.

"Robert! Why . . . oh, Robert! I didn't expect you until to-morrow! Oh! I'm so glad!" She started to clasp her arms about his neck, but her hands were pushed away and Robert stood straight and tall, the furrow between his eyes deepening.

"My dear, if you please!" Anger and indignation flushed his face. "Look at yourself! Your hair . . . your dress!"

Isabel brushed away the bits of cut grass that clung to her skirt with a frightened air.

"Oh! Robert, I'm sorry. But don't be cross, please don't," she begged. "And don't scold me. I'm so happy that you're home again." Impetuously she stood on tiptoe and kissed him. But there was no response, no answering kiss. "It's seemed such a long time without you. The days are endless when you're away. Did you have a nice time? What was London like? Did you see anyone?" Her questions came breathlessly.

"Isabel, I wish you would think just a little more of me . . . of my position," Carlyle said coldly, heedless of the questions. "I wish you, please, to remember that you are my wife. And as my wife you should never place yourself in the undignified position in which I have just found you. Now go to your room . . . at once! Go and make yourself presentable. I've brought a guest from London."

"A guest! Oh, Robert, who? Is it anyone I know?"

"Yes, it's Francis Levison."

"Francis Levison!" Isabel's voice rang out happily, her eyes shone. "Oh, my dear, how sweet of you. Oh, I'll be so glad to see him. Where is he?"

"He's in the drawing-room at present, but . . ."

Like a child, Isabel was running across the lawn before Robert could reach out his hand to stop her. Forgotten was the scolding of the moment ago. Forgotten everything, save that here was Francis Levison, from London, with news of old friends, news of the Continent. Along the corridor Isabel sped and burst into the drawing-room, her hair flying, her dress grass-stained, her collar awry. She was too excited to see the looks of amazement, of dismay, that spread over the faces of those people gathered about the tea table.

"Francis Levison! This is a surprise!" She went toward the man, who arose and took her hand, pressing it. "I'm delighted to see you again! How are you? When did you arrive in London?"

"And I'm delighted to see you, Lady Isabel." Levison had already caught sight of the upraised eyebrows, the looks that flew from one woman to the other, and he was trying to warn Isabel, to keep her out of trouble.

"Have you met . . ." Isabel began, turning to Cornelia and the others. And then she realized what she had done; realized her disheveled appearance; realized that Cornelia was not missing one detail of the entire scene and knew that she was storing it up for future use. Her cheeks became scarlet, and in wild confusion she tried to arrange her collar, pat her hair.

"I . . . I'm . . . you must pardon my appearance," she stammered. "I've been romping with the baby . . . out there . . . on the lawn."

"I'm certain Mr. Levison will excuse you, my dear," Carlyle's voice came sharply from the open doorway.

Isabel stared at her husband. Never had she seen him look so stern, so determined.

"Oh, yes, yes," she smiled nervously. "I can imagine how I must look! I'll join you in a moment. You'll pardon me, Francis?"

"Of course." He gave Isabel's hand a pat that was meant to reassure her, and the gesture was not lost on any person in the entire room.

Isabel hurried into the hall, conscious of the

silence that was there behind her; conscious of the tongues that were waiting to wag; conscious that all eyes were following her. Swiftly she ran up the stairs and went to her bedroom.

"Joyce, Joyce!" she called.

"Yes, milady." Joyce came hurrying in anxiously.

"I've left the baby on the lawn," Isabel said calmly and was surprised at the quietness of her own voice. "Please go to him."

"Yes, milady." Joyce went bobbing off.

Isabel closed and locked her door and threw herself onto the bed. Tears of anger, indignation, and chagrin welled into her eyes, spilling down over her cheeks. She began to sob. Robert had no right to speak to her in that manner, she cried to herself. She had been doing nothing wrong. And he had reprimanded her as though she had been a naughty child caught in the act of stealing jam.

Of course, she probably shouldn't have run into the drawing-room with her hair and clothes in such a state. But that was no reason for him to humiliate her. What would Francis Levison think? Francis Levison . . . back again, after three years. And here . . . here, at East Lynne. She sat up abruptly. What fun it would be, hearing all the bits of gossip and news he would have to tell. He would know everything that was happening in London.

She mustn't cry, now. It would only make her eyes red. She choked back the sobs. And she wanted to look her best this evening. Wanted to look her best so that Francis should know that she was happy at East Lynne . . . happy with Robert . . . with her baby. Because she was . . . she was, she told herself fiercely. Robert was right. She really should not have run into the drawing-room looking such a fright. After all, she was Robert's wife!

CHAPTER VI

ISABEL had dressed carefully for dinner. Francis Levison shouldn't see that there had been any change in her. She had brought out a dress she had ordered months before, but had scarcely worn, because there had been few occasions upon which to wear it. The soft, sky-blue satin bodice fitted her slender figure perfectly; the wide skirts fell in swelling ripples about her feet; the little sprigs of pink rosebuds that gathered the flounces into drapes were the color of her cheeks. And into the knot of golden hair that lay softly upon the nape of her neck she had woven a little garland of the flowers.

The vicar and his wife had been pressed to stay for dinner in honor of the guest's arrival. The Hares, Sir Richard and Barbara, had been dispatched a hasty note. They had turned up, bringing with them a guest, Sir Tobey Mansfield, a drooping, elderly man with drooping white mustaches, who scarcely uttered a word. Levison's sharp, quick eyes had missed very little as they had gathered about the table. He noted the charming, quiet girl, who was introduced as Barbara, and who seldom spoke; he heard Sir Richard discussing his live stock; listened to the vicar and Cornelia deep in a conversation concerning

68

A Fox Movietone Production.

East Lynne.

ISABEL CONTEMPLATES HER HAPPINESS AS WIFE OF ROBERT CARLYLE AND MISTRESS
OF EAST LYNNE, HIS BEAUTIFUL COUNTRY ESTATE.

the church and parish. But most of all, he had
watched Isabel.

Perhaps the change in her seemed greater because of the three years that had intervened since
their last meeting; perhaps he was more conscious
of all that must have happened than was Isabel
herself. At any rate, he missed the light-hearted
ease, the ready laughter that he had once thought
of as belonging to the girl. Girl . . . she seemed
a girl no longer. She was a woman who had become saddened somehow, had been repressed.
There was little of the spontaneous talk, the
brightness that had once been hers.

Isabel was trying . . . trying hard. But all
the time she was conscious of Cornelia's cold
scrutiny, of her watchful eye, her listening ear.
It was hard to say meaningless little things where
every word was weighed, every syllable counted.
And she felt that Levison noticed all this . . .
noticed it even as he talked to Carlyle of business affairs in London; as he politely asked Barbara questions about the countryside. And it
was with a distinct feeling of relief that she rose
and followed Cornelia into the drawing-room with
Barbara, to be joined shortly afterwards by the
gentlemen.

Now Levison lounged in a corner of the room,
his hands behind his back, surveying the group
and thinking . . . thinking. Carlyle stood before
the fireplace talking to Sir Richard. The vicar
and Sir Tobey had settled to a glass of port and
a game of chess, and both white heads nodded
drowsily before the board. On a Chesterfield

sofa, Cornelia spread her voluminous skirts, Mrs. Hartledge on one side of her, Barbara on the other. Isabel wandered about like a butterfly looking for a flower upon which to alight, and finally seated herself at the piano.

Her fingers ran lightly over the keys and soft little cadences of melody trembled through the room, like an accompaniment to the droning conversation of the women on the Chesterfield, to the harsher voice of Sir Richard, the smooth tones of Carlyle. Droning, buzzing, humming, like sleepy insects and tired birds. Quiet, still and deep. An evening at East Lynne. Levison frowned. It wasn't any wonder . . . wasn't any wonder, he said over and over again to himself.

His eyes met Isabel's. She smiled and went on with her playing. Not a sign of any sort did she give.

"I tell you, there's been too much rain this summer," Sir Richard's voice overcame all other sounds. "Bad for the hay . . . bad for the hay!" He shook his head. "Bad for the cattle. All the tenants are complaining."

Carlyle nodded. "It's the same everywhere in the country," he agreed. "No doubt they'll blame it on the conservative party, as usual."

Both voices rose in laughter at this sally. Quite unfunny, Levison was thinking. The weather . . . the conservative party . . . the cattle . . . it all seemed so futile to him.

"Speaking of cattle, are you showing at the fair this year?" Carlyle was asking.

"Wouldn't miss it, my boy, wouldn't miss it!"

Sir Richard said heavily. "I've got three fine heifers, and one of 'em's going to take that blue ribbon. Are you showing?"

"Perhaps," Carlyle nodded.

So this was what happened in East Lynne, Levison told himself. This was what Isabel had, evening after evening, day after day. This was the reason that her friends had fallen off, one by one, until there were no more week-ends at East Lynne, no more parties, no more balls. To give a ball in this atmosphere . . . Levison shuddered. Carlyle himself was a good sort, but this Miss Cornelia. He turned his attention to the Chesterfield.

"I visited poor Mrs. Hanson to-day," he could hear Barbara saying. "She's suffering terribly from a cold."

"My dear!" Mrs. Hartledge leaned forward and put her hand on Barbara's arm as though the very life of Mrs. Hanson depended upon her words. "There's only one cure for a cold in the head. You must tell the good soul to take her red flannel petticoat and tie it crosswise over her head."

"And drink a basin of onion gruel," Cornelia added.

Levison took a deep breath and raised his eyes ceilingward. Worse . . . worse . . . worse than he had imagined! He shook his head. Frankly, he decided, he was bored, quite unutterably bored. What a life to lead, especially after one had known gayety and gladness and beauty. This was all so drab, so narrow, so petty.

"Your move!" The voice of Sir Tobey made him turn his head.

Drowsily the vicar opened his eyes and studied the board. Now it was Sir Tobey's chance for a little nap. He took a sip of port, leaned back and closed his eyes.

Levison felt Isabel's gaze upon him. He realized that she had been watching him for a moment, and he prayed fervently that she could not read his thoughts. But he noted that she smiled in a sympathetic way, a knowing way, as though she had understood what was passing in his mind. And even so, why shouldn't she understand? She belonged to his sort of people. Surely she could realize to some extent his feelings.

The music trailed off slowly and Isabel rose. She came across the room, and stood before Levison, smiling.

"I know you're dying to smoke," she said softly. "Why don't you come out on the balcony?"

"Thank you." Levison sighed a deep sigh of relief. "You've rescued me from an early grave."

He crossed the room behind her and stepped out through the opened doors into the moonlight night. He took a cigar from his pocket, lighted it carefully, and sent a long curl of white smoke drifting lazily out into the darkness. The new silver moon made patches of bright light on the lawn, gleaming on the trees and bushes. The air was soft and still. Scarcely a leaf stirred.

The faint, sweet scent of climbing roses mingled with the fragrance of the tobacco.

Isabel seated herself upon the wide balustrade and stared out across the park. The chirping of the crickets sounded louder as the drone of voices in the room blended into murmurs and mumblings. A frog croaked, a hoarse, rasping croak. She felt Levison's eyes looking at her, studying her.

"I hope the excitement of this evening won't be too much for you," she said at last. There was a slight tinge of sarcasm in her voice.

Levison laughed lightly. "It is rather gay and abandoned, isn't it?" He tried to keep any feeling out of his words. He didn't want to hurt her, to make her uncomfortable.

"Oh, this is a really spirited evening," she contradicted, and still the sarcasm was there. "Especially in contrast to some of them. But then . . ." She shrugged her bare shoulders. The moonlight made her neck and arms like alabaster.

She was beautiful, Levison told himself. As beautiful as ever. There was almost no change in her face. But he had never before heard sarcasm in her voice.

"Your husband tells me you like the country," he said suddenly. "We were talking of you this afternoon."

"Oh, I don't mind it," she returned, but the words didn't ring true. "I've grown quite accustomed to the quietude of East Lynne. I have

my baby, you know. And he keeps me rather
busy. He's such a darling. You must see him to-
morrow.''

"I'd like to."

There was a slight pause. "I suppose, too,
some of your friends run down from London oc-
casionally,'' Levison broke the silence.

Isabel frowned. "Well, at first they did. And
then, one by one. . . .'' She looked away as
though hesitating to continue in her confession.
Then her words came in a rush. "One by one
they dropped away. I tried to entertain. I
wanted to give dinners and balls. But even the
young people from around here don't come to
East Lynne any more. I suppose, though, that's
usually the case.''

Levison glanced over his shoulder into the
drawing-room. Carlyle still talked intermittently with Sir Richard, who teetered back and
forth on his heels and now and again yawned
openly. The vicar and Sir Tobey were both nodding over the chessboard. Cornelia, Barbara, and
Mrs. Hartledge still seemed able to find matters
to discuss which were worthy of their interest.
Barbara, he noted, looked more animated than
she had at dinner.

"I think I understand,'' Levison nodded.

"Oh, but after all, you know there really is
a great deal to do here,'' Isabel went on hastily.
Somehow, she felt that she had revealed too
much. He mustn't see that she was unhappy, that
her once full life was almost empty save for her
child. "We have fairs and charity bazaars, and

there are some dances. . . ." Her voice trailed
off. "But tell me about yourself. What have
you been doing these last three years? It has
been three years, hasn't it?"

"Yes, it's been three years, Isabel. Does it
seem as long as that to you? It seems three
thousand years to me . . . since I felt England,"
he added quickly. "It's three years ago this
month."

"But where have you been? What have you
seen?"

"I've been almost everywhere . . . seen almost everything," Levison laughed. "But, like
everything else, the diplomatic service becomes
mere routine. I may be in the Balkans one month,
and in Russia the next. I've spent quite a bit of
time in Berlin and Budapesth, and some in Paris.
I've been to Turkey, Greece . . . all over the
Continent."

Isabel sighed pensively. "That makes for variety, at least."

"Variety? Oh, I don't know." Levison raised
his eyebrows quizzically. "It's interesting at
first, seeing strange places, getting to know
strange peoples. But after a while one begins
to long a little for familiar things, familiar language, familiar faces. You have a desire to come
back to roast beef and Yorkshire pudding. You
can't live forever on *Coupe de fruit de Champagne.*"

"And you can't live forever on roast beef and
pudding," Isabel parried, and then wished she
hadn't said that. "At any rate," she hurried on,

"your days are not the same. You see different places, meet different people, people who are interesting, who do things."

"I thought you said you liked the country," Levison returned, and there was a funny little smile about the corners of his mouth.

"I do . . . of course, I do," Isabel protested a little too vigorously. "But it's nice to hear of things that are happening in the outside world, too. And you must have had romance. . . ."

"Romance? What do you mean?"

"Oh, come now," Isabel teased. "Surely you haven't drifted from one capital to another without having some romantic adventures. You've fallen in love a thousand times, I'll wager, if you'll only confess it."

"I've never fallen out of love," Levison said abruptly.

Isabel started. She could feel her whole body growing rigid, tense. Her eyes met Levison's for the briefest space of time and then the long lashes veiled them. She felt frightened. She mustn't allow Francis to say things of that sort. She knew what he meant. It was so obvious. But she mustn't . . . she mustn't listen to him. It seemed an eternity before she could force the sounds from her lips, although it was only the matter of a fleeting moment.

"Will you be in England long?" She spoke at random, choosing the only question she could think of on the spur of the moment. But it didn't matter. Anything, to change the subject.

As though bowing to her will, Levison answered quietly. "No longer than it takes to settle my uncle's estate. Possibly a few weeks. Your husband knows the business angle of it more thoroughly than I do."

"Then why must you go back to London on Monday? Stay here for a few days. We'd be delighted to have you."

"That's very kind of you, Isabel. It was kind of your husband to invite me here in the first place. I'd like to stay, but I'm afraid it would be an imposition."

"That's utter nonsense," Isabel shook her head. "It's been years since we've seen each other. I want to hear more about you . . . I want to hear the news of London. We have so few visitors. Surely, you'll stay? Oh, Robert!"

"Here you are!" Carlyle appeared in the doorway, standing there for a moment, and then stepped out onto the balcony.

"Will you join me?" Levison held out a cigar.

"Thank you, no," Carlyle refused.

"I'm trying to persuade Francis to remain for a few days," Isabel turned to her husband. "Perhaps you can help."

"Oh, but you must stay," Carlyle turned to his guest. "Of course, we can't offer very much entertainment, I'm afraid, but there's some very good fishing, plenty of horses, and dogs. And some beautiful walks."

"But, my dear," Isabel turned impulsively to her husband. "You've forgotten the Hunt Ball.

It's next Tuesday. The invitations are out, and I don't think Cornelia has sent regrets . . . yet. Francis could go as our guest"

"That sounds interesting," Levison agreed, more because he noted Isabel's evident delight at the mention of the ball than anything else.

"I'm sorry, dear," Carlyle said with an air of finality. "But in the excitement of having Levison with us, I forgot to tell you. I have to be in London on Tuesday trying a case in chancery."

"Oh, but can't you possibly postpone it, Robert?" Isabel's brows puckered and her mouth pouted. Her eyes looked like a great collie dog's begging for a morsel. "Can't one of your associates try it for you?"

"I said, my dear," Robert repeated, "it was a case in chancery. No one can handle that but myself."

"Oh!" There was hurt and pain in Isabel's cry. Something like the whimpering of a whipped animal.

Levison longed to take the girl in his arms and comfort her. But he held steadily to his glowing cigar and tried not to see the tears that he felt were rising in her eyes.

"Will you excuse me, please?" In a second Isabel had turned and vanished.

Carlyle frowned. How like Isabel to run off that way. She was always doing something without thought or reason. A little disappointment and she behaved like a baby. She gave way to her emotions entirely too easily. He felt a little ashamed that Levison should see his, Carlyle's, wife acting so childishly.

"It's too bad that I must disappoint her," Carlyle said apologetically as though trying to excuse Isabel's conduct. "It's the one event of the year she looks forward to. But what can I do? It's vitally important that I try that case on Tuesday."

"If I might make a suggestion," Levison began. "Your sister undoubtedly would like to go. I'd be very glad to stay on here and to escort them both to the ball. Perhaps that might take off a little of the edge of disappointment."

"That's a capital idea," Carlyle exclaimed heartily. "Cornelia ordinarily doesn't care for that sort of thing. She's not very much interested in balls. But I'm certain I can persuade her to go."

Levison puffed in silence at his cigar. He glanced into the drawing-room and saw that Isabel had already disappeared, her figure just dimly visible in the hall beyond. She was turning toward the stairs. Well, perhaps this might give her a little happiness.

Isabel, looking neither to right nor to left, rushed up the stairs and to her room. She dabbed at her eyes with her lace handkerchief. It was cruel . . . cruel of Robert. Not to have told her until this evening. And she had been hoping and looking forward to this ball for such a long time. She did want to go. It was one of the few events of the entire year, one of the few times when she saw some of her old friends.

"Oh, milady, is something wrong?" Joyce came into the room, her eyes wide.

"No, Joyce, no." Isabel tried to control her quavering voice. "What do you want?"

Joyce noted the sign of tears, and her heart went out to her mistress. "I . . . I heard you come to your room, milady. I thought perhaps you wanted me."

"No, I don't need you, Joyce. You may go."

"Very well, milady. But if your ladyship has time, perhaps you wouldn't mind looking in the nursery. I can't get Master William to go to sleep somehow."

Isabel sighed. "I'll go to him now." She hurried from the room.

Behind her marched Joyce, muttering uncomplimentary remarks concerning Miss Cornelia and her "doin's."

As Isabel opened the nursery door a gurgle of laughter reached her ears. William was standing at the foot of his crib, holding onto the railing, and dancing up and down.

"You're a bad boy!" Isabel went to the child, holding out her arms. "Aren't you a bad boy?" But her voice was full of love, rather than chiding.

The child shook his curly head, and then put his arms about his mother's neck.

"Now, you lie down and go to sleep," Isabel commanded, placing the baby in the crib. "And shut 'em eyes . . . shut 'em tight." She drew the covers up about the chubby neck. "And handies under the covers!" She tucked in a pink hand. Then she seated herself by the crib, bending over the child.

She began to hum a fragment of a song. Bits of the words drifted out over the sleepy room.

"When other lips and other hearts . . .
    Their tales of love shall tell . . ."

She watched the child sinking rapidly into dreamland under the spell of her soft voice. She leaned closer and kissed the pink fingers that curled about the blanket; laid her face gently against the soft baby cheek. Forgotten were the scoldings of the day, forgotten the disappointment of the evening, forgotten everything save the little form that lay there quietly, blinking blue eyes up at her until they went shut for the night.

CHAPTER VII

ISABEL stood before the pier glass, turning this way and that, surveying herself with critical approval. To-night was the Hunt Ball. To-night she was going to dance . . . and dance . . . and talk nonsense . . . and be thoroughly and delightfully happy once again. She felt a little pang of regret that Robert shouldn't see her looking so resplendent; a little pang of regret that she would not waltz the last, lingering waltz with him. But Robert was always so busy. If he were accompanying her, they'd probably leave long before the last waltz, so that he might not be tired for the following day.

Anyhow, it was nice to be going somewhere, and Cornelia had been a perfect dear to agree to attend the ball. Cornelia didn't care for dancing and the new waltzes caused her to raise shocked hands in the air. But if Cornelia didn't go, Isabel couldn't go. It wouldn't be exactly proper for Robert Carlyle's wife to attend the Hunt Ball without her husband and in the company of another man unless she had a duenna of sorts with her. And certainly Cornelia was more than a duenna of sorts; she was a chaperone made to order. No breath of scandal, no hint of gossip could fly about making trouble if Cornelia lent her approval to the plan.

Isabel clasped her hands together and turned once more to survey the short train that Joyce was so carefully draping. The new dress was perfect, she thought. The white petticoat of tulle with silver stripes glimmered through the over-skirt composed of alternate bands of tulle and white satin. Little garlands of pink and blue roses looped up the draperies, and tiny silver stars sewn over the wide skirt and bodice showed bright in the flickering candlelight.

"Oh, Joyce," Isabel exclaimed for perhaps the tenth time in as many minutes. "You will promise to keep an eye on Master William, won't you? Don't let anything happen to him."

"Don't you worry about him, milady. You just enjoy yourself." Joyce smiled up at her mistress, as happy in the prospect of the other's good time as though she were going to the ball herself.

"And be sure to see that he stays asleep. I'll just take a peep at him before I go." It was so seldom that Isabel left the child that he occupied a good share of her thoughts, full as they were of the prospect of the evening's entertainment.

"Now, milady," Joyce soothed. "He's going to be all right with his old nurse. I'll take care of him. Oh, your ladyship'll have such a good time," she sighed. "Every dance taken . . . there won't be a more beautiful lady there to-night than your ladyship!"

"Oh, Joyce, Joyce," Isabel laughed. "You do spoil me. But I know I'm going to have a good

time. There, now, you may go. And please look
in at Master William."

"Yes, milady." Joyce rose from her knees and
proudly surveyed her mistress. "I'll go right
away." She hurried from the room.

Isabel drew up a chair before her dressing
table, seated herself, and prepared to put the
finishing touches to her toilet. She patted her
cheeks a little to increase their pinkness, and
ran her tongue over her lips to bring out their
natural redness. Carefully she smoothed rice
paper over her nose and chin and forehead to
remove any little vestige of "shine" that might
linger there. Her skin was fair, and white, and
smooth, and she told herself that she was glad
she didn't have to use that liquid "enamel" as
so many women did.

She patted into place the wavy hair that had
been brushed until it shone like gold; patted the
curls that fell softly against the curves of her
neck. Then she took a strand of pink and blue
satin twisted together, twined it about her head,
and secured the ribbon with a tiny diamond ai-
grette. Opening her jewel box she drew forth
the great diamond pendant and the diamond earrings that had been her mother's. She fastened
the earrings to the golden loops in her ears and
clasped the pendant about her neck.

Then Isabel rose, a thing of gold and silver,
of glittering, shimmering beauty. As she gazed
once more at her reflection in the pier glass she
wanted to dance. She felt so happy, so gay. She
took a great feather fan from its box and opened

it out, fluttering it back and forth. Once again she fancied herself back in London, at Lady Townsend's, ready for a ball. Why, it was years and years and years and years since she had felt this way, she told herself breathlessly.

In the midst of a little *pas seul* the door opened abruptly. Cornelia stood in the opening, a drab brown dressing gown clutched about her. Isabel stopped short; stared at the grim apparition in bewilderment.

"Why, Cornelia, you're not dressed yet," she gasped.

Cornelia shook her head. "I've a violent headache. I'm afraid we shan't be able to go to the ball."

"Not go to the ball?" Isabel caught her breath. Her mouth opened, her forehead wrinkled in stunned bewilderment. "Not go to the ball," she repeated slowly.

"No, I'm sorry. I know how you've looked forward to this, but I'm entirely too ill," she answered flatly.

"Oh, but please!" Isabel was trying to be solicitous, striving to hide the shock, the hurt, the disappointment she felt. "Let me try to do something for you," she begged. "Isn't there something you can take? Perhaps a bromide . . ."

"They never do me any good. Nothing does me any good," Cornelia refused firmly. "I must go right to bed."

"But . . . but, Cornelia," Isabel faltered. "Think of Mr. Levison. He'll be so disappointed.

He stayed over just for this ball, so that we could go. And we can't go without you. Robert only consented because you promised to chaperone.''

"I did not promise him I wouldn't have a headache," Cornelia averred sternly.

And without another word she turned and left the room, closing the door behind her.

Isabel stared at the closed door until she could feel the misty tears clouding her eyes. Not go to the ball! And after she had so looked forward to going, had been so happy in planning for it. Her first ball in almost a year. And she had so few opportunities, so few chances to snatch a little pleasure. Why . . . why . . . why did Cornelia have to be ill on just this evening! Why did Cornelia have to have a headache!

She couldn't go without Cornelia, Isabel told herself. What would people say? What would they think? Of course, all the country round knew that Francis Levison was the house guest of the Carlyles. But that wouldn't stop jealous, catty tongues from wagging. Ladies did not do such things, not the wives of men like Robert Carlyle. There were some women in London who might do that sort of thing, but their reputations were already the property of the scandalmongers. Why, oh why, did Cornelia have to have a headache?

Listlessly, Isabel walked to her dressing table and dropped her fan on top of it. Slowly she sat down and stared at herself. Just a moment ago she had been reveling in the thoughts of the delights the evening would bring. Now, it was

gone . . . all gone. With heavy fingers she
reached around and began to unclasp the neck-
lace about her throat. A tear spilled over an
eyelid and ran down one pale cheek. Why did
Cornelia have to have a headache this evening?

Cornelia always seemed to have a headache
when . . . when . . . Isabel's pretty mouth drew
into a thin line. Cornelia always had a headache
when she didn't want to do something. That
was it! Might just as well say it. Cornelia
hadn't wanted to go to the ball. She didn't want
Isabel to go to the ball . . . didn't want to do
anything that might give her a little happiness.
It was Cornelia . . . always Cornelia, who interfered.

Cornelia had brought that headache upon herself, if headache she did have, Isabel reflected
bitterly. More than likely it was another excuse.
Cornelia resented anyone having any pleasure.
She had determined that Isabel should not go
to the ball. And she had found the means to
keep her at home. Well, she wouldn't keep her
at home! She, Isabel, would go to the ball!

Her fingers trembling, Isabel picked up the diamond pendant and clasped it again about her
neck. She'd go to the ball in spite of Cornelia.
It wasn't fair to try to keep her sitting at home
day in and day out. If Cornelia had really been
ill, that might have been a different matter. But
she was convinced that her sister-in-law was
shamming shamelessly. It wasn't the first time
that such a thing had happened.

Isabel wiped her eyes carefully and patted them

with a thin film of rice power to hide the traces
of tears. With something of the spirit of the
Lady Isabel Vane of old she rushed to the bed
and seized the white ermine jacket that Joyce
had so carefully laid out for her. She thrust her
arms into the puffy sleeves and drew the black-
tailed collar about her throat. She'd go to the
ball. She wasn't doing anything actually wrong.
Cornelia shouldn't keep her at home. She hurried out into the corridor and made her way down
to the hall where Levison waited for her.

As she reached the bottom steps her feet faltered. Perhaps she shouldn't go through with
this. Perhaps . . .

"How lovely you look!" The sincerity of
Levison's tone, the frank look of admiration in
his eyes, held Isabel spellbound.

She was a girl again. She was starting out
to her first ball. Her heart thumped with excitement, her cheeks glowed with the thrill of
a true compliment. It was glorious to have someone appreciate you and to say so. And Francis
. . . Francis looked so straight, and tall, in his
formal black and white evening dress, the frills
on his shirt front soft and gleaming in the candlelight.

"You're perfectly beautiful!" He took her
hand and led her down the last two steps.

They stood in the hall, the soft, mellow light
all about them.

"Oh, Francis," Isabel began. "Cornelia's ill.
She's got a headache. But I don't think she's
really got a headache at all. She doesn't want

me to go to the ball and she's using that as an excuse. But I want to go . . . I do want to go." Her words tumbled out haphazardly.

"If you want to go, I'll take you," Levison said quietly.

"Upstairs," Isabel went on as though she hadn't heard the man's remark, "I tried to think. At first I felt that I shouldn't go at all. If Cornelia were really ill, I should stay at home. But she's not! She's not! She's only making a pretense. It's not wrong for us to go alone. There's nothing harmful in it. And I've been so anxious . . ."

"Why, of course, there's no reason why we shouldn't go to the ball, Isabel." Levison patted the girl's hand that clung to his coat sleeve. "I'll do whatever you like . . . whatever you think best. I'd be very disappointed if we didn't go, but you mustn't allow any thought of my feelings to color your decision."

"That's very kind of you, Francis." Isabel's head rose higher and her chin took on a determined line. "We'll go."

Levison stopped to take his hat from the table, swung his long, satin-lined opera cape over his shoulders, and offered his arm to Isabel. Together they went out into the soft, June night where the carriage waited for them.

Neither of the two said very much as the high-stepping horses pranced along the open road. The moonlight filtered through the leafy branches of the great trees and made patches of shimmering light on the dirt highway. Hedges of wild,

pale pink roses lay like fairies' shrouds over the
greenery. The air was sweet with the scents of
a summer night.

Levison watched the girl beside him, saw her
staring straight ahead, thoughtful, her face mo-
bile in the light and shadow. Her features were
beautiful. A tender, lovely face, yet with all its
tenderness, it had strength and something of re-
lentless purpose about it. If only matters had
been otherwise three years ago. If only he could
have made his decisions, everything might
have been different. But he couldn't, and
now he must sit in silence and watch . . . and
wait.

Through the trees came long beams of bright,
yellow light, shining from the open doors and
windows of an ancient castle. As the carriage
drew nearer the strains of music drifted out to
meet it. The sound of chattering, laughing voices
filled the air. The horses stopped before a doorway over which burned a big gas lamp. The
groom jumped down from the box. A butler
stood to one side, ushering in the guests.

There were introductions, and bows, and hand-
shakings, and then Isabel felt herself being drawn
onto the dance floor. She was in Levison's arms.
The lively rhythm of a polka made her feet light
as thistledown. She was floating on pink clouds.
It was all like a delicious dream, and she wished
that it could go on and on, and that she would
never waken.

With no assistance from Levison her dance
program was filled; even all the "extras" and

encores were taken. She was in the midst of a
group of men one moment; the next she was
whirling about on the floor. Her low, clear
laughter rang out; her words fell on eagerly
attentive ears. Her favors were sought as though
she were once again the Lady Isabel Vane attending a ball in Mayfair.

The light, the color, the gayety went to her
head like sparkling wine. It was good . . . good
. . . good to be happy and free; to forget, even
for a brief instant, the heart hurts of East Lynne;
good to get away from the depressing atmosphere
that seemed to emanate from Cornelia's swishing
skirts. It was good to be young, and to float on
air, and to laugh, and talk and dance.

So engrossed was Isabel in her new-found happiness that she did not see the raised eyebrows
of many of the elderly dowagers settled in the
gilt chairs that lined the walls of the ballroom;
she did not hear the little, whispered questions
and comments of some of her own neighbors. She
was still laughing and chattering when Levison
found her, the center of a group of men gathered
on a balcony, to take her out onto the floor for
the last waltz.

And then they were in the carriage again, wend-
ing their way homeward. Isabel settled more
deeply against the cushioned seat and snuggled
down into her coat. She half closed her eyes,
as though to see once more in retrospect the vision
of the ballroom, the dancers, the lights, the color.
A little smile played about the corners of her
mouth; a happy, contented smile.

"Tired?" Levison spoke at last, breaking into her reverie.

Isabel opened her eyes, looked up at the man beside her and smiled. "Tired?" she repeated, shaking her head. "Oh, no. But still bewitched . . . enchanted! Do you know, as I was dancing, time began to turn back very gradually and I was in Mayfair again. It was just as though everything had been transported back . . . back. . . ." Her voice trailed off dreamily.

"Dancing in a dream!" Levison said softly.

"Yes, that's it!" Isabel smiled again, her eyes kindling with light. "Dancing in a dream! A beautiful dream. There were moments when I felt that it was a dream, and then, I wanted to sleep . . . and just stay asleep."

"I felt it, too. It was wonderful, dancing with you again. Time turned back for me, as it did for you. I remembered all the times we had danced together; all those last waltzes of ours." He paused, sighing. Then: "But such moments are not for me." And his voice was sad.

Isabel stirred slightly as though vaguely conscious of something from the outside world intruding upon her innermost thought.

"Why?" she asked lazily.

"Because of the bitterness of the awakening."

"I'm grateful for anything," she said softly.

They fell silent again, as though words grated harshly on the quiet night. A still, hushed solemnity descended about them. All the tranquil beauty of a golden moon wrapped them in a cloak of silence. No leaf stirred. No bird called out. They might have been driving up and up into the azure blue, sailing over enchanted islands.

"You know, as I watched you to-night, I found I couldn't take my eyes off you," Levison said at last. "I've never seen such a change in anyone."

Isabel's laugh rang out. "Really? How do you mean?"

"It was like seeing a miracle," Levison explained. "A flower that had drooped come to life and bloom again. The first day I arrived at East Lynne you were so different from the way I had remembered you. You looked so . . . so stifled, so drooping. And then, to-night, when you came down the stairs you were lovely. But when I watched you dancing there, you were radiant."

"Gracious! Have I really changed so much?" Still dreamily Isabel asked the question. It didn't seem to matter whether she had changed, or hadn't, at this moment. Everything was sublime. She wanted to reach out her arms and hold the night close . . . close to her breast; to keep it forever.

"You have changed, Isabel. When I first met you, I realized that you were lovely . . . beautiful! But to-night! To-night, you were more beautiful than I've ever seen you before."

Isabel looked up startled, a puzzled frown on her face.

"I hope I haven't offended you," Levison apologized.

Isabel laughed. "Offended me? Mercy, no. Pray keep on talking."

"I would," and Levison laughed too, "but I believe we're home."

The carriage drew up before the main doorway of East Lynne.

CHAPTER VIII

For a few silent moments they stood before the heavy, iron-hinged door, Lady Isabel and Francis Levison, lost in the beauty of the summer night. It seemed to both of them that once they entered the house the magic spell which had slowly been woven about them would vanish into thin air. East Lynne, with all its ancient beauty, its memories, was not conducive to dreams. Once within the still, dark hall, reality would settle over them like a pall. But neither put such thoughts into words. They were such strange, light, little thoughts that they could scarcely be revealed in words.

As they waited there came a slight creaking of bolts and the door swung noiselessly on its hinges. There was a small crack, through which a glimpse of Joyce's capped head was vouchsafed them. Then the crack became wider.

"Oh, Joyce!" Isabel stepped into the hall, Levison behind her. "Thank you for waiting up for me. Is Master William all right?"

"Quite all right, milady," Joyce answered in a whisper. She drew her mistress aside, still speaking in a low tone of voice. "I didn't know how your ladyship was goin' to get in, what with the door barred an' all. So I stopped down here.

I left the candles burnin' in the drawin'-room, an' a lamp there.''

"Thank you, Joyce. Don't wait any longer for me. I shan't need you any more to-night. And it's late now.''

"Yes, milady.'' With a little bob of her head Joyce silently disappeared.

Isabel led the way into the drawing-room where the candles still flickered in their sockets, sending wavering shadows over the heavy, carved walnut furniture. Not a sound, not even a rustle of a curtain disturbed the ghostly stillness. It was like a world apart, after the brilliance of light and music, the clatter of voices, the revelry of the earlier evening.

Levison threw off his cape, flung it over the back of a chair, and laid his hat on the center table. "Well, Isabel,'' he said gently, "did you enjoy the ball?''

"Oh, it was glorious . . . glorious!'' Once more her eyes seemed to be looking into the far, far distance; once more the corners of her lips dimpled in happy reminiscence.

"Allow me.'' Levison began to remove Isabel's wrap, his fingers lingering caressingly on the soft, white fur, warm from its contact with arms and shoulders. A faint, sweet perfume clung about the wrap; the same perfume that had drifted gently about his face when he had danced with Isabel; a subtle, compelling perfume, yet light and fresh as the smell of new violets and damp leaf mold.

"You know, Isabel,'' he said as she took the

jacket from him, "you've matured . . . you've
become a woman. At first it seemed as though I
were watching you change back into the girl you
were. But it isn't that. You're much deeper,
much stronger, much lovelier than ever before.
You're the loveliest woman I've ever seen."

Isabel laughed. "Really?" She placed the fur
jacket over the arm of a wing chair. "And after
all your adventures with Continental beauties?"

"After all my adventures with Continental
beauties," Levison repeated seriously, "if you
will insist that I've had adventures. Which I
haven't. But after all my wanderings, after all
the women I've met, I still think you're the
loveliest."

"I shan't listen to another word!" Isabel's
voice was light and bantering. "You're out-
rageously wicked!"

"You've no idea how hard I've struggled to
give that impression," he retorted quickly.

His voice was as light, as bantering, as Isabel's
own. But beneath the airy badinage ran an un-
dercurrent of serious meaning. It was delicately
veiled, that seriousness, but Levison knew that it
was there; knew he meant what he had said, and
yet he would scarcely admit it, even to himself.
He knew that there were a great many things he
wanted to say to this "loveliest of women," and
he mustn't . . . he mustn't, he told himself
fiercely.

He realized now, as never before, that he really
loved Isabel. When he had known her during
those earlier years, he had had a great affection

for her, an admiration for her youthful beauty.
He had, he admitted, been in love with her. But
he had never put his love into words. He hadn't
spoken because he realized that his career, such
as it was, was better made alone until he had become established. He hadn't wanted the respon-
sibilities of a wife and a home. Selfishness?
Yes, he knew that there was a certain amount of
selfishness in his attitude.

But this evening as he had watched this beautiful woman, saw her in the arms of other men;
gazed upon the full power of her radiant, matured splendor, he knew that he loved her as
he would never love anyone else. And yet, how
could he speak? She was another man's wife.
She had her child, her home. He mustn't say
anything that would disrupt her life. If he had
been a fool, he told himself bitterly, he must pay
for his foolishness.

"Don't tell me it was a struggle!" Isabel's
laughter brought his wandering thoughts back to
the drawing-room of East Lynne. "I have never
seen anyone as popular as you were this evening."

"I? Popular?"

And Levison, too, laughed. "Why, it was all
I could manage to arrange three dances with you.
I did my best, but your admirers were always
at your heels. I spent my evening among the
dowagers. When they've turned sixty, they're
at least appreciative of attention."

"And how long have you been a philanthropist?
Playing the gay cavalier to your elders! That

doesn't sound like the Francis Levison I knew.
Oh, no!" She wagged a flippant finger at the
man. "I very much doubt the truth of that statement."

"Not really! I must say, however, regardless
of my darling dowagers, the young men seem to
like you," he persisted. "The whole thing ap-
pears to be out of balance."

"Something for a diplomat to adjust," Isabel
suggested. "Oh, I'm sorry. There's brandy
here, if you like." She gestured toward the
decanter, set about with glasses on a gate-leg table
which Joyce had thoughtfully arranged beside
the Chesterfield.

"Thanks." Levison took the glass stopper
from the decanter and slowly poured out some
of the mellow, golden-brown liquid into a fragile
glass. It made a gurgling, melodious sound. He
held the glass cupped between the palms of his
hands, warming it.

Isabel walked over to the long windows, pulled
back the draperies, unloosed the catches, and
threw open the casements. The moonlight
streamed in upon her, lighting up her face, playing upon the gold in her hair. She took a deep
breath, inhaling the fresh, night air. The thrum-
ming of insects, the chirping of crickets, broken
intermittently by the deep basso of a frog, sounded
loud and clear in the midst of the stillness.

Once again she could see the balconies and
terraces, bright in the yellow, mellow gas light;
hear the orchestra, the violins and deeper cellos
singing as the whirling figures moved in rhythm

about the great ballroom; feel the warmth of people around her, the pressure of a hand against
hers, an arm encircling her waist in the dance.
Her fingers interlaced, held to each other tightly,
as though they would grasp this one evening and
hold it forever.

"What a glorious night!" Isabel spoke softly,
almost to herself. Then, as though suddenly conscious of another's presence, she turned her head,
smiling at Levison. "Do come and look at it.
Isn't it exquisite?"

Levison set his untouched glass of brandy back
on the table and went to the windows.

"It is magnificent," he said quietly. "A night
for dreams. It's all a dream!"

"No! No! I won't have it that way!" Isabel
returned passionately. "It's not a dream at all!
It's real. I'm in London again." Her eyes half
closed as she wove her vision. "It's a warm,
April night . . . gossiping and laughing in the
moonlight. Goodness me! What have I to do
to-morrow? There's a luncheon at Lady Townsend's . . . a reception later at Lord Trevor's.
Perhaps I shall see Francis Levison . . . the fascinating Francis Levison. I hope so . . ." Her
voice trailed off.

"Charming, my dear. Perfectly charming,"
Levison applauded.

Together they stared out over the park. The
old chestnut trees with their white torches of
blossoms gleamed silver in the night. Tiny petals
trembled and went fluttering to the ground like
snow. Faint perfume of clover and meadowsweet

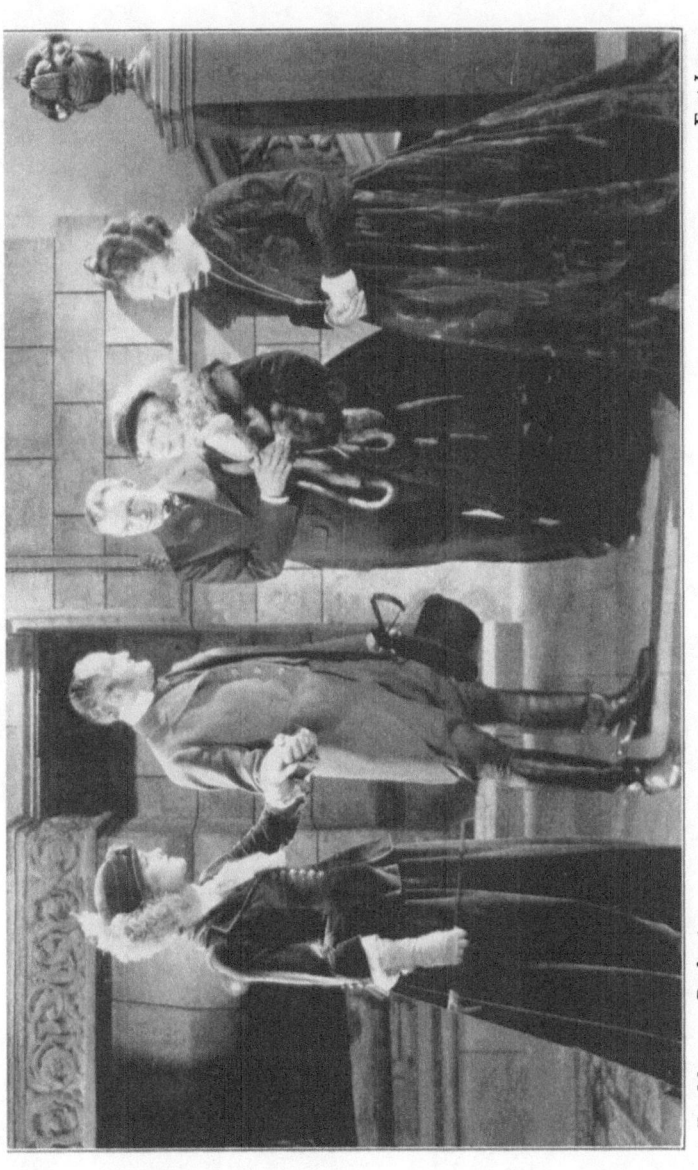

A Fox Movietone Production. *East Lynne.*
SIR RICHARD HALE AND HIS DAUGHTER HAVE RIDDEN OVER TO EAST LYNNE TO MEET
THE BRIDE OF ITS OWNER, ROBERT CARLYLE.

was wafted gently from the fields, scenting the air
with sweetness.

"You know," Levison said suddenly, "it re-
minds me of a night at Richmond three years
ago" He turned to look at the woman beside
him. "I wonder if you remember?" he questioned
softly.

Isabel hesitated, then nodded. "Yes, I remember," she answered thoughtfully.

"I wonder if you remember what you told me
that night?" Levison continued. "That you were
to be married."

Married! That was the evening she had told
Francis that she was to marry Robert Carlyle.
How long ago that seemed, Isabel reflected. It
all came back to her now with a swift rush of
feeling. There had been a dinner, and after the
dinner she had wandered into the conservatory
with Francis. They had sat on a wide bench, the
windows all opened to the night and the fresh
spring odors drifting lazily across their faces.

Francis had been so attentive that evening.
And her engagement to Robert hadn't yet been
announced. She remembered how she had lingered over the idea of telling Francis the news.
After all, she had decided, it was only fair that
he should know. They had been very good friends
. . . there were even times when she felt that his
interest might be just a little more than friendly.
Yes, she should tell him.

She remembered that he had taken her hand
. . . that was before she had mentioned her engagement. He had talked a lot of silly nonsense

. . . said a lot of pretty things. And then, suddenly he had become more serious. That was
always Francis' way. She had realized the change
almost immediately. His face had come close to
hers. She could still feel his lips brushing her
hair.

"I'm going to be married to Robert Carlyle,"
she had told him simply.

Then he had sat there beside her, for a long
time, saying nothing. Just sitting and thinking.
She didn't know exactly what she had expected
him to say, but she hadn't expected this silence.
It had made her uneasy, a little nervous. She
recalled that she had felt glad when Lady Townsend had wandered into the conservatory and
broken the tension with some slight remark.

"I remember," she repeated, very slowly. "I
remember . . . that you said nothing."

"Perhaps the bitterest tragedies of our lives
arise from words unspoken." The distress in
Levison's voice made Isabel look at the man beside her.

"I've thought of that night again and again,"
he went on. "I've lived it over a thousand times.
Isabel, the most pathetic figure in life is the man
who places his career above the woman he loves."

She raised her hand as though to silence him.

"No! I must explain!" He disregarded her,
his words coming quickly. "That same pathetic
figure was fool enough to believe that love could
come into his heart and mean nothing . . . suf-
ficiently conceited to think that he could come back
and casually meet the woman he loves, and as

casually say good-by. But Isabel, I can't! Isabel . . . I . . ."

Isabel could feel her fingers locking and unlocking. Her hands were like ice. Her heart was hammering until it seemed to be rising to suffocate her, to choke her. She knew that the man at her side was leaning toward her; knew that his hands were groping for hers; knew that his breath was hot against her face. And yet she could make no movement.

"But I never dreamed . . ." she managed to gasp, somehow.

And then came a flow of words that beat upon her brain, stormed in her ears.

"How could you? I never intended that you should. I thought I could ignore my feelings . . . crush them . . . forget them. I tried . . . tried all these three years. But wherever I went, whatever I did, I could still see you, remember you. When I danced with other women, it was you I was holding in my arms. When I kissed another woman, it was your face that came before my eyes. Don't you understand, my dear? Oh, don't you understand? I love you . . . love you more than anyone else in the world!"

Suddenly she was in his arms. His lips were pressed against hers, crushing them; against her eyes, her cheeks, the warm hollows of her neck. She was drowning; the roar of the sea resounded in her ears; the waves covered her, taking her breath. She was sinking, sinking, into a black oblivion. Her body trembled, quivered, lay still and quiet. And then the waves parted.

"Francis! Francis!" Her voice was little more than a hoarse whisper. Her fingers clutched at his coat sleeves. She swayed. Suddenly she pushed him back . . . back, away from her. Her breath came in short gasps.

"Don't! Oh, don't!" she moaned. Her hands went to her eyes, as though to brush away the mistiness. All at once she seemed to realize what had happened. With a frightened cry she fled across the room. Out into the dark hall she sped, up the stairs, down the corridor, until she reached the haven of her own rooms. She wrenched open the door, pushed it behind her, and sank breathlessly into a chair.

In her mad flight, terrified at her own thoughts, she had not noticed the door of Cornelia's room swinging open a little wider than it had been; she had not seen the figure that waited there, half concealed, watching her. The figure remained stationary for some time. No lights showed from the room. Only the flickering oil lamp that burned all night in the corridor lighted the scene, making a yellow globule of color against the wainscoted walls, throwing all else into dim, dark shadow.

Down in the drawing-room Francis Levison very slowly closed the windows and replaced the catch. Like a person in a dream he walked to the table, picked up the oil lamp Joyce had left, and went out into the hall. For a little while he stood at the foot of the stairs, as though he, too, were trying to clear his mind. At last, with a sort of stately, measured tread, he began to ascend the stairs. And in his preoccupation, he did not see that door to Cornelia's room closing until only the merest crack was left open; and behind that crack a pair of all-seeing eyes.

In her sitting room Isabel stared at herself in the long pier glass. Was this really herself, looking back at her? What had happened? What was it that had taken place in the drawing-room? Surely she couldn't have been so rash, so absolutely insane! Yet her lips burned still with Levison's kisses upon them. Her face was hot. She was trembling. She tried to steady herself by gripping the arms of her chair, but her fingers were weak and futile.

As she sat there the door opened. She jumped to her feet, her hand against her mouth to stifle the cry that rose to her throat.

"Francis!" she breathed. "Are you mad? Why did you come here? You must go . . . go immediately!"

Carefully Levison placed the lamp he had been carrying upon the center table.

"I'm sorry, Isabel. I didn't mean to intrude," he said quietly. "But I had to see you again . . . had to talk to you for just a moment, at least. I didn't come to apologize . . . exactly. I'm sorry that everything's happened as it has. But I won't take back what I said downstairs. I love you. I love you more than anyone else. Isabel, I can't let you go. Don't you see? I can't come back into your life this way, and then walk out of it, not knowing whether . . ."

"Please, Francis!" There were tears in Isa-

bel's eyes, but her head was high and her voice
was brave. "There's no point in discussing anything. I'm sorry for all that's happened. . . ."

"I'm not," Levison said stubbornly. "I'm glad.
Because now at least I've told you what I should
have told you years ago. Isabel," he took a step
toward her, holding out his hands, "you do love
me! You must love me a little. I can't go away
without you. Nothing else matters, now. We'll
go away together . . . somewhere, it doesn't
matter!"

"Oh, can't you see this is all so impossible?"
Isabel wailed. "I don't love you. I tell you I
don't!" Her voice rose in angry determination.
"I love my husband, my baby. Nothing can take
me from them. I love Robert, I tell you. I
love him."

"You don't, my dear, you don't! You're only
trying to make yourself believe that you do.
You're not happy here; you never will be. I want
to make you happy. I'd do anything in the world
for you."

"The only thing you can do is to go away. Go
away as soon as possible!"

"I won't go, Isabel . . . not this way." Two
steps and Levison was taking her in his arms.

Frantically Isabel pulled away. "No! I won't
listen to you!" She put her hands to her ears,
shielding them from his words. "I won't listen.
You're mad . . . absolutely mad to think of such
a thing. I can't stand it! You must go! You
must!" She dropped into a chair burying her
face in her arms. Suddenly she began to cry, all

her pent-up emotions finding an outlet in her tears.

"Isabel! Isabel, don't!" Levison was on his knees beside her chair, stroking her hair. "You mustn't cry, my dear. I'll go if that's what you want. If I've hurt you in any way, I'm sorry. I'll do whatever you like. I hadn't meant that this should happen. I hadn't intended to say anything. I knew the first moment that I saw you here that I loved you. But I was going to go away without telling you."

"Oh, if you had . . . if you only had," Isabel sobbed.

"I'll try to forget that it's ever happened," Levison promised. "But I shan't be able to do that. I'll always remember you. I'll always remember a night in June, and the scent of clover; a balcony, and you in the moonlight."

Slowly he rose to his feet. "I'll be off to London first thing in the morning. Good-by, my dear." He bent over and kissed the golden hair. "Good-by. And I wish you happiness . . . always . . ."

CHAPTER IX

SWIFT moments went slipping by. The tall clock in the hall chimed the half hour. East Lynne lay buried in a vast, far-reaching silence. The clock in the hall struck two. And still Isabel sat huddled in the big chair in her sitting room. The candles had flickered out, one by one, until only the lamp on the center table remained, shedding its meager glow of light that left the corners of the room in darkness.

Round and round and round her mind went in weary circles. Isabel felt like a squirrel in a cage, making unceasing motions, yet never arriving at any destination. She was desperately tired . . . too tired to rouse herself, and yet she couldn't stop thinking. Why did all this have to happen? Why had life suddenly become such a complicated affair, she asked herself over and over again.

Just that morning everything had seemed so simplified, so delightful. Then, she had been living in expectation of the evening, waiting and anxious for its enjoyment, its happiness; and now she could wish that the evening had never been. Why had Robert had to go to London on this very day? Why did he always have to attend to business? It seemed that more and more

108

business occupied him, kept him from her. It hadn't been that way at first.

And then the coldness that had been slowly growing upon him until he seemed another person. He wasn't the man she had married, Isabel told herself brokenly. He was so entirely changed. He had been a charming, smiling, interesting young barrister. And within three years he had become settled and severe; sometimes even harsh, and he gave her a feeling that he had thoroughly matured and aged, and now wanted very little of life save his business interests and his few stodgy friends.

And yet she loved him, she told herself fiercely. She did love Robert. It was only seeing Francis Levison again, being fascinated by him as she had been fascinated when she was a girl. She didn't love Francis. The dancing, the music, the lights . . . all had worked that illusion in her for the moment. As though a magic spell had been cast over her, she decided. That was what had made her listen to Francis at all. If Cornelia had only gone to the ball with them!

But then, a great many things might be attributed to what Cornelia did or didn't do. Robert had changed as soon as he had come back under his sister's influence. It was Cornelia who had made life so drab and so gray that she, Isabel, had reached out into strange places for a little color, a little brightness. It was Cornelia who dominated, interfered; never quite obviously, but she was always there, a personage to be taken into consideration.

The clock in the hall struck the half hour. Wearily Isabel dragged herself to her feet and went over to the mantelpiece. The clock there proclaimed the hour of half-past two. Isabel shivered. Slowly she went into her bedroom, closed the door, and began unhooking her dress. She crossed the room and sat down at her dressing table, taking off her diamond pendant and her earrings, placing them in their case.

Somehow or other she managed to get out of her dress at last. The white satin and tulle billowed out on the floor. She looked down at its pale beauty and shuddered. She had been so happy when Joyce had slipped it over her head and arranged its folds. But that was years ago, that had happened! And yet it wasn't. Only six or seven hours ago, that was all.

With a dreary sigh Isabel pulled her nightgown over her head, blew out the lamp, and slipped into bed. The cool, clean sheets soothed her fevered body. But still she couldn't sleep. Her mind raced on and on. Should she tell Robert what had happened? Should she or shouldn't she? She didn't know what to do.

Robert had seemed to be growing away from her. She couldn't go to him and begin an explanation. He wouldn't understand. It would be better, perhaps, to say nothing; better if she'd stop thinking about the matter entirely. Francis would be gone in the morning; she wouldn't see him again. It would only upset Robert to know. And what did it all matter, anyhow? Nothing . . . nothing!

It was just an event that had arisen from a set of circumstances. Nothing could be done about it now. If she were in love with Francis, then things might be different. But she wasn't. There was only Robert, and her baby. And the baby meant more to her than anything in the world. It was the baby she must think of and plan for. And with the thought of the child taking possession of her mind, Isabel fell into a troubled sleep.

She was running . . . running . . . running. Through woods and over meadows, she was running. Something pursued her. She couldn't make out the figure, but she knew that she must escape. She mustn't allow it to catch her. She was breathless, panting, but still she kept on. She scratched her hands, her ankles on the brambles, but that didn't matter. And then the figure behind her disappeared. And she had reached the ravine. But now she couldn't stop. With a scream she felt herself falling . . . falling. . . .

Joyce was shaking her shoulder, speaking to her.

"It's half-past nine, milady," Joyce was saying. "I brought you some breakfast."

Isabel sat up abruptly. Half-past nine! Morning! Joyce pulled back the heavy drapes and the gray light of a gray morning seeped feebly into the room. Rain dripped from the window ledges and trickled along the panes in rivulets. Gray, and misty and chilly!

"There, now, milady." Joyce came back bringing a breakfast tray and placed it on Isa-

bel's lap. "Are you all right?" she questioned
anxiously.

"I'm afraid I didn't sleep very well, Joyce.
I've a little headache." Isabel stared at the tray,
wondering, vaguely, how it had ever got past
Cornelia's watchful eyes. Cornelia didn't hold
with having breakfast in bed, and said so in no
uncertain terms. One stayed in bed when one
was so ill that the doctor ordered it. Otherwise,
meals were served in the dining room, and nowhere else.

"Miss Cornelia had her breakfast at seven
o'clock this morning," Joyce informed her mistress. "She's been out in the garden ever since.
So I just thought I'd let you sleep a little longer,
milady, knowin' you might be tired after the
ball."

At the mention of the affair, Isabel winced.
But she attempted to make a brave showing. She
poured out a cup of tea and sipped the steaming
liquid.

Joyce puttered quietly about the room, making
a pretense of shaking out the white satin gown
that had lain all night on the floor, hanging it in
the wardrobe; and all the while anxious to hear
something of the ball. She liked to talk to her
mistress, was devoted to her interests, but this
morning the Lady Isabel seemed in no mood for
talking. She was probably tired from dancing so
long, "the pretty dear," Joyce told herself.

"How's Master William, Joyce?" Isabel asked
finally.

"He's fine, milady," Joyce smiled in answer to

the question. "It bein' too wet to take him out
this mornin', he's playin' in the nursery."

"Has there been any message from Mr.
Carlyle?"

"Miss Cornelia expects him by tea time, milady. And . . . oh, yes, Mr. Levison was called
to London early this mornin'."

Isabel bit hastily on a piece of toast to try to
hide her shaking hands. So Francis had kept his
promise. He was gone. And she'd not see him
again. Certainly, he'd never return to East
Lynne, after all that had happened. Undoubtedly, he'd go abroad . . . stay somewhere on the
Continent, as soon as his business in England was
completed. But it was all over, now; finished.

Somehow, she didn't know quite how, the
morning passed. But there was no sight of Cornelia. She was "busy in her room" was all that
Isabel learned from Joyce. Probably pretending
to recuperate from her headache, which was
rather unlikely, since she had been up and about
in the garden at seven o'clock. Probably "dis-
ciplining" her, Isabel reflected, for having gone
to the ball unchaperoned. That would be the
first thing Cornelia would tell her brother.

Robert would scold her, of course. But she had
gone, and there was no getting out of that. If
only she hadn't. If only she could go to Robert
and tell him the entire story. Half a dozen times
she went over the episode, trying to think how
she might make him understand what had occurred. She hated secretiveness; hated anything
that was not honest and sincere. But Robert

would discuss everything with Cornelia, and Cornelia would see only the worst side of the situation, and she would influence her brother.

No, the best thing to do was to keep her silence. After all, it wasn't her right to betray Francis. Nothing had really happened. Francis had told her that he loved her, but when she had asked him to leave, he had gone. He had been quite fair to her, in the end. The least said, the better. She must put the whole affair out of her mind.

The gray drizzle of the morning turned to heavier rain and sent Isabel to the nursery to entertain William. Like a child herself, she sat cross-legged on the floor, her skirts billowing about her, building houses of blocks and tumbling them over, laughing and clapping her hands when the tall towers trembled and collapsed. The worries of the night crept from her mind and lost themselves in the baby's prattle. The outside world became only a hazy dreamland.

But the outside world, to Cornelia, was neither hazy nor a dreamland. It was a grim reality. With a stern, implacable face she sat by the window of her sitting room . . . the window from which she could command a view of the driveway which led to the main entrance. A piece of knitting in her hands, at which she did not trouble to look, kept her fingers busy. But her eyes were free to watch for her brother's arrival. And at last her vigil was rewarded.

Before it was in sight, Cornelia's sharp ears caught the sound of crunching carriage wheels

on the gravel. She dropped her knitting, rose,
and stood in the middle of the window. An en-
closed carriage came into view, the horses dripping with rain. The carriage slowed down,
stopped before the main entrance. She could see
Dodson, a big umbrella shielding him from the
rain, open the carriage door, and then Robert
alighted. Cornelia started for the stairway.

"Hello! Where is everyone?" Carlyle's voice
resounded through the hall.

Swiftly, her skirts swishing, Cornelia came
down the stairs, her face set in stern, hard lines.
Without a word she went to her brother, offering
her cheek for his usual kiss.

"Well, Cornelia," Robert began. Then he
noted that something was amiss. "What's the
matter?" he frowned. "Why are you looking at
me like that?"

Cornelia was silent for a moment. Then:
"Mr. Levison left early this morning," she reported pointedly. "He said to tell you that he
had received a telegram calling him back to
London."

"Well?" Robert's voice was questioning.
"What's wrong with that? Undoubtedly some
business matter."

Again Cornelia paused long enough to allow
the import of her words to take effect. When she
did speak it was as though she were measuring
each syllable, weighing it in a balance.

"Something happened in this house last night
. . . something unspeakable!"

Without further ado she led the way to the

drawing-room, opened the doors, and stepped inside.

"What happened?" Carlyle was beside his
sister, half frightened by her severity.

Cornelia carefully closed the doors behind her
brother and then motioned him into the room.

"I say, Corney, what's up?" he demanded.

"Robert, I don't quite know how I'm going to
tell you," Cornelia began, seating herself in a
wing chair and folding her hands across her lap.
"It's terrible . . . terrible! To think that such
a thing should happen, here, in my own home!
Under my very eyes!"

"But what has happened?" Carlyle persisted.

"It's Isabel . . . and that . . . that Mr. Francis Levison!"

"Isabel? And Francis Levison? I must say,
Cornelia, I don't quite understand. What do you
mean?"

"I . . . oh, Robert, can't you understand?
How can I explain? How can I tell you? It was
too dreadful!"

"Look here, Cornelia!" Carlyle seized his
sister's shoulder, almost shaking her in his per-
plexity. "What are you trying to tell me? What
did Isabel do?"

"Robert, that man . . . that man," and Cornelia mouthed the words. "That man was in
Isabel's room last night!"

"Cornelia!" Shock, anger, and indignation
all fought for supremacy.

"Yes, it's true!"

Carlyle choked back the utterance that rose to

his lips. The blood drained from his face, leaving it an ashen gray.

"Cornelia!" he repeated harshly. "Do you realize what you're saying?"

Cornelia bridled. "Most certainly I realize what I'm saying. I've always known that this would happen. I warned you, Robert; I told you in the first place . . ."

Robert started toward the bell rope. "We'll see what Isabel has to say about this."

"No, Robert, wait a moment!" Cornelia jumped to her feet, catching her brother's arm. "Please allow me to tell you just what happened. No doubt she'll attempt to deny everything. But I tell you I saw it with my own eyes. I want you to listen to me. Then you may ask Isabel to explain matters . . . if she can."

"Very well, Cornelia," Robert submitted to be led back to a chair. "I'm sure I don't understand, but Isabel . . ."

"I'll begin at the beginning. I had one of my headaches, Robert, and I was forced to tell Isabel that we couldn't go to the ball because I was ill. Disregarding me entirely, your wife attended the Hunt Ball, unchaperoned, with Mr. Levison."

"She shouldn't have gone, of course, but . . ."

"Oh, Robert, if that was only all I have to tell you." And Cornelia took a deep breath and plunged into her revelations. "I was still awake when they returned. I simply couldn't sleep because of my headache. I heard Joyce let them in. They went into the drawing-room, and there they stayed for . . . well, for goodness knows

how long. I could easily hear Mr. Levison talking and . . . well, Robert, I simply can't repeat
what he said."

"Surely, Cornelia, you've made some mistake."

"Mistake! Rubbish!" Cornelia snapped. "I
could hear him as plainly as I hear you. He told
her that . . . that he loved her, and always had
loved her. I know that he kissed her. And then,
Isabel ran upstairs and went to her room. I heard
her running, and so, of course, I opened my door
to see what was the matter. But she didn't stop.
She went flying past, and a few moments later
Mr. Levison came upstairs with the lamp, and
walked straight into her room!"

"Cornelia!" Carlyle leaped to his feet, his
face set and hard. "Do you realize that you're
speaking of my wife?"

Cornelia sighed. "I'm sorry to have to tell you
this, Robert, but it's the truth. If you care to
ask your wife for an explanation, I should be
glad to hear what she has to say myself."

"Ask Isabel for an explanation? Most certainly I shall." Carlyle once more reached for
the bell rope and jerked it.

He began pacing back and forth across the
drawing-room. Levison . . . and Isabel. It
couldn't be! Yet Cornelia had seen everything.
And Cornelia wasn't one to make up a story.
Certainly not anything as serious as this. There
must be some explanation of the affair. But what
explanation could there be? What conclusions
could be drawn from such a scene? What conclusions save the obvious!

"You rang, sir?" Dodson discreetly waited in the doorway.

"Yes!" Carlyle turned to the butler. "Is Lady Isabel at home?"

"Yes, sir, I believe her ladyship is in the nursery with Master William, sir."

"Will you please tell her that I should like to see her in the drawing-room?"

"Very good, sir." Dodson hurried off, closing the doors behind him, frightened by the look he had seen on his master's face. Judging by that, Dodson told himself with an air of authority, her ladyship was in for a bad time of it.

Back and forth . . . back and forth across the drawing-room Carlyle walked, his mind in a whirl of doubts, beliefs, hopes, and fears. That Isabel could do such a thing! It was too monstrous, too awful. Yet he had Cornelia's word for it. Cornelia had seen Levison entering Isabel's room. Isabel had always liked Levison. He remembered now that those two names had been coupled together by Mayfair before he, Carlyle, had been engaged to the girl.

If Levison had taken such advantage of his hospitality, Carlyle was thinking, the man was a low cur, a scoundrel of the first water. He hadn't known Levison very well, but he had always liked him. Surely . . . surely, even if Isabel had been foolish enough to allow this man to make love to her, she couldn't have . . . He tried to stop his mind from dwelling on that angle of the affair.

If only there were some explanation, he said

over and over again. But what could there be?
He could visualize Isabel running to her room;
visualize Levison walking up the stairs, the lamp
in his hand; up the stairs, down the corridor,
opening the door. . . .

CHAPTER X

ISABEL started in surprise as a discreet knock came at the nursery door.

"Yes?" she called out. "Come in."

Dodson opened the door. "Mr. Carlyle is in the drawing-room, m'lady," he began.

"Oh, thank you, Dodson," Isabel interrupted hurriedly. "Will you tell him that I'll be down in a moment?"

"Yes, m'lady. He told me to say that he would like to see your ladyship there."

"Very well, Dodson."

As the door swung shut on the retreating butler, Isabel jumped up, ran to the small oval mirror which hung above the mantelpiece and smoothed her hair. She pulled the bell rope, and then went back to the mirror to arrange the lace collar about her neck. She shouldn't be scolded again for looking disheveled. Another knock at the door, and as Isabel answered, Joyce entered the room.

"You rang, milady," Joyce bobbed.

"Yes, Joyce," Isabel nodded. "Mr. Carlyle's returned. I wanted you to stay with Master William."

"Yes, milady."

Isabel hurried out, never noticing the worried frown that clouded Joyce's usually placid face.

For Joyce had seen the master's return and then she had heard the sound of raised voices proceeding from behind the closed doors of the drawing-room. And, according to Joyce, "Miss Corney was stickin' her fingers in the pie again, an' no good would come of that."

But the moment Isabel opened the drawing-room doors she realized that something was wrong. Cornelia stood facing her, an almost malignant glow of triumph on her countenance. Robert's face was white and drawn, his lips a mere hard line. Slowly she closed the door behind her, trying to smile in welcome at her husband. But she felt as though she had been frozen stiff. She could scarcely move her feet to cross the room.

"I'm so sorry I wasn't downstairs to meet you, dear," she began. "But I was in the nursery, playing with William."

Carlyle made no gesture of greeting. The muscles of his face never relaxed. When his words finally came, his voice was harsh; his hands clenched and unclenched in an effort to control his emotions.

"Isabel," he said slowly, "Cornelia has just told me . . ." He stopped as though unable to continue with the cruel accusations in his mind.

Swiftly Isabel stepped to her husband's side, her hand raised in a little gesture of placation.

"Oh, please, Robert." She tried to smile, but her lips were stiff. "If we're going to discuss the right or wrong of my going to the ball without your sister, can't we do so alone?"

"No!" Carlyle retorted decisively. "My sister remains." He paused, as though considering what he should say next. Finally he went on. "And I'm not concerned with the ball. I'm only concerned with what happened afterwards . . . here! In this house!"

The unexpectedness of her husband's words caught Isabel off her guard. Her hand went to her throat in alarm and consternation. She stared at Cornelia. What had the woman told Robert? What did she know? What imputations had she brought to her brother? Cornelia must have seen something, heard something last night. And no matter what had happened, Cornelia could and would put only one interpretation on anything . . . the worst.

Cornelia was returning Isabel's stare, and it seemed to the girl that her sister-in-law's face had taken on a new look of spite, even hatred. But it was a vaunted spite and hate; a look that was plainly indicative of "I told you so." It was as though Cornelia had been anxiously awaiting the moment when she might be able to accuse the girl of a wrong which had had its birth in her own mind. And Isabel felt a contempt for the woman which her open countenance could not conceal.

"I'm sorry you had to hear about that from someone else," Isabel said simply, looking at her husband. "I wanted to tell you myself."

In the dead silence that fell upon the room Cornelia's disdainful sniff of disbelief sounded like a knell. For one brief moment Isabel felt

that she could fly at her sister-in-law and shake
her . . . slap her . . . scratch that ugly face.
For the moment she was a primitive woman, de-
fending herself, her husband, and her child from
the brutal attack of a wild beast. And then she
was back in the drawing-room at East Lynne,
facing Robert and Cornelia.

"Well," Carlyle waited for the explanation.

"You're making it very difficult for me to explain something that really has no importance,"
Isabel began with unaffected candor. "I don't
know what Cornelia has told you, Robert, but
there is nothing that I am afraid to confess.
When Francis and I came back last night we
went out on the balcony . . ."

"And he . . . he kissed you!" It was not entirely anger and indignation that forced Carlyle
to repeat his sister's words. There was jealousy
. . . a jealousy that he felt for his wife when he
thought of her in the arms of another man.

Isabel started. It made her seem so guilty, that
reproach, because she knew that it was true.

"Yes, he kissed me," she acknowledged quietly.
"But Robert, can't you see that I'm trying to
make you understand? It was moonlight. I
could still hear the music of the dance. I was
filled with excitement . . . the romance of the
night. I was a girl again, back in Mayfair. Now
that I look back upon it, it all seems so silly."

She waited, watching her husband. And as
she watched, she came to realize that he, too, believed as his sister believed. All his innate puri-
tanism was rising to the fore; all the masculine

in him rushed to the defense of the sanctity of
his home. What could she say, what could she
do to make him credit the truth of her state-
ments?

"I give you my word, Robert," she said, shaking her head. "That is all . . .. it all meant
nothing."

"It meant nothing that he followed you to your
room," Carlyle's voice cut like the lash of a
whip.

So! That was what Cornelia had reported to
her brother. That was what Cornelia was thinking of. How vile! How unspeakably vile!
Isabel told herself angrily. That she should be
accused of such a thing! She didn't hold herself
completely free from blame. She should never
have allowed Francis to kiss her. But that her
own husband should even listen to such a story
against her was almost incredible.

It was Cornelia who had implanted the germs
of suspicion in Robert's mind. It was Cornelia,
and Cornelia alone who would be able to weave
a story like that in such a way as to make it
sound possible and true. And it was a cheap and
vulgar thing to do. Isabel could feel the nails of
her fingers cutting into the palms of her hands
as she clenched her fists spasmodically in her
rage and disgust for the woman. She turned
away from her sister-in-law contemptuously and
addressed only her husband.

"Yes, that's true," she spoke with a kind of
treacherous calmness that hid the surging vol-
cano within her. "Francis did come to my room.

He begged him to go away with him. He said
that he loved me . . . always had loved me. I
told him that he was mad . . . that I loved you,
my baby, my home. I asked him to go away. I
never wanted to see him again. He understood,
and . . . he left. That's all."

"And you expect me to believe that?" Carlyle's
voice was low and hoarse.

Isabel drew herself up in indignation. Robert
didn't believe her . . . didn't believe that she
was telling the truth. It surprised her, frightened her. Yet why should she be surprised, she
asked herself. Surely, by this time she should
know that Cornelia had wanted to believe nothing
but the worst, and had passed on her beliefs to
her brother. Then why should Robert think anything else? Suddenly Isabel felt old, and tired
. . . very tired, as though she had been fighting
a long, losing battle.

"No," she shook her head with a weariness
that combined hopelessness and desperation.
"No! How can I expect you to believe me after
you have listened to her?" She glanced at Cornelia and then away again quickly. "It's always
been her word against mine . . . her orders
against mine. . . ."

"How dare you say such a thing?" For the
first time during the ugly, tedious interview Cornelia spoke, drawing herself up with an air of
righteous dignity. "I never interfered!"

For one brief instant Isabel closed her eyes,
afraid of what she might say or do. Never interfered! Those words burned in her brain. A

brief vision of past indignities suffered at the
hands of this woman rose before her. The many
times when she had had her own orders to the
servants countermanded . . . had been forced to
do without gowns for herself and clothes for
William . . . had been humiliated in the presence
of others. Then her anger flared, and now, for
all that past, she spoke.

"How can you say that!" She whirled on Cornelia, her face white, her eyes burning like live
coals. "You interfered with every move I made
. . . every breath I drew! You drove out my
friends, ruled my house! I've never been mistress in my own home. From the moment I came
to East Lynne you began to try to rule me as
you've ruled everything else here. You've dominated me and my child."

"Robert!" There was a choked gasp from
Cornelia as she turned to her brother for help
against this attack.

"Yes, I'll speak, now," Isabel went on, disregarding her husband's warning gesture; Cornelia's interjection. "You've crushed every im-
pulse, destroyed every bit of romance that was in
me. I've never been a free, human being since
I entered this house. I came here, a girl, and I
wanted to be happy. I did everything in my
power to make you like me. I wanted you to like
me for Robert's sake. But you . . . you made
my home a prison . . . until the very air seemed
to press down and smother me."

"Isabel, if you . . ." Carlyle tried to interrupt
the tirade.

"And you!" Isabel turned on her husband accusingly. "You, my husband, stood by without a word, without doing one thing, and said nothing. Because I was your wife I was supposed to change completely . . . to become subdued . . . drab . . . old . . . like she is!" She pointed to Cornelia. "Well, I tried. I did my best! I . . ." Her voice broke; she choked back a sob that rose in her throat.

"Oh, Robert," she sighed, "can't you see that you're as much to blame for what happened last night as I am?"

"How dare you say that!" Now it was Carlyle's turn to become indignant. "How dare you blame me . . . for . . . for last night!" He rasped out the words as though they were poisonous.

A little softness crept into Isabel's voice. She was pleading, now; pleading because she knew that she had right on her side, because she knew that it was hard for this man she loved to understand her.

"I blame you," she answered, "because you never tried to know the woman you married. Why, if you had loved me half as much as I loved you, you would have seen how unbearable my life here has been. But you've never given one real thought to my happiness. When you brought me to East Lynne, I was happy . . . full of romance. I wanted a little youth, a little brightness about me, that was all. You were a lover, then, Robert, considerate, kind . . . then suddenly, over-

night, you changed. When you came under her
influence again, you changed. . . ."

"I'll not hear another word against my
sister!" Carlyle interrupted, turning to Cornelia
and placing his hand protectingly on her arm.

"Oh, yes, you will!" Isabel's slow, melodious
voice became resonant, deep, flooded with tense
emotion. "She's made my life a constant humili-
ation. I've done nothing . . . nothing, I tell
you! Nothing that should make her hate me, try
to accuse me of things that have not happened!
Ever since I came into this house she's been trying to turn you against me. She's been planning
. . . waiting . . . hoping for the moment when
you would drive me out!"

She faced Cornelia, her voice breaking hysteri-
cally. "Well, you're not going to drive me out.
Because I'm going . . . I'm going, you understand! But I'm going of my own free will . . .
right now!"

Her voice choking with the long pent-up sobs,
Isabel turned and ran from the room. Ran . . .
and ran . . . up the stairs, down the corridor to
her own room . . . ran inside, banging the door
behind her. She jerked at the bell rope; paced
the floor impatiently. She'd leave East Lynne
. . . East Lynne that hated her; had made her
life one long, drab stretch of misery. She'd leave
these people who accused her . . . accused her
of doing something she would have scorned to
do. She'd leave these evil-minded, horrible
people . . . never see them again.

"You wanted me, milady!" Joyce appeared in the doorway.

"Yes . . . yes!" Isabel spoke hurriedly. "Get the baby ready, Joyce. We're leaving right away!"

Joyce stared, her eyes round with amazement. "Leaving? Why . . . why, what's happened, milady?" she stammered.

"Don't ask questions!" Isabel snapped. "Get Master William ready. Pack a few things for him. We're leaving at once!"

"Yes, milady." Swallowing her questions, Joyce bobbed and scurried off.

Isabel ran to her bedroom, opened a long wardrobe and from the bottom shelf seized a traveling bag. She threw it on the bed and opened it. With feverish energy she pulled open drawers of dressers and cupboards, snatching a dress here, toilet articles there, and tumbling them all helter-skelter into the case. Her jewel box containing her mother's jewels, a photograph of the baby, a pair of tiny shoes . . . all went in at once. She snapped the bag shut.

She took a hat from the closet and jammed it down on her head. She wouldn't stay any longer at East Lynne where she wasn't wanted. If Robert would rather have his sister than her, then he should have his sister. It had always been Cornelia's wishes against hers . . . always would be. Well, at last Cornelia had had her way. She had succeeded in turning Robert against his wife. That was what she had been trying to do for three years. She'd done it!

Isabel found a cape, flung it about her shoulders. She'd take the baby and go . . . it didn't matter where. But they'd go. She wouldn't be hurt any more. She'd have her child, and nothing else would matter. If Robert didn't love her any longer, why should she stay on at East Lynne? And Robert couldn't love her, or he wouldn't have listened to those hideous lies of Cornelia's. She snatched up the traveling bag and ran toward the nursery.

As she reached the nursery door she halted abruptly. In front of the half open door stood her husband, his form blocking the entrance.

"You can't go in there," he said quietly, nodding toward the baby's room.

"What do you mean?" Isabel gasped. "William is going with me. Joyce is packing . . ."

"William is staying here," Carlyle returned frigidly.

"He's not! He's mine! And I'm taking him with me! You can't stop me!" Isabel caught hold of her husband's arm, trying to push him to one side, trying to get past him. But he merely shook off her clutching fingers.

"I can stop you," he warned, and his tone was ominous. "You forget that the law is on my side."

"Law?" Isabel frowned, not comprehending the meaning of her husband's words. "What has the law to do with me . . . or my child?"

"Everything!" Carlyle answered shortly.

"I . . . I don't understand!"

"The laws of England can take any child from

such a woman as you! Laws were made to protect the sanctity of the home, the honor of the
family.''

Isabel swayed slightly. In her hysterical condition she could scarcely grasp the full import of
Carlyle's words, yet she realized that he was
making dreadful accusations against her . . .
those horrible accusations spawned by his sister's
imagination. But what did it matter what he
said, or what he thought? She must have the
child; that was the only thing of importance.
She must get William and take him with her.
Again she tried to push her way into the nursery.
Again Carlyle's arm thrust her back.

"But . . . but I've done nothing!" Isabel
tried to moisten her dry lips with her tongue. A
cold feeling of stark terror was creeping over
her. Never before had she seen Robert so pale,
so defiant, so stern. He was like a piece of
crystal, cold to the touch, even. And he wouldn't
allow her in there where the baby was . . .
wouldn't allow her because he thought she had
done something wrong. But she hadn't . . . she
hadn't! She must make him understand that she
hadn't, so that she could have her child.

"Robert!" she pleaded. "Listen to me, Robert! You must believe me! I've told you the
truth . . . I told you all that happened. Robert!
You've got to believe me!"

She was shaking him, shaking him with all the
strength born of hysteria. She could hear William in the nursery, calling for his "mummy."
She could hear the high, baby voice calling her.

A Fox Movietone Production.   *East Lynne.*

ISABEL IS INTRODUCED, TO CAPTAIN LEVISON, AND FIND THAT THEY WERE FRIENDS SOME YEARS AGO.

Then Carlyle reached behind him and pulled the door to, shutting off the sound of that little voice. Frantically Isabel clung to her husband's arm. The satchel dropped from her hand.

"You can't keep William away from me," she sobbed. "You can't! He's part of me. I couldn't live without him."

"You should have thought of that before," Carlyle reminded her grimly.

"Oh, I didn't mean all I said downstairs," she began to plead. "I didn't mean all I said about leaving. Really, I didn't. I was hurt, and angry. But I couldn't go without him, Robert. I couldn't go alone!"

"You haven't anything to say about it." Carlyle's face was set in hard lines, but he kept his hands behind his back to conceal their trembling. "You've outraged my name, my honor, my love for you. You've forfeited all rights of motherhood . . ."

"But I'll not leave this house without him!" Isabel broke in defiantly. "You don't have to believe me. I can't help what you think. You can turn me out, you can do what you like, but you can't take my baby from me. You can't punish me like that. I'll do anything you say. I'll go anywhere you tell me . . . if I can only have him."

"No! What you did once, you'll do again," Carlyle forced the harsh judgment from between set teeth. "He must never know anything about what has happened. You're going out of his life forever."

"No! No! No!" Isabel's voice rose in a sharp scream. "You can't do that!"

"You have made your decision." There was dreadful finality in Carlyle's tones; the finality of a judge pronouncing the sentence of death. "You are leaving this house alone. You will never come back. There isn't a court in England that will believe your story."

The door of the nursery opened and closed, and Carlyle was gone. For an instant Isabel stood there on the threshold, overcome with stupefaction. Her breath came in short, choking gasps. You are leaving this house alone . . . alone . . . alone! The words sang and danced in her brain. The air about her was swimming in a sea of blackness. Alone . . . alone . . . alone! She fell against the door, beating upon it with futile, strengthless fists.

"William! William!" She called over and over again. But no sound came. Silence spread about her. "Robert!" she cried. "Robert!" But only the echoes answered her. Her hands were numb, but still she beat the unresponsive wood of the door. Beat . . . and beat . . . and beat . . . against the awful stillness that encompassed her.

CHAPTER XI

THICK, impenetrable fog hung heavily over the harbor of Dover. Evening closed down, yet it was not darker than the day had been. From morning on the yellow gas lamps along the quay had been lighted, but their beams could not dispel the misty pall that covered streets and houses, cliffs and rocking vessels. Pavements were damp and the roads wet with tiny, trickling streams that settled in the gullies of the cobblestones.

Drip . . . drip . . . drip! The moisture collected and ran in thin rivulets down windowpanes, dropped dispiritedly from porch roofs, clung dejectedly to bare branches of trees as though gathering sufficient energy to roll off onto the heads and shoulders of pedestrians. People moved slowly, groping their way, unable to distinguish shapes and forms, bumping into one another, turning corners carefully for fear of losing themselves in this vast, sickly green atmosphere.

Out beyond the breakers the sea tumbled restlessly, moaning and keening its eternal dirge. The buoys kept up a constant mournful conversation, their doleful bells answering each other back and forth. The hoarse groans of foghorns sounded, now deep and despairing as the boat came nearer; now like the eerie wail of a banshee

135

as the waters of the English Channel bore off the craft, carrying it toward the shores of France.

In the harbor the small fishing schooners lay anchored, bobbing up and down like corks. Heavier boats rocked back and forth in ceaseless rhythm. From time to time a scraping, grinding rasp marked the jostling of one vessel against the side of another. Creaking sounds told of windlasses being raised and lowered. The odors of damp hemp and tar, of salt air and decaying fish vied with each other in a race for supremacy.

On one of the larger vessels innumerable gas lamps attempted to liven the gloom. Straggling passengers bound for Calais made the precipitous journey up the swaying, creaking gangplank and mulled about on the decks, hurried to the bar, settled to the salon, or headed for their staterooms. Porters struggled with luggage, piling it in heaps here and there to be stumbled over and sorted. Voices that seemed to come out of the nowhere rose and fell in ghostly cadences.

Up the gangplank and into the midst of the confusion came the Lady Isabel Carlyle, clinging to the arm of her father. A heavy chiffon veil concealed her features and protected her face from the cold dampness. As she stepped onto the deck she pulled the fur-lined cape she was wearing closer about her and shivered. Lord Mount Severn began poking among the piles of luggage with his stick.

"Are your boxes here, Isabel?" he questioned

with some asperity. "Don't want 'em to get lost,
you know."

"They'll be all right, Father," Isabel answered
tonelessly, her voice as dreary as the evening
itself.

What did boxes matter? What did anything
matter now? Her life was finished. Decisions
had been reached and there was no turning back.
Everything seemed inevitable, hopeless, colorless.
If East Lynne had once been drab, it stood out
at present as a bright spot by comparison to the
dullness that lay ahead. But it was no good
thinking of that now.

"I'll see you to your stateroom," Lord Mount
Severn suggested. "Steward! Here, steward!"
he called out as an attendant brushed by.
"Where's Room 27?"

"This way, sir." The man motioned for
Mount Severn to follow him.

Taking Isabel's arm, Lord Mount Severn
piloted his daughter through the stacked luggage.
Up a short flight of steps they went, down a long,
white corridor that smelled of gas and oil, paint
and sea air, until they reached the proper cabin.
The attendant threw open the door, fumbled for
a match and lighted the gas lamp. The yellow
flare disclosed a built-in wooden bunk, a wash-
stand with pitcher and bowl, a small table and
one red plush chair decorated with red fringe
that had faded to a lighter shade than its original
color.

"Anything else, sir?" The steward waited.

"Yes, bring me a brandy," Mount Severn ordered. "Sure you won't have a little brandy,
Isabel?" he turned to his daughter. "Do you
good."

"No, thank you, Father." Isabel shook her
head.

"Very well. One brandy, steward."

"Yes, sir." The attendant backed out, closing the door behind him.

Isabel loosened her cape and began to remove
the heavy veil that swathed her head. Lord
Mount Severn sank into the plush chair, dropped
his gloves, stick, and hat onto the floor and un-
fastened the collar of his caped mackintosh.

"I think you're doing the wisest thing," he
began, "in getting out of England until this
scandal blows over. It's been a pretty sorry
affair." He shook his head morosely.

Isabel, still holding her cape about her, seated
herself on the edge of the ship's bed.

"I'm not leaving England because of the scandal," she spoke a little sharply. "I'm not even
thinking of what people are saying. I'm going
away, hoping to forget. I must forget!" She
rested her tired head on the palm of her hand,
her elbow on her knee.

"What a frightful affair!" Mount Severn persisted. "Divorce . . . notoriety . . . the papers
full of it! It's going to be a bit awkward for
me, you know. There'll be raised eyebrows wherever I go."

"Haven't there always been raised eyebrows?"
Isabel suggested bitterly.

"Well," her father grunted, "they'll be raised higher than ever, now."

"I'm sorry, Father," she said. But if he'd only stop talking about it, she thought. If she could only get away where there was some peace, some relief from the ceaseless round of questions and talk and evil gossip. If she could only be left alone until she should be able to assuage the torment of these nerve-racking months just past.

In one way she did feel genuinely sorry for her father. It was, as he said, "a frightful affair." And he had had to face the publicity, the town talk that had blazed from one end of Mayfair to the other. But she had had to do the same, and to face it with a heart full of sorrow. She was paying, and paying all too dearly, for her one little piece of folly.

A knock at the door interrupted her reflections. As Mount Severn called "Come in," the steward entered with a tray carrying a bottle of brandy and a glass. The man arranged the articles on the table and poured out the drink. Mount Severn took the brandy, slid a shilling across the tray, and sent the attendant off.

"I tell you, Isabel," he grumbled, sipping the liquor. "The trouble with you is you've too much pride. You should swallow it. I did. It gagged me, but I swallowed it. There are times when it doesn't pay to be too proud, you know. You should have taken Carlyle's money when it was offered to you."

Isabel's trembling fingers played nervously

with the chiffon veil that she pulled across her lap.

"I couldn't!" she shook her head. "I've enough of my own to last for a little while. I'd rather not discuss that, if you please."

Something in the tone of her voice made her father silent on the monetary situation. During that frightful trial for divorce, Isabel had learned several things, and one was that Lord Mount Severn had been receiving money from Carlyle. Her husband had been supporting her father since the marriage. That seemed almost the last straw. She hated to think of it, and yet she knew that her father would probably go on accepting his monthly allowance as long as Robert sent it.

She, herself, had refused the settlement her husband had offered to bestow upon her. She couldn't accept money from anyone who believed her to be what Robert evidently did. What she should do when her own money was gone, she didn't know; hadn't even thought about it. Money seemed such a small matter, and as yet she had had no time to look ahead. Just now, it was bad enough that one member of her family should touch the Carlyle money.

"And that fellow Levison!" Lord Mount Severn rambled on. "I should horsewhip the scoundrel!"

"Oh, please, Father!" Isabel stopped him quickly. It was all right to take such a grand attitude of paternal protection, she told herself sarcastically, but it would have been a lot better to have adopted that attitude earlier.

"All right! All right!" Mount Severn said testily. "I shan't say any more. But I dislike seeing you going away alone. I'd go with you myself, but I've been invited to Scotland for some shooting. I don't care for the shooting, as you know, but the dinners are rather good."

"Don't worry about me. I'll be all right. Nothing really matters."

"Then you're certain there's nothing I can do for you?" Mount Severn set down his empty glass and began to gather up his gloves and stick. "If you want anything . . ." He reached for his hat and got to his feet.

"Yes, there is one thing you can do for me, Father," Isabel began anxiously. "When you can, try to see my baby and write to me about him, please."

"Oh, don't worry about the baby," her father said easily. "Carlyle'll take good care of him."

"Yes, so His Lordship said when he rendered the verdict," Isabel returned scathingly. "Justice trying to be consoling."

The loud hoot of a whistle sounded through the corridors.

"There's the last warning, my dear. I must be off." Lord Mount Severn opened the cabin door.

"I'll come out on deck with you." Isabel rose and followed her father down the stairs and outside toward the gangplank.

"Good-by, dear . . . good-by, Isabel . . ." Father and daughter kissed perfunctorily, and Mount Severn hurried down the passage, turning to wave once. And then he was lost in the fog.

Isabel stood at the railing, trying to peer through the mist. The clanking of chains, the voices of the sailors as they pulled in the plank, the rattling throbs of the engine all intermingled in a confusion of sound. Good-bys and bon voyage messages came from the quay. Slowly the ship began to pull away from its moorings. The faint gas lights on the streets of Dover were growing fainter in the fog. Only the noises familiar to the boat, the sights and sounds on board, remained.

"Isabel!" The low repetition of her name brought the girl around with a start. In the yellow light she saw a familiar figure taking shape beside her.

"Francis Levison!" Amazed, she turned to greet this unexpected companion.

"Isabel," Levison said softly. "I heard you were leaving England to-day. I couldn't let you go without telling you how sorry I am that I was responsible for what happened. I had to see you again. I had to apologize. I'd have tried to see you before, but I knew that for your sake I shouldn't. But I can't tell you how sorry . . ."

"It doesn't matter. It's all over," Isabel's voice was terribly tired.

"But I must talk to you," the man hurried on. "I'd give anything if I could undo all that's been done. Please believe me, Isabel, my dear. I'd give anything in the world to bring you and Carlyle together again."

"That would be impossible. I never want to

see him again. I never thought anyone capable
of such heartless cruelty.''

''And not only he, but everyone! At the trial,
when I was testifying, telling what really happened in your room that night, someone laughed.
I could have killed him. Then it came to me that
the world didn't believe what we said. It only
wanted to believe the worst.''

Isabel sighed. ''What does it matter what the
world believes, now?''

As she stood there at the rail the sickening
thoughts of all that had happened rose to confront her. Once again she could see the crowded
courtroom, the whispering, nodding heads and
sneering faces. It was quite true that nobody
had believed what she said. It had all been as
Carlyle had prophesied. The court didn't believe
her story . . . couldn't believe that a man had
come to her room for no other purpose than to
say that he loved her. She shivered.

Cornelia had given her testimony. Cornelia,
the good, the righteous woman, the worker in her
church parish, honored and respected for her in-
tegrity by the community in which she had lived
her entire life. And always . . . always harping
on the damning evidence of that kiss on the balcony. If a woman, a young married woman with
the responsibility of a child, could so far forget
herself as to allow any man other than her husband to kiss her, then she could go to greater
lengths. That was the argument.

Of course Francis had told his story . . . told
it in a perfectly straightforward manner. But

Francis Levison was a gentleman, or so the court
believed, and the only natural thing for any gentleman to do under the circumstances was to lie
in an attempt to shield the woman in the case.
According to all codes he had done the proper
thing, and had done it very well. But that didn't
impress the bench, when it came to handing down
a verdict.

It was Carlyle who had the sympathy of the
court, of the newspapers, of the people. It was
his good name which had been besmirched by a
faithless wife. It was for the child's own protection that it should be taken from such a woman
and placed in the custody of its father. Oh, yes,
the laws were made to protect the sanctity of the
home, Isabel reflected grimly. But they were
laws made by men, for men, and not for women.

"Perhaps you feel now that it doesn't matter
very much what the world thinks," Levison was
saying gently. "But you still have your life to
live. There is only one way to do it. You must
forget."

"I left England because I wanted to try to forget," Isabel explained. "Oh, Francis, I must forget! I must! I must! But all I can do is think
of that horrible trial. And then, the realization
that I've lost my baby!"

"Isabel! Don't, my dear, please!" Levison
laid his hand on her arm. "I can't bear seeing
you so unhappy, and knowing that it's my fault.
What are you going to do? What do you want
to do? You must let me help you. I feel responsible!"

Isabel shook her head. "It wasn't your fault
. . . it wasn't my fault . . . it was everybody's
fault. Everybody's!" she repeated passionately.
"If everything had been different, all this
wouldn't have happened. As I look back on it
now I can see where I might have changed some
things at the very beginning. But whether that
would have done any good, I don't know. That's
what makes it all seem so hopeless."

"I understand, my dear. You tried to destroy
the very things in your nature that made you *you*.
You see, I know you, Isabel. You tried to destroy the gayety, the laughter, the happiness,
that was you, and you couldn't. Why should
you change?"

"I don't know." Isabel leaned back against
the railing, closing her eyes. The cold air stirred
the golden hair that showed beneath the little
velvet hat, whipping tendrils of curls against her
cheeks.

The boat was rocking up and down, sending
the passengers scurrying for the safety of the
salons. The long-drawn wail of the foghorn
sounded dismal blasts that were repeated and
flung back by other craft on the sea. The white-
capped stewards lurched with each roll of the
ship, steadying themselves against the walls of
the corridors as they went backward and forward, distributing boxes and bags. Only long
signal lights cut through the ghostly darkness
that had settled over the channel.

"How did you happen to be on board this
boat?" Isabel said suddenly.

"I came because I had to talk to you," Levison
explained again. "All during the trial I knew
that I didn't dare try to see you. That would
only have made matters much worse. So I kept
out of your way. But now that it's all over I
want to make whatever amends I can. I watched
you come on board with your father. I waited
until he left, because I didn't know what he
might think if he saw me here. I couldn't think
of you going off alone."

"It doesn't matter," Isabel repeated. "I'll be
quite all right."

"It does matter, my dear," Levison protested.
"It matters a great deal. You're too young to
feel that way. All this has been horrible for you,
I know. But as time goes on you'll be able to
look at it a little differently. You'll forget . . ."

"If I could . . . if I only could," Isabel
moaned.

"You will forget! Once you're back in an
atmosphere that you know you'll be able to forget. You need all the things you had before your
marriage. I know it sounds cruel to say it now,
but you need laughter . . . you need the light-
hearted freedom you once had. Let me restore
those things to you, Isabel. In Vienna, in Paris,
wherever you wish. There's nothing I wouldn't
do to make you happy. Let me try?"

Isabel shrugged her shoulders, staring out into
the night, scarcely heeding the man's words.

"Fog!" she shuddered. "Fog, getting into
our lives . . . our hearts . . . our souls!"

CHAPTER XII

VIENNA . . . the world's capital of gayety! Sparkling music and stolen kisses, twinkling feet and laughing eyes, the clank of swords and the clink of glasses, the perfume of a hundred flowers, the scent of a hundred perfumes, a blare of color, a blaze of light, the swift darkness of wooded parks, love and intrigues, a whisper here and a nod there and an army marches, the glitter of a wine garden's lamps through the leafy trees, the clatter of carriages along the broad streets, the ceaseless buzz of carefree voices . . . Vienna!

In an open fiacre, open to the soft breath of late spring air, open to reveal short glimpses of the sparkling stars, rode the Lady Isabel Carlyle and Francis Levison. Other carriages, crowded with laughing, shouting merrymakers, passed them at every turn. On the sheltered walks lovers strolled, arm in arm, whispering softly, sighing deliciously, deliriously happy.

"Flowers . . . for Madame . . ." A little flower girl with a tray almost as large as herself ran after the carriage, calling out her wares in her native tongue.

The fiacre stopped at a busy corner. Breathlessly the child thrust her tray at Levison. The man slipped a coin into the flower girl's hand and took a great bouquet of yellow violets from the midst of flaming roses and deep blue corn flowers. He placed the violets in Isabel's lap as the carriage drove off again.

"Or would you rather have had the roses?" he questioned.

"Oh, no, these are lovely," Isabel buried her face in the coolness of the yellow velvety petals with their outlining ruff of broad, green leaves.

In the softness of the street lamps Isabel looked almost ethereal. There seemed to be no change after all her mental anguish. She had flung back the white ermine collar that trimmed the light mantle she wore against the slight chill of the evening, and the fur made a soft, warm background for the golden curls that clung in profusion about her neck.

It seemed impossible to Isabel, when she allowed herself to think of it, that almost two years had passed since she had gone from East Lynne. Almost two years, and yet, to all outward appearances she was the same. There was a time when she felt that she did not dare to look at herself in a mirror, so certain she was she would not see gazing back at her the reflection she knew so well. Surely such intense suffering would leave its mark.

It was during her sojourn in Paris that she couldn't look at herself. She had gone on with Levison, staying in the French capital while he was there, too weak to depend upon herself for anything; her brain too benumbed to function normally. Levison had proffered the strong arm upon which she could lean; had held her hand tightly in his when her reason had seemed to totter and she was certain that she was going mad. He had watched over her, looked after her, neglected his own affairs to care for her.

Then slowly, with his aid, she had forced herself to take command of her thoughts; had blotted out the vision that had so persistently risen before her eyes. Over and over again he had told her that she must go on living. People didn't die from such sorrows; they only lapsed into melancholia. She had to go on living, and the only way to go on was to force herself to forget by taking an interest in other things. He was being sent on a mission to Vienna . . .

And so with desperate resolution she applied all her energies to the task of making herself forget. Youth has strength, has Nature herself to assist in the processes of forgetting. So Isabel had recklessly flung herself into the midst of the gayest crowds, the liveliest parties which Vienna could offer. With an abandon she had never realized she possessed she entered into the wild, mad festivities of the young military set of that wildest, maddest city of the Continent. And the young, mad military set took her to its bosom.

The beautiful young Englishwoman had easily captured the fancies of romantic officers. Little whispers of her past life were bandied about, but she danced divinely, her gowns were gorgeous, and she was altogether charming. So what did the past matter? And always in attendance upon her was the handsome member of the British Diplomatic Corps, Francis Levison, whose protection warded off the possibilities of any other liaison.

"Was there any further news to-day?" Isabel turned to Levison, breaking the silence. She hated silences that left her free to think; she must talk, or listen to others talking.

Levison shook his head. "Nothing further," he answered. "But any day, now, I'm certain we'll hear of a declaration of war. France has been actually preparing for two years; she won't wait much longer. There's too much jealousy between France and Prussia."

"Do you still think France will begin the invasion?"

"The Minister of War has announced that he has four hundred thousand men ready to place on the frontier." Levison shook his head. "Four hundred thousand men, with cartridges enough to withstand the offending Germans for years to come. Napoleon the Third has already satisfied himself that Northern Germany can only place some three hundred and thirty thousand men on the Rhine. So now it's merely the matter of a pretext."

"But England? What will happen there?"

Levison frowned, looking quickly at the woman beside him. What made her ask that? Surely, she could know nothing. But of course she didn't, he reproved himself for his fright.

"I think England will have nothing to do with the quarrel," he said easily. "From all I hear, this will be war between the German states and

France. But why are you so interested?" He tried to make his tone casual.

"Oh, I don't know," Isabel shrugged. "I suppose it's merely because everybody's talking about war. What shall we do, you and I, if France does begin an invasion?"

"Return to Paris, I think. We'll be safer there. Perhaps we may have to return."

"Have to return? Why? What do you mean?"

"Oh, nothing . . . nothing at all," Levison answered quickly. "I may be sent back if war's declared, that's all."

"Oh, I see."

Once again Levison looked at Isabel, but she was staring, quite oblivious to his presence, up at the bower of trees that lined the broad avenue, her mind busy with her own thoughts. What did it all matter anyhow, she reflected bitterly. What did war, or peace, or invasions have to do with her? It would be just the same, her own life, whether it was one thing or the other. War couldn't replace the things she had lost; it couldn't give her back her baby, her home, her peace of mind. Nothing could do that for her.

Like gleaming pearls among the dark, moonlit leaves the domes and columns of the Dommayer Casino now stood out in soft relief. Candles gleamed fitfully, casting their mellow radiance over the numberless little tables beneath the trees of the famous gardens. The wild strains of Tsigane music throbbed mournfully, wailing of

sorrow and sudden death, and then flared to a
reeling crescendo of strange, almost insane
hilarity.

"Here we are." Levison stepped down from
the fiacre and assisted Isabel to the ground, in-
structing the coachman to wait for them.

"It's quite crowded to-night," Isabel observed
as, on Levison's arm, she made her way through
the drifting maze of humanity.

"This way." Levison piloted the girl along a
meandering walk toward a fantastic pavilion de-
signed after the Chinese.

Through the trees they could see the main
pavilion where the symphony orchestra played
night after night the music of Johann Strauss and
Lanner. Beyond lay a platform where dancing
couples whirled and pivoted to the tunes of the
most famous waltzes of the world. At the little
tables sat groups of two and three and four, sipping wine, whispering, laughing, flirting. Waiters
with trays and bottles hurried in and out. The
popping of champagne corks sounded with the
frequency of repeating rifles.

At the entrance to the Chinese pavilion Isabel
stopped for a moment, surveying the members of
the party there. Officers, resplendent in their
colorful uniforms, formed the majority of the
group. Scattered among them were several
women in evening dress, their jewels dazzling,
scintillating in the light of the gas chandeliers and
the added brilliancy of innumerable candles. Then
one young officer, catching sight of Isabel and
Levison, jumped to his feet. The others followed.

"Ah! Good evening!" There was the click of heels, deep bows, and the men trooped forward to kiss Isabel's hand. Everybody tried to talk at once. French, English, and German filled the air. Welcomes, and laughter, and the popping of corks, the clink of glasses. Until at last Isabel found herself seated at the table between two officers, with a third arranging her mantle on the back of her chair, a fourth handing her a glass of champagne.

The officer on her left seized his glass and touched its rim against the bottom of hers.

"To love!" he called out.

"To you," Isabel returned, laughing.

"No . . . no . . . no! To you!" The officer on her right clinked his glass against the side of hers.

"All right! To me!" Isabel raised her glass in the midst of the others, and then drank.

Farther down the table Levison sat talking in furtive whispers to the tall, elderly man beside him. But now and again his gaze wandered to Isabel. He had noticed her quick acceptance of the wine; watched her glass being filled and refilled. Yet there was nothing he could say; nothing to do. Evening after evening was spent in the same way, drinking, dancing, talking, and always, he knew, in the hopes of being able to forget, even for one brief moment, the past.

Isabel looked as lovely as ever, he told himself. That spring green color of her gown was becoming. She was beautiful . . . far more beautiful than any of the other women here. Hers was a more natural beauty. But in these glowing lights he could see what it was that had changed her. Her eyes were bright, too bright, and where, before, they had been soft and appealing, now they were almost hard. There was a coldness in their depths that held terrible, frozen secrets.

And her mouth . . . the mouth that had been so sweetly childish, seemed to show a strain at its corners. A strain, that was it; that was what made her eyes cold, and gave her mouth that touch of grimness. She was fighting . . . fighting to live, to get what she could out of what was left to her of life. Hour after hour she was forcing herself to talk, to laugh, to go on as best she could.

Isabel looked up and saw Levison staring at her. She waved to him and went on talking to her attentive officers.

"What is that?" she questioned abruptly, as the music began a spirited dance.

"It's the gypsy song to love," one of the men told her. "It's from the Strauss opera, 'Zigeuner Baron' . . ."

"And Herr Strauss is conducting, himself," another man pointed out as the conductor-composer waved his baton.

A ballet of brilliantly costumed gypsies appeared on the platform and began a wild csárdás. Back and forth the lithe bodies wove in strange gyrations; stamping heels clicked, forms whirled in writhing contortions. The oil lamps of the footlights created a second ballet of shadows that leaped and fluttered in ghostly ecstasy. Then a mad burst of applause resounded through the gardens. The orchestra broke into a quiet waltz.

"I believe this is my dance." Levison's voice startled Isabel from her reverie. She arose, placing her hand on his arm.

"Will you excuse me?" she smiled back at the officers.

"But I am not going to allow you to forget that it is the next dance which you have to me promised, Madame," one of the men reminded her in his heavily accented English.

"I shan't forget," Isabel called back. "I'm looking forward to it."

Out on the dance floor, beneath the sparkling chandeliers with their millions of prisms, dancing in Levison's arms, Isabel suddenly shivered as though she were cold. How many times in these last two years had she danced . . . and danced. Round and round they circled. It was like her life, she thought. Always going around in the same circle. And to-night . . . somehow, to-night she couldn't get that idea out of her mind. Around and around in a circle. Where would it all end?

"Hadn't we better think about going home?" Levison asked as they danced. "It's almost three o'clock."

"Oh, no, not yet," she pleaded. "I don't want to go yet. And I've promised so many dances. Let's stay just a little longer."

"If you dance with everyone you've promised, we'll be here until daybreak," Levison returned. "I'm rather tired, myself. Another thing, my dear, you can't keep up this pace. Lately you've been going entirely too hard. You'll drop from sheer exhaustion."

"Oh, please don't lecture! You know that's the only way I can sleep . . . sheer exhaustion. I shouldn't sleep if we left now. I must keep on. It's only when I've worn myself out I can sleep."

"Are you . . . regretting things? It's not very flattering to me."

"No . . . no!" Isabel laughed, a forced, brittle laugh. "I'm happy to-night. You've always said you wanted me to be happy."

"I never said I wanted you to be selfish."

"But I don't want to be selfish!" Isabel looked up at her partner wistfully. "I never want to be selfish. Please," she coaxed, "let's not go home just yet."

"Well, as you like."

The music stopped, there was a burst of applause, and then Levison led Isabel back to the Chinese pavilion. Once more her admirers gathered about her, raising their glasses, humming snatches of songs, presenting compliments. How long could she keep this up, Levison wondered. He felt weary enough to sleep for months on end. But Isabel seemed as tireless as though she had an unlimited supply of strength and energy upon which to draw.

"Oh, who is that?" Isabel's exclamation brought the attention of the members of the group to the central pavilion.

"Ah, that is a countrywoman of yours, Ma-

dame," one of the officers informed the girl.
"Madame Neilson, the prima donna. You must
have heard her at Covent Garden. She is the
guest to-night of Herr Strauss."

"No, I've never heard her," Isabel answered.
"I know of her fame, of course. I hope she sings
as sweetly as she looks."

One of the officers screwed a monocle into his
eye and regarded the woman who was being led
onto the center of the stage by the composer.

"They never sing as sweetly as they look,
Madame," he said gravely.

A clatter of applause, the hum of dying conversation, of subdued laughter, as Herr Strauss,
bowing, introduced the guest of the evening.
Madame Neilson smiled out over her audience and
then gave a little nod to the conductor. The orchestra members settled their instruments; the
conductor lifted his baton; and the strains of
gentle music filled the gardens, then died into a
low accompaniment as the singer's voice took up
the aria from "The Bohemian Girl."

"When other lips and other hearts . . .
Their tales of love shall tell . . ."

Isabel set down her glass, staring at the woman
on the stage. The familiar chords, the well-
known words, struck into her very being. She
brushed her hand across her eyes, feeling all the
while that she must be dreaming. Why, that was
her song . . . her own song; the one she loved
because Robert had loved it; the one she had sung

as a lullaby to her baby. Did Robert still love it, or had he put it out of his heart, as he had put her out? Did anyone ever sing it to her baby now?

"In language whose excess imparts
The pow'r they feel so well . . ."

She had sung that song in the Townsend drawing-room the first evening she had met Robert. That was the evening, as he told her later, when he had realized that he loved her. She was back in Mayfair again, surrounded by her friends. Robert was sitting across the room, talking to Lord Townsend. But whenever she looked up she found him watching her. His eyes were upon her, no matter where she turned.

"There may, perhaps, in such a scene
Some recollections be,
Of days that have as happy been,
And you'll remember me. . . ."

Remember! Remember, Robert! It was his voice calling out to her. His voice, and she was at East Lynne. He was bending over her as she sat at the piano. She could feel his very nearness. He reached out his hand to place it over hers. No! No! No! It wasn't! It wasn't Robert! It was the officer on her right, and his hand was over hers.

She scarcely knew whether she screamed aloud or not, but all at once she realized that every-

body at the table was looking at her. She could
feel the color draining from her face. All about
her objects began to swim in a haze. She clutched
at the table edge for support. Her teeth bit into
her white lips. She must keep herself from falling . . . falling . . . into that black, abysmal pit
that yawned before her.

Swiftly Levison was at her side, catching her
by the shoulder, supporting her.

"What is the matter, Madame? Are you ill?"
The officer at her right jumped to his feet, the
other men following his example and crowding
about her chair.

"No . . . no!" she managed to gasp. "I . . .
I'm tired," she whispered, and there was a world
of pathos, of sadness, in her voice. Her eyes
turned to Levison imploringly. "I'm so tired.
Let's go . . . go home."

"Of course, my dear." Tenderly Levison drew
the mantle about her shoulders and helped her
from the chair. She stood, white and shaken,
groping for his arm. He caught her hand and
put one arm about her waist. "You will kindly
excuse us?" He nodded to the group.

Little murmurs followed their course as they
made their way into the darkness of the night.
Eyes looked at them curiously, for a moment, and
then turned back to the singer on the stage. And
over all, ringing in Isabel's ears, haunting her,
torturing her, came the last words of the song:

"And you'll remember, you'll remember . . . me."

CHAPTER XIII

Isabel tossed restlessly in her bed, turning this way and that. It must be noon, she thought, looking at the tiny strands of light that managed to creep around the edges of the drawn curtains of her windows. And yet she hated to ring the bell for her maid; hated to awake to face another day. If she could only keep on sleeping! But it was so warm. She pushed back the satin coverlet and drew a deep breath. Then she pulled the bell rope at the head of her bed.

It was already July, and still Francis remained in Vienna. That was strange, she reflected, frowning. Last season they had gone to the Swiss Alps to escape the heat. And yet why should it be strange? She tried to convince herself that everything was all right. Francis couldn't go anywhere with everyone expecting France to declare war on Prussia at any moment. It was only a matter of hours until the declaration would be made, he had told her.

A knock sounded on the door, and a maid appeared. "Good morning, Madame," the girl curtsied.

"Good morning, Marie. Is there any post?"

"Yes, Madame. Several letters. Shall I open the curtains?"

"Please. And then bring my chocolate."

"Yes, Madame." Marie drew the heavy portières that kept out the morning light, tying them
back with their cords, and disappeared.

Isabel blinked as the bright sun came through
the long lace curtains, flooding the room with its
hot light. She buried her head in the pillow,
shielding her eyes. Would there be a letter from
England, she wondered desultorily. Each morning, month in and month out, she pondered that
question, watching and waiting for a little note,
a word, which would give her some news. But
this morning . . . surely, there'd be a letter this
morning.

"Your chocolate, Madame." The maid was
arranging the tray on the bedside table.

"Oh, thank you." Isabel sat up dully, propped
the pillows behind her, and reached for the newspapers and the letters that lay beside her cup
and saucer. She tossed the papers to one side
and hastily ran over the little sheaf of envelopes.
With a quick intake of her breath she dropped
them all save one . . . one that bore the hand-
writing she loved to see; the dear, familiar English postage stamp.

Her fingers trembling, Isabel tore open the en-
velope and straightened out the one-page letter.
Her eyes hastily scanned the few lines written
in a cramped, old hand. Then she reread the
letter, this time more slowly.

"My lady:" Her lips unconsciously formed
the words as she read them. "This is to tell
your ladyship I received the birthday gift you
sent for Master William. I did not dare give it

to him; if Miss Cornelia knew it, it would cost
me my place, but I did give him the kiss. He is
well and I hope your ladyship is well and happy.
Your obedient servant, Joyce."

Slowly Isabel folded the letter, holding it close
to her breast. The hot tears dimmed her eyes.
Dear, faithful Joyce! She did her best, but it
was all of no avail. Of course, she might have
known that Joyce wouldn't be able to give William the little toy she had sent him. Cornelia
would discover its source with those prying ways
of hers. But William was her own baby . . . her
very own. How could they dare to do such a
thing!

Yet she knew that Robert was simply making
good his word. When he had told her that she
had made her decision and that she should go
forever out of the child's life, he had meant it.
But it was cruel! Cruel! No mention was ever
made of the Lady Isabel in the household at East
Lynne. The servants had been forbidden to
speak to William of his own mother. All that,
she had learned from the few letters Joyce had
managed to send her.

"Oh, Madame!" The sound of Marie's startled
voice made her look up. "You have receive the
bad news! Someone is dead?"

Isabel nodded, her face white and strained.
"Yes, Marie," she said slowly, "someone is dead
. . . dead to me. Someone I love more than anything in the world."

"I am so sorry, Madame." The maid came
to the bed and patted the pillows sympathetically.

"Is there something I can do? Perhaps you have a little chocolate, no? You will feel a little better," She picked up the cup and handed it to her mistress.

"Thank you, Marie." Isabel took the chocolate, grateful for the girl's sympathy. "But there's nothing you can do . . . nothing anyone can do. I'll be all right. Just leave me."

"Yes, Madame." Hastily Marie went on tiptoe from the bedroom, shaking her head sorrowfully; wondering what could have happened to her young English madame.

For a long time Isabel sat propped against the pillows, oblivious to the noises that sounded from the street below, until her chocolate was cold and her hand felt cramped from holding the cup. Then the grating of a key in the lock of the drawing-room door aroused her. That would be Francis, and her eyelids were red and her hair still uncombed. She put down the cup and jumped out of bed.

Quickly she crossed the room and opened the drawer of a small, gilt escritoire. From behind a hidden partition she took a little bundle of letters tied with a piece of blue ribbon. She held them for a moment as though she derived some comfort from touching them. Then she slipped the newest letter in with the others.

It wouldn't do any good to allow Francis to see the note from Joyce. She had shown him the first few when they had arrived, but they made him angry. He felt that she allowed herself to dwell too much upon her home and her child. Once he had flown into a temper because, as he later explained, he was jealous of Carlyle, and that if she really meant what she said about trying to forget everything that had happened, she wouldn't communicate with her former home.

A tap at the door and Marie entered, closing the portal behind her.

"Monsieur is arrive, Madame," she announced.

"Thank you. Will you brush out my hair a little, Marie?" Isabel seated herself before the lovely, satin-draped mirror of the gilt dressing table, and began to pat a creamy liquid into her skin, smoothing it over her face and neck with little pads of cotton, while Marie brushed the long, waving hair that fell about in profusion over the white shoulders.

In the drawing-room Levison paced back and forth nervously, now stopping at the bay window to look into the street below, now listening anxiously for sounds from Isabel's room. He picked up a cigar from the humidor on the long, carved table, lighted it, and then extinguished its glowing end almost immediately. Should he tell her . . . shouldn't he tell her? The questions seesawed in his mind, unanswered.

If he told her, it would be difficult to make her understand; there was so much explanation and so many reasons as to why he didn't want to go into that explanation. If he did, there were a great many things which might hurt her. If he tried now to tell her why he had acted as he had,

A Fox Movietone Production.
A QUIET EVENING AT THE ESTATE OF ROBERT CARLYLE, EAST LYNNE.

East Lynne.

she would think that he was reproaching her.
And he didn't want to cause her that unhappiness. No, the best thing to do would be to offer
a superficial reason for what was about to occur
and say nothing more.

It had been a bad morning, taking it all around.
He'd been a fool. But it had been partially Isabel's fault. Still, he mustn't say that; he mustn't
hint any such thing. Isabel was extravagant;
not exactly extravagant, but she never had known
the value of money. He reviewed the entire
scene, walking back and forth, his hands clasped
behind him.

The British Ambassador had sent for him. He
had waited in the small anteroom, knowing fairly
well what was coming. Then he had been admitted to the audience room. His own Ambassador, a member of the French Embassy, an official
in the Austrian government and two Austrian
generals were there to confront him. He had listened to the accusations leveled against him and
had made no answer. There was nothing he
could say.

"The Government of Her Most Excellent Majesty the Queen of the United Kingdom of Great
Britain and Ireland," he could still hear the
formal words of the British Ambassador ringing
in his ears, "is grateful to the Foreign Secretary
of His Imperial Majesty, the Emperor of Austria-
Hungary, for the information it has received concerning the unethical conduct of a member of the
British Embassy in Vienna."

He had stood there, silent, while the Foreign Secretary bowed. Then the Ambassador had turned to him, his voice chill as steel.

"It is my unpleasant duty to remind you," he had begun, "that, as a member of the British Embassy in Vienna, you have violated the confidence imposed in you by a foreign and friendly power. You have taken advantage of your position in an attempt to disturb the peace of this country by fomenting public opinion on behalf of the French Government in its crisis with Prussia.

"Your conduct is doubly reprehensible," and here the Ambassador's voice had cut like a whip, "inasmuch as you have accepted payment for this. Fortunately, your own government was saved embarrassment by the early disclosure of your perfidy. I shall ask for your immediate resignation and the surrender of your papers. You will not be permitted to return to England."

He had merely bowed in token of the fact that he had heard and comprehended the reasons for his dismissal.

"There is a train leaving Vienna to-night for Paris," the Ambassador had suggested. "After to-day, the Embassy can offer you no further immunity from arrest. That is all."

He had bowed and left the room. Well, what else was there to do, he asked himself. It was true, all that the Ambassador had said. He had needed the money; he had been in a position to help the French Government, and he had known many officials who could buy his help. And he had sold. Now, he had to get out. Well, at least he'd establish Isabel in Paris before war was declared. And he wouldn't tell her anything more than he had to.

"Good morning, dear," Isabel came into the drawing-room, into the midst of Levison's thoughts, a delicate pink peignoir about her shoulders, its creamy falls of fluffy lace half concealing, half revealing the whiteness of her arms and throat. She went to him, kissing him.

"Oh, they're lovely . . . the flowers." Over his shoulder she saw the big bouquet of pale pink roses he had brought in and placed on the table. "You never forget, do you?" She took his face in her hands and kissed him again. As she turned toward the flowers, he caught her hand.

"Isabel," he said hastily. "I . . ." then he stopped, regarding the girl seriously. "I want you to tell me the truth. Are you happy? Are you happy with me?"

Isabel stared, puzzled. "Why, of course I'm happy," she said at last.

"And you haven't any regrets? You must tell me, Isabel."

There was a slight pause as he waited for her answer. Regrets, she was repeating to herself. What did it matter whether she had any regrets or not? Regrets wouldn't bring back her child; wouldn't undo the harm that had been done. All the regretting in the world wouldn't change Cornelia's nature and make East Lynne into another place. It wouldn't change Robert's attitude, either.

And as for regretting her life with Levison

. . . well, she had accepted that when there had seemed to be no other way out. He had been kind to her, far kinder in many ways than Robert ever had been. He had been thoughtful, had tried to make things easier for her when he knew how she was suffering. In all fairness to him, she felt that he had done what he could, and she was grateful for that.

"No, no regrets." And she attempted to smile. But his peculiar manner continued to perplex her. "Why do you ask?"

"Isabel, if something happened in my life . . ." Levison pressed her hand anxiously. "If something happened . . . if I couldn't continue to give you the things I always want you to have . . . the things you should have . . ."

"That wouldn't make any difference to me!" Her head went up, her chin high, and her voice was steady.

She realized now that something, indeed, had happened. Seldom had she seen Francis as serious as this. But what could he mean? What could make him ask such a question? The war! Perhaps that was it. War had been declared. But what would the war have to do with his affairs; how could it affect him seriously, unless England became involved? And why should he think such morbid thoughts?

Levison, noting the bewilderment on the girl's face, tried to laugh reassuringly, but the laugh wouldn't come. He dropped her hand and turned to the decanter and glasses on a taboret, pouring himself a drink of brandy and downing it at one gulp.

"Whatever is the matter, Francis?" Isabel frowned.

He hesitated, and then in a low voice answered her question. "I've been . . . gambling," he said.

"Gambling?" Isabel repeated. "But . . . you mean, you've been playing for high stakes?"

"For high stakes!" Levison's mouth twisted crookedly. Well, he might as well get it over with; tell her at least a part of the story. "I've been gambling with my career . . . my future. I've lost."

"I . . . I don't understand."

Levison turned to the window and stood there, staring down at the street below. Suppose he did tell Isabel everything? Suppose he told her that he had been dismissed from the diplomatic service for giving aid to France when his own country was remaining neutral, using his position to gain money from a foreign power? What would she think of him? She'd probably hate him . . . hate him for his treachery, his disloyalty.

Suppose he told her that he had very little money left? It was one thing to put a hypothetical question; another to state bald facts. Would she turn against him, leave him, when he was down? Isabel wasn't that sort. But she had been reared to expect certain of the luxuries of life. If he couldn't give her those luxuries,

would it make a difference in her attitude toward him?

There had never been any question of money
between them, and he hated to raise that question
now. Isabel had had a little of her own, but he
had taken care of all the heavy bills, and those
bills had run up in the most appalling manner.
Isabel knew that he wasn't wealthy. She might
have been a little more careful, more considerate.
Yet he mustn't blame her . . . he mustn't! She
had been so unhappy, and he was partially to
blame for her unhappiness. She had so many
other troubles weighing upon her.

But if she had tried a little harder to put those
troubles from her, he reflected with a twinge of
jealousy, this might not have happened. If she
had been more interested in him, in his career,
instead of constantly bemoaning the loss of her
home and her child, she would have seen that his
affairs were growing desperate. Yet would she?
She knew nothing of business matters, and he
wouldn't have told her. No, it was again as much
his fault as her own.

"Francis, won't you tell me what's worrying
you?" Gently Isabel took the man's arm, standing beside him, looking up at him.

"I suppose I should be a little more courageous
about it than I am," he said slowly. "I weighed
all the possibilities of failure before I started. I
tried to imagine how I'd feel if I lost out." He
took her hand from his arm and went to pour
himself another brandy.

"What are you talking about? What has happened?"

Levison swallowed the brandy. His hand trembled slightly as he put the glass back on the taboret.

"Do you remember once I told you that all my life I'd been rotten and weak underneath? Well, there's no doubt of it now. The wonder of it is that I've lasted as long as I have. I am rotten and weak. I've tried to hide it, but . . ." He reached again for the brandy. Isabel caught his hand.

"I don't know what's happened," she said firmly. "But whatever it is, brandy's not going to help it."

Again he shook her off, poured the drink and swallowed it quickly.

"I must do something . . . I must do something." He began to pace the floor, muttering to himself. "A man without a country!"

"What do you mean?" Isabel caught his words and they frightened her.

"Oh, never mind now," he gestured impatiently. "I'll tell you later." Still he walked, back and forth, back and forth, back and forth, like a caged animal seeking some outlet from its torture. Suddenly he stopped in front of Isabel and grasped her shoulders so that she faced him.

"You've tossed your life in with mine," he said roughly. "So far, so good. But I can't guarantee anything from now on. Do you understand? I don't know what will happen. I can't promise you anything at all. It's not too late for you to turn back . . .''

"Oh!" Isabel's cry was almost a moan. It hurt her to feel that Francis should think she was that sort of a person. "How can you say that? It's not too late for me to turn back! Do you imagine for one moment that because you're in some sort of trouble, I'd leave you? When I told you I'd stay with you to the end, did you think I didn't mean it?"

"But now it won't be the same," Levison tried to explain. "Things will be different. You must understand that. Our life will be changed. To-night I leave for Paris."

"For Paris?"

"Yes," Levison nodded slowly, watching the girl.

There was a slight pause. Then Isabel looked up, her blue eyes unwavering. "Very well," she said simply. "I'll be ready." Not a question; not a reproach.

Impulsively Levison took her in his arms, kissing her. "You dear, dear person," he murmured over and over again. And his eyes were misty with tears.

CHAPTER XIV

France required now only a pretext for a quarrel. All Europe sat back, expectant. Meanwhile the distracted Spaniards were searching among the royal families of the Continent for a king. They chanced upon the Prince Leopold of Hohenzollern. France, separated from Spain by the Pyrenees, intimated that she would not approve of the occupancy of the throne of Spain by any member of the house of Hohenzollern. But King William of Prussia disclaimed all knowledge or responsibility in regard to the proceedings of his relative. The relative refused the vacant throne firmly. France's pretext for declaring war was lost.

Germany had not been idle. The famous spy system of the Herr Doktor Stieber had been at work in France. Stieber, himself, came and went in his many guises, including that of a Greek capitalist. A thousand German women had found their way into French households, acting as servants; as chambermaids in hotels where French officers and notables stopped. Hundreds of German "farmhands" seeped into France; hundreds of young secretaries who had been taught how to open sealed envelopes and seal them again without detection. From Stieber's minutely detailed reports Field Marshal

Von Moltke had already formulated the plan for the invasion of France. Germany wanted Alsace and Lorraine.

Two more veiled messages regarding the Prince Leopold and Spain were exchanged, and on July 19, 1870, the formal declaration of war was delivered at Berlin.

France was mobilizing. Along narrow, winding streets and on either side of wide boulevards, flags and buntings, wreaths and flowers decorated the fronts of tumbling, ancient house and white, palatial mansion alike. Everywhere sounded the tread of marching feet, gay feet, light feet, ready feet. The strains of the "Marseillaise" flooded broad avenue and blind alley; filled street corners and cafés. "On to the Rhine . . . the Rhine . . . the Rhine!" France and Germany were at war.

Throughout the length and breadth of the city no subject was discussed save the war. The strength of France, so the French had been led to believe, was carefully built up; organization was faultless; supplies of clothing were inexhaustible, "not even a gaiter button" was missing; the cartridges were enough to push back the Germans and cross the Rhine; there were whispers of that "terrible *mitrailleuse*," whose power was now to be revealed. The Emperor, Napoleon the Third, enfeebled through illness, did not want war; but it was claimed that his rule had been expensive and that his foreign policy had brought disgrace. So Paris grew en-

thusiastic and shouted: "On to the Rhine!"
And the provinces blindly acquiesced.

On the little iron balcony on the second floor
of an ancient, once-beautiful home, stood the Lady
Isabel and Francis Levison. The laughter and
shouts of the crowds on the street below were
augmented by the cries and songs of the group
of people within the apartment. A piano was
noisily strummed, glasses were held high, and
toasts were drunk to the anticipated victories of
the French army. The French army couldn't be
defeated!

As another champagne cork popped, Isabel
turned wearily and stepped into the room. An
elderly artist in baggy corduroys leaped forward,
bowing, offering his glass to the girl. Isabel
shook her head, smiling. But a poet, distin-
guished by the fact that his hair curled about
the collar of his shirt which stood open at the
throat, was noisily insistent.

"To La Belle France!" he sang out. "To La
Belle France! To her spirit that never, never
dies! To her soldiers! To Victory . . . pretty
mistress of a thousand battles! To the down-
fall of Prussia!"

The man at the piano banged the keys and
set the "Marseillaise" to a waltz tempo, im-
provising the bass to fit his own version of the
melody. Two actresses, whose heavily jeweled
hands sparkled in the morning sunshine, began
to sing the words, executing little dance steps,
raising their ruffled skirts and petticoats until

the tips of kid slippers showed, the heels gleamed softly, and slender ankles were displayed to the light of day.

"Bravo! Bravo!" shouted the pianist.

"To Victory! To Victory!" the cry rang out.

"My friends!" The artist raised his voice to make it heard above the bedlam. "Everyone predicts that the war will be over in three months!"

"Booh!" Hisses and catcalls greeted his statement. "Yes . . . no . . . yes . . . no longer . . . easily . . . three weeks . . . three days!"

"I do not believe it will be over in three months!"

"What?" The entire group screamed in chorus.

"I believe it'll be over in three weeks!"

"Bravo! Vive la France!"

"I drink a toast to the new Paris!" the artist insisted. "Triumphant in war . . . gayest capital in the world! Where shall we go? Let's all go to the cafés! We're missing all the excitement! Who's coming?" He banged his glass on the table.

"We'll all go!" the actresses decided. "Come along, Piggy," they prodded the musician into activity. "We'll take you."

"And me?" The poet turned out his empty pockets significantly.

"Yes, everybody," they called, laughing.

Isabel toyed with the glass of champagne she held in her hand, watching the bustle and activity, the screaming gayety of these Bohemian friends.

Suddenly she swallowed the wine, shuddered, and stepped a little to one side as though to efface herself. But one of the women stopped her.

"We'll all go together, my dear. Where's your hat?"

"I'm afraid you'll have to excuse me," Isabel murmured.

"Oh, very well!" The woman shrugged. "And you, chérie?" she called to Levison.

The man glanced sharply at Isabel, frowning a little, and then shook his head. "I'll join you later," he promised. "Wait for me. Where shall I meet you?"

"We'll go to Antoine's. Don't be too long!" With a wave of her hand, the actress started for the door, crowding the others along with her, calling out farewells.

As the door banged on the last departing guest, Isabel sank into a chair, and surveyed the room. A broken glass lay beneath a chair. The table spread that had once been a piece of beautifully worked tapestry was stained with wine. The top of the grand piano showed little white rings where damp glasses had rested too long. A cigar, or match, had burned a round hole in the upholstery of a chair back.

It was all like her own life, Isabel reflected dully. Everything falling to pieces, little by little, crumbling into ruin. The paint on the paneled walls needed renewing. The delicate gilt chairs creaked shakily when one sat upon them. The portières were frayed at the edges; the lace curtains carelessly mended, the net drawn to-

gether by a hasty needle. A large alabaster
statute of the God of Love, standing in one
corner, showed a chipped wing and a missing
finger.

And these people . . . these people who came
to see them here, who drank and smoked and
laughed and talked, and fluttered away as lightly
as they had come when the supply of wine was
exhausted! They were an entirely different sort
from any Isabel had ever known. They were
the hangers-on of the real artistic set of Paris.
None of them was a true, a serious worker or
thinker.

"Well, you evidently don't care for our Bohemian friends," Levison interrupted the girl's
thoughts, his voice cynical.

"No, I can't say that I do," Isabel answered
truthfully.

"Well, neither do I." Levison went to a decanter on a side table and began to pour himself
a glass of brandy. "But beggars can't be
choosers. At least you could be decently polite
to them. We can't live like a couple of hermits."

"Of course not," Isabel agreed hastily. "And
they help one to forget."

Levison gulped his liquor. He was annoyed,
a little angry with Isabel for declining to go out
to the cafés. If she didn't like these friends of
his choosing, why didn't she find others more
interesting to her? He had told her before they
left Vienna that things would be different, and
she had made her decision; had come on with

him to Paris. Then why couldn't she be sensible
about their present situation?

He didn't blame her entirely for her dislike
of these pseudo artists. But why make a scene
about them? They were well enough in their
way, and lack of money made it impossible to
try to keep up with a more exclusive and expensive set. How could Isabel expect to be received
in her own circle, when she was ostensibly living
as Madame Levison and everybody knew the circumstances of the case?

And as for the diplomatic circles, they were
closed to him. He had hoped to be able to attach
himself in some way to the French Government
and thus replenish at least to some extent his
rapidly diminishing funds. But the French Government would have none of him. It was so secure, so confident in its own power, that his few
rather feeble services were negligible. But if
matters continued this way, he'd soon be at the
end of his rope.

"Will you please order another bottle of champagne?" Isabel asked finally, anxious to turn the
subject away from these friends.

"Champagne?" Levison raised his eyebrows,
and sniffed sarcastically. "So, you must have
an expensive wine, too, to help you forget. Did
you ever happen to think, my dear, that champagne costs money? Other women have been
known to ease their troubled consciences on a
cheaper wine."

"Oh, please!" Isabel raised her hand in a

gesture of hopeless distaste for the insinuation.
"Let's not be common! Above everything else,
let's not do that. Besides, I don't want it for
myself. I hate it . . . loathe it."

"So you don't want it for yourself? For
whom, then? A visitor?" Again that meaning
smile that was so suggestive.

She hated Francis, hated him when he was
in this mood, Isabel told herself with a sudden
revulsion of feeling, a swift flash of the truth
penetrating her mind. He had changed; he was
drinking entirely too much; he was never actually
sober these days. And when he drank he became
ugly; he said things that he never would have
uttered before. He had never been this way in
Vienna.

"Yes, I'm expecting a visitor," Isabel nodded
wearily. "My father. I wrote to him and asked
him to come here. He cabled that he'd arrive
to-day."

"Your father? Here?" Levison was startled
out of his mood. "Why? Why did you write
to him? You never told me anything about it.
Was it such a secret? Why did you do that?"

"Well," Isabel began evasively, hoping to put
a stop to the scene she felt might ensue. "I
merely want to see him. That's all. He's my
father."

"Oh, you want to see him!" Levison spat out
the words sarcastically. "It didn't occur to you,
I suppose, that I might have been consulted . . .
that I might not want to see him! You seem to
manage a great many things quite easily without

taking me into consideration.'' He poured another brandy.

With a sense of utter futility, of inability to cope with Francis when he chose to adopt this mood, Isabel rose from her chair and went to the window, turning her back on the room. Tears of mortification filled her eyes. But it would do no good to say anything. She had scarcely been able to understand his attitude since they had left Vienna. Always before he had been kindly considerate, but now he seemed to delight in cruel speeches, cheaply vulgar and thinly veiled hints and aspersions.

It had all come about in these three weeks that they had been in Paris. Francis even looked dissipated now. There were lines about his mouth, and his eyes were haggard. Little bags of flesh hung flabbily beneath his eyes. She knew that he was worried over finances, that his work in the diplomatic service had somehow come to an end, and she was sorry for him in his trouble. But he never told her anything of his affairs; never mentioned their flight from Vienna and even refused to allow her to discuss it.

She had tried to help, she reminded herself. But she didn't know how to live economically. That flat . . . they had taken it because it was fairly cheap, she knew. And she bought no clothes. But they had to live. Wasn't that what Francis himself had told her when he had met her on the channel boat? One had to go on living; one didn't die of sorrow. Too bad; that might be the solution to everything.

But as for Francis, he had no right to say to her the things he had said. She resented as much as he did having to live in these surroundings, having to associate with these people. They had both placed themselves beyond the pale when they had begun their new life together. Francis knew it. She knew it. And she had never made any mention of that issue. It was a tacit agreement, that was all.

Francis had never suggested marriage to her, even after the final decree of divorce had been granted. As she looked back on it now, she realized that never once had he proposed to her. Even at East Lynne, when he had urged her to go away with him, he had not mentioned marriage. Well, why should he, she asked herself. She doubted very much whether she would have married him, even had he wanted it. The ties that bound her to East Lynne were stronger than any other attachment she could ever make. She didn't want others.

"So your father's coming here," Levison said loudly.

Isabel faced about, her fingers pulling nervously at a looped silk cord that draped the front of her pale green gown. He was still surly, and she could see that the rims of his eyes were an angry red. She said nothing.

"Oh, well," Levison went on when she didn't speak. "Perhaps he'll return the money I loaned him the last time I was in England. Miracles have happened!"

"Please! Aren't you forgetting yourself?"

Isabel retorted sharply. She could feel the blood mounting to her cheeks, and she shut her teeth together tightly in an effort to control her emotions.

Levison shrugged his shoulders, smiling cynically. "Perhaps I am," he answered lightly. "But may I suggest, my dear, that champagne will not be strong enough for your father. It takes something with a little more body to it for anyone with his capacity. Oh, no! Brandy for his lordship! Cognac! Yes . . . yes, indeed!" He poured a glass of the liquor for himself and raised it, looking at Isabel over the top.

"Now, if you'll excuse me," he drained the glass, set it back on the table, and reached for his hat and stick, "I'll take myself off. A bit indelicate, what, for an erring lover to intrude between a devoted father and daughter." He reached the doorway and paused, looking back as he settled his hat on his head.

"Old Mount Severin!" He grinned. "Huh! Do you know, my dear, he once read me a lecture on reaping the whirlwind? Fancy that!" The door banged shut behind his departing figure.

A flood of resentment against such conduct swept over Isabel, leaving her cold and shaken. Weakly she dropped into a chair, her hands falling listlessly to her sides. What difference did it make, after all? But it was so unfair, so hateful of Francis to make a point of reminding her of her father's weaknesses. Surely she wasn't responsible for Lord Mount Severn. Rather, he should be responsible for her.

But he never had been, Isabel reminded herself grimly. He had come into money; everything had been handed him. He had never done a stroke of work in his entire life; never shouldered a responsibility. He had even managed to squander the money that should have been hers. He had accepted money from her husband, and now she heard that he had been borrowing from her lover. It was disgusting, revolting, the whole affair. Yet in a little while, her father would be here.

Would it do any good, she wondered dully, talking to her father? She rather doubted it, but she had felt desperate when she had written, asking him to come to her. Such a little distance separated her now from England. And she wanted so much to hear news; wanted to know how matters stood at East Lynne. Perhaps . . . perhaps things might have changed just a little. The feeble spark of hope still burned. But she must know . . . she must be certain.

A knock at the door made her sit up straight in her chair. Could her father have arrived already? She called out and a servant in shabby livery entered, bearing an ice-filled bucket with the long, thin neck of a bottle protruding from it, and a tray with fresh glasses.

"Monsieur ordered the wine to be served here," the man spoke in French.

"Thank you, Pierre. Will you put it on the table? And arrange the room a little."

"Yes, Madame." The man straightened the tapestry on the center table and placed the tray with the glasses and the bucket, wrapped with a heavy napkin, on top. Sketchily he went over the room, picking up the fragments of glass, re-arranging the chairs and giving some semblance of order to the place. Then with a hurried bow he departed.

Isabel leaned against the window frame, watching the street below, looking up and down for some sign of her father. He should be here at any moment, now. If only he weren't the in-effectual, careless person that he was! But at least he would bring news, and that was something to be thankful for. And perhaps he might . . . he might just be able to do something.

What she hoped to hear of East Lynne Isabel didn't quite know. She didn't dare to allow her-self to think what she really wanted to hear. She had long since had word that Carlyle had secured the final decree of divorce. But time might have worked a little change in his attitude. She hated to feel that he was so bitter against her; that he believed Cornelia's accusations against his own wife.

It was all such a hopeless muddle. Isabel's head dropped against the portières. This life she endured at present couldn't go on much longer. There would be some end to it. And what to do when that end came, she realized that she didn't know.

CHAPTER XV

A BATTERED carriage drawn by a pair of lean
chestnut horses rumbled over the uneven street,
jolting and jerking Lord Mount Severn, who
clutched at his gold-handled cane and tried to
cling to the battered upholstery of the seat. He
wondered impatiently why on earth Isabel had
been so insistent upon seeing him; why she had
wanted him to come to Paris. He hated the crossing and he wouldn't live on the Continent under
any circumstances, he grumbled.

He was still grumbling when the carriage finally
came to a stop before that row of genteely im-
poverished dwellings where Isabel and Levison
had their flat. He glanced around and sniffed
disdainfully.

"This the place?" Mount Severn prodded the
coachman with his stick and waved toward the
house which bore the number Isabel had sent
him. He spoke in English, refusing even to attempt French, holding that it was the Frenchman's own fault if he didn't understand.

The cabby jumped down and entered into a
voluble explanation, also waving toward the
house.

"Very well! Very well!" Mount Severn interrupted curtly, stepping down onto the walk.
"Appalling neighborhood, what? Slums, I should

say." He looked about a second time, uncertain
and a little dubious.

Another volley of French set him to hunting
for his change wallet. The coachman was silent
as the Englishman carefully counted out francs
and centimes, placing them in the waiting palm.

"There you are, my man." Mount Severn
stepped jauntily up to the door and pulled at the
big bell knob. A clatter resounded throughout
the house and another clatter broke forth on the
street as the cab driver counted his money. A
barrage of imprecations, threats, and pronounce-
ments fell upon Mount Severn's non-understand-
ing ears.

An aged concierge opened the door at last and
waited patiently while the English gentleman explained his errand. Silently he led the way up
two long flights of thinly carpeted stairs and
pulled the bell. A slight tingle resounded and
then the door was flung open.

"Father! Oh, Father, I'm so glad to see you!"
Isabel's arms were about his neck and Mount
Severn was kissing his daughter and patting her
shoulder.

"There . . . there . . . there . . . there!" he was
muttering, a little uncomfortable in the presence
of so much emotion. Isabel always was too emotional, he reflected. Exactly like her mother.
"Well, my dear, how are you?"

"Come in, dear." Isabel led her father into
the drawing-room, closing the door. "It's so
good to see you . . . so good to see anyone from
home."

"Yes, yes," Mount Severn agreed testily. "So I should imagine." He gazed about the room, noting its shabbiness, its pitiful pretenses to luxury and beauty.

Well, it must be true, then, all that he had heard, he reflected. Levison's money was gone and his career as a diplomat was over. Otherwise he wouldn't be living in such quarters as these. It was a shame, but he didn't know what could be done about it. He did hope Isabel wasn't going to ask for financial assistance. That would be too embarrassing.

"Do sit down, Father. This chair's comfortable." Isabel was pulling out an armchair, the only one that looked as though it would bear any weight without falling to pieces.

"Thanks," he grunted, laying his hat on the side table and then seating himself. "Paris! Same old smelly Paris! Always at war . . . always fighting with some country or other. I didn't know whether it would be safe to travel here. I loathe the place. Don't see how you stand it, my dear. I wouldn't have come, but for you. Of course, blood's thicker than water."

A little, wistful smile overspread the girl's face. "You've always said that, haven't you? But I did hate asking you to make the trip. Only I wanted to see you so badly."

"Humph!" Mount Severn cleared his throat. "I'll have to return to-night, you know. Why did you send for me? I haven't any money." Better explain right away, before he was asked,

he thought. Dreadful shame, though, seeing Isabel reduced to this.

"I'm not going to ask you for money," the
girl hastened to reassure her father. Of course
that would be his first idea, that she was in dire
financial straits and had called on him for help.
What else could he think, seeing her in such
surroundings? For a moment she felt ashamed;
felt a hatred for herself, for her father, for
Francis. But that moment passed, and again she
was eager to talk, to find out what she wanted
to know.

"What I really need is your advice, Father,"
she explained. "But first, tell me . . . have you
any news of East Lynne? Have you seen . . .
have you seen anyone from there? What is
happening?"

"Humph!" Mount Severn twisted about nervously in his chair. "Of course, you've heard
that the final decree of divorce was awarded to
Carlyle?"

"Yes . . . yes, I heard that long ago," Isabel
nodded impatiently. "While we . . . that is, I
was in Vienna. I read it in one of the English
newspapers. But I don't mean news of that sort.
You . . . you haven't seen Robert? That is, I
mean I thought perhaps he might have forgiven
me . . . a little. Perhaps he's not so bitter
against me, now. Maybe time has softened him.
Maybe in his heart he's sorry for what he did?"

Her words came in a torrent of sound. Anxiously she was watching her father's face, scan-

ning every feature to try to read the answer to
all her faint, flickering hopes. And as she watched
she grew frightened, terror gripped her. For
there was no encouragement in the way her father
was shaking his head; no consolation in the grim
compression of his mouth. Her breath caught in
her throat.

"Why do you do that?" she cried out in desperation. "Why do you shake your head?"

Mount Severn hesitated for an instant and then
spoke abruptly. "My dear, did you think that
you could escape gossip? Did you think that news
of you would not travel back to England? Have
you been laboring under the delusion that the
world was making an exception of you and your
. . . ahem . . . your indiscretion? Your . . .
uh . . . continuous indiscretion?"

"I never thought of it," Isabel returned
simply. "I . . . why . . ." She stood up,
straight and tall, her chin raised, her whole attitude one of defiance. "After all, what I have
done is my affair, and mine alone. How should
anyone dare to criticize me! I've made what I
could out of my life. I've gone on living it, facing
it; I've set up no pretenses; I've asked no
favors!"

"Perhaps not," Mount Severn said quietly.
"But the cruelest truth is that we cannot live
our lives apart from the opinion of the world."

"Oh!" The painful wail escaped involun-
tarily. "But do you . . ." she wavered, fearful
of hearing the answer to her question, yet forcing
herself to ask it. "Do you think Robert knows?"

Mount Severn's eyebrows flew up in surprise.
"Knows? Undoubtedly he knows. The purpose
of gossip is to wound." Uneasily the man arose
and walked about the room. This whole interview was painful, quite painful. He wished he
were well out of it. His eyes lighted on the decanter of brandy on the side table.

"May I?" he asked, reaching for the glass
container.

Isabel looked up, startled. "Oh, yes, yes, of
course. Help yourself. But there's some wine
cooling there on the table. Wouldn't you
prefer . . ."

"No, thanks," Mount Severn interrupted
hastily, pouring out the brandy. "Much rather
have this. The crossing was a little rough. I
feel a bit upset. This'll settle my stomach."

"Of course," Isabel acquiesced dully.

That was what Francis had said. It was
brandy for his lordship! Champagne was too
light. Well, let him have the brandy. Francis
was right. For that matter, her father was right,
Carlyle was right, the whole world was right.
It was only she who was wrong. Everything she
had ever done had been wrong. Even the most
innocent things could be distorted until they were
made wrong.

And the gossip . . . the wagging tongues
anxious and greedy to seize upon the slightest
morsel! How they must have delighted in picking her to pieces. She shuddered. She had never
thought of it in that way before. She hadn't
realized that her conduct was giving rise to murky

speculations, hard criticism. She had never
thought of herself as the sort of woman the world
branded her. Why, she wasn't . . . she wasn't.
She had just gone on living.

Yet, after all, where was the dividing line to be
drawn? When she had been perfectly blameless
and stainless, Cornelia, Robert, the whole world
had pointed the finger of scorn at her; had accused her of doing what she had never even
thought of doing. It was Cornelia, and Robert,
and all the people like they, who had forced her
to become what they believed her to be. Then
who was at fault? Who carried the guilt on his
shoulders?

It wasn't that she was trying to elude the responsibility of her actions. She blamed herself
as much as anyone else for all that had happened.
But it was so easy for those others to criticize;
others who had no temptations, no desires, no
love of life. If she hadn't had that love of life,
she might have settled into the groove at East
Lynne, passively accepting her fate. She would
have had no desire for brightness, for laughter,
for love.

But she had. And the desire had been born
in her. Then how could she escape from it? She
had tried. But because a series of events had
occurred she had become the scapegoat. And
there was no one who had believed in her. No
one wanted to believe her. Only Francis had held
out a helping hand; only Francis, who knew the
truth of her story. And now even he was

changing. Suddenly she felt very weak and very much alone.

Lord Mount Severn maneuvered another brandy and looked at his daughter quizzically.

"May I inquire why, after all these months, you suddenly become interested again in East Lynne?"

"Oh, but I haven't suddenly become interested in East Lynne!" She felt a sense of wonderment at her father's lack of understanding. That he should think that through all these months she had forgotten her child, her home!

"I've only tried to forget! Night and day I've tried to forget." Her fingers laced and interlaced as she talked, living over again these months of horror. "Don't you see, I've never forgotten, no matter how hard I've tried. No matter what I've done, nothing could actually blot out the past.

"Oh, there were times," she hastened on, eager to make him see what she meant, "when I thought, perhaps just for one evening, that I had forgotten. But I had to pay for every moment of that forgetting ten times over. A little peace, and then for days, weeks, it would be worse than ever. I've almost gone mad! I couldn't sleep. I used to try . . . and try. And then I'd get up and go out on the boulevards in the rain and snow and slush. And I'd walk . . . walk as fast as I could, as far as I could, trying to tire myself out; trying to exhaust myself."

She shook her head. "But I couldn't. I couldn't! Sometimes, when I could scarcely stand on my feet, suddenly out of the mists of the night my baby's face would come to me . . . like that.'' She reached out her hands as though to touch the face that constantly rose before her. She sighed brokenly.

"It's silly to say it, I know, but I could feel his breath on my lips. Oh, I don't know what to do. I don't know what to do!''

She rose and began to pace the floor nervously, fighting back the tears, clenching and unclenching her hands, the nails biting into the palms unheeded.

Mount Severn, slightly upset by this emotional outburst, tried to think of something comforting to say. "Uh . . . ghastly mess, isn't it?'' he managed after a bit. He hadn't realized that his daughter had been so wrought up over the divorce; he had never thought she felt this way about it.

Isabel scarcely heard her father's remark. There was one question she must ask him; one thing she must know. And she was desperately afraid of what his answer might be. Yet she must find out. She had sent for him because she wanted to find this out. She tried to make her voice light; tried to conceal its trembling.

"And Robert?'' She stopped beside her father, watching him. "I suppose he will marry again?'' Now, it was over. Now, she'd know.

Mount Severn drew a deep breath of relief. If that was all she had wanted to ask him! "Undoubtedly,'' he returned. "As a matter of fact his engagement to Barbara Hare has already been announced. I believe they're to be married shortly. Very quietly, you know, but after all . . ."

"Oh!" Isabel gasped, and turned away quickly. She went to the window, staring down at the street. The sounds of voices were carried up to her, but she didn't hear them. Carriages rattled by; on the boulevard beyond soldiers marched to the strains of military music. But she didn't see anything. Robert was going to marry Barbara Hare. Well, Cornelia had got her way at last.

Robert, married to Barbara Hare! Barbara, that sweet, quiet girl the mistress of East Lynne. Barbara taking the place that had once been hers; taking her place in her baby's affections. Barbara would have William; she'd have her baby; another woman would hold the child in her arms, and perhaps he'd learn to call this strange woman "mummy." She could hear the childish voice ringing out.

"After all, my dear," Mount Severn rambled on, "Carlyle has the right to marry."

Frantically Isabel turned on her father, her eyes blazing. "I'm not thinking of Carlyle!" she burst out. "I'm thinking only of my child. What does it matter what Robert does, as long as it doesn't affect my baby. But don't you see, he'll bring that woman to East Lynne. She's going to take my place in my baby's heart. He'll grow up, and never know me. Maybe if I met

him later on, I wouldn't know him! Think of it!
My own child, and I wouldn't know him . . . he
wouldn't know me!''

The tears filled her eyes and streamed down
her cheeks. ''My God! My God!'' she moaned.
''I can't stand it! No matter what I did, that
isn't fair. Robert must know that isn't fair. He
was cruel to me . . . cruel! But that doesn't
matter any more. It's my baby that matters.
He mustn't grow up, never knowing his mother
. . . never seeing me!

''Oh, can't you understand? Can't you understand?'' She flung out her arms despairingly.
''Maybe if Robert knew how much I've suffered
he'd relent a little. If he could only know how
I wake up with my baby's fingers clinging to
mine! And now another woman's to take my
place, to tend him, be close to him, love him.
She'll make him love her. He won't know me!''

Her voice broke. Pitiful sobs racked her slender body, shaking it as the wind shakes a tender
sapling.

''There, there, my dear.'' A little awkwardly
Mount Severn patted his daughter's shoulder.
''I only wish there was something I might do.
Don't take on so.''

''Oh, but there is . . . there is something you
can do.'' Isabel turned a tear-stained face to her
father, seizing his hands and clinging to him for
support. ''That's why I sent for you. I want
you to go to East Lynne. I want you to see Robert. You must see him, talk to him, plead with

A Fox Movietone Production. East Lynne.

ISABEL, UNABLE TO STAND THE INSINUATIONS OF HER
HUSBAND, PREPARES TO LEAVE EAST LYNNE.

him, reason with him. You must! You must, Father. Beg him to let me see my child!"

"But, my dear!" Mount Severn spoke sharply, a little annoyed that his daughter should demand anything so out of the question. "That is impossible. You know the man. There are ten generations of puritans behind him. He'd never listen."

"He must be made to listen!" Isabel pleaded with a desperation born of awful terror. "You must tell him that I know I did wrong. Tell him that I admit the justice of everything he has ever said against me. What does it matter what he thinks about me? What does it matter what the world thinks about me? My life is finished. Robert can think what he likes.

"Tell him I make no defense for my actions in the past. Tell him I was wrong . . . he was right. Make him understand I'm willing to do anything he says. I'll do any penance, no matter what. I'll crawl in the dust on my knees if he'll only let me see my baby once more . . . let me touch him . . . just hold him in my arms. I can't stand it any longer. You must make him understand!"

She stopped, exhausted by her outburst. Her father put his arm about her and gently led her to a chair.

"Will you do that? Will you go to East Lynne?" she begged.

"Yes, of course, I will." And for the first time Mount Severn was deeply touched; for the first time he understood a little of what Isabel had suffered. "I'll do what I can. I'll go to Carlyle. I'll tell him what you've said. I don't think there's a man on this earth who could refuse you what you ask." And his tone was sincere.

Isabel sighed brokenly, but this slight hope buoyed her up. "Oh, my dear! You don't know how much I appreciate that! I'll be so anxious until I hear from you. Everything in my life depends upon you."

"I'll not fail you," Mount Severn promised faithfully.

Isabel rose shakily and went to her father, kissing him. "Thank you, dear. And now, please don't waste any time. Take the first train out. And cable me as soon as you see Robert, won't you? I'll be waiting. Think of me, sitting here, waiting . . ."

"All right, my dear." Mount Severn patted his daughter's hand consolingly, even a little affectionately. "I'll do my very best." He took up his hat and stick and once more kissed the girl. "Good-by, my child," he said tenderly.

"Good-by, Father." She opened the door for him and saw him walk down the hall. Finally she closed the portal, leaning wearily against it. If he could only do something . . . if he only would do something.

But in the darkness of the corridor Lord Mount Severn stopped to look back, shaking his head in doubt.

CHAPTER XVI

Six weeks later the Emperor, Napoleon the Third, was a prisoner in the hands of the Germans and the long siege of Paris, which marked the Franco-Prussian War, was begun.

A series of tragic and unexpected failures had met the French at every turn. Where the Emperor should have found himself at the head of four hundred thousand men, perfectly disciplined and equipped, he discovered, to his alarm, that his troops numbered but two hundred and twenty thousand, many of whom had not been drilled at all in the use of the breech-loading musket. The officers who were familiar with the *mitrailleuse* had been carelessly drafted off to other duties.

Supplies which had been, seemingly, so carefully tabulated, were wanting. There was a shortage of money and food which struck terror to the bravest heart. True, there were vast accumulations, but they had been piled up in two or three grand depots, and now it was found that they could not rapidly be delivered. There were transport wagons at one point, but the wheels for those wagons had been stored at another point. So that many days elapsed before carriages and wheels could be assembled to transfer the stores. The artillery had no horses; it was obliged to borrow from the cavalry. The only maps provided were maps of Germany.

The plan of the French had been to cross the Rhine before the Germans could gather the necessary troops to prevent them. But with the lack of forces, the incompleteness of supplies, the plan was hopeless. At Saarbrück the Emperor was driven off and forced to fall back toward Metz. At Speichern the French held an almost impregnable position on the heights, but hours of heavy fighting, with lamentable slaughter, sent them beaten and disorderly from the field. Fourteen days had sufficed to bring forth four hundred and fifty thousand German soldiers, the states of the south marching with their countrymen of the north, forgetful of their internal quarrels.

In quick succession came the two bloody but indecisive battles at Rezonville and Gravelotte, where vain attempts were made to break through the German lines. The march to Metz was blocked and the French were driven northward toward Sedan, driven through the dark night with heavy rain miring the roads. The Germans began their attack. Marshal MacMahon was borne from the field, wounded. Long, hard hours of frightful battle. And the French were scattered, captured, or driven back into Sedan.

Soldiers and citizens ran riot in the streets. Arms were thrown away, regardless of orders. Food, and shelter from the withering fire of the German guns were sought. People were trampled down; the panic-stricken wagoners forced their way through the town. And over all, the ceaseless bombardment of the German guns. Until the Emperor, vainly seeking death by exposure in the field, ordered the flag of truce to be hung out and surrendered himself to the King of Prussia.

His first entrance into German territory was made as a prisoner of war.

The way to Paris was cleared of all obstacles. Now the roads resounded with the tread of the advancing Germans. The heavy wagons rumbled through French territory, on to Paris. In that city the captive Emperor was deposed and a Republic set up. The new government planned a vigorous defense. But the Germans completely surrounded Paris. Communications with the outside world were cut off. Supplies grew lower and lower. Famine faced the defenders. The occasional boom of bombarding guns came as a reminder that the Germans were waiting.

The streets were thronged with wounded, disabled, and dying men . . . men who had escaped and made their way back to Paris, or had been brought with the German armies. Citizens were struck down by the guns surrounding the city. Every public building, every private home, became a nursing and dressing station. Everywhere the blood of France and Germany ran red. A month, two months. Winter set in. Fuel was exhausted. Freezing, starving human beings turned into vicious animals, fighting for existence.

During these bitter, savage days Isabel went to the little post office which had been converted into a dressing station for the wounded to do what she could for the unfortunate. Her hours were spent tearing strips of cloth in bandages, making crude dressings, and waiting upon the stricken soldiers who lay on pallets on the floor. Having something to do, something with which to occupy her hands, gave her a little relief from her own thoughts.

No word had yet arrived from her father . . . no word of the outcome of his interview with Robert Carlyle. But each day she waited expectantly, hope lighting up her eyes, and then dying again as the postmaster shook his head in answer to her question. Whether her father had actually seen Robert she couldn't know. He had promised, and she didn't think that he'd break that promise to her, but then, in his usual, careless way, he might have put off the interview; might have made one feeble attempt and given up entirely.

Of course the matter of getting messages through at such a time as this was entirely problematical, with postal communications being sent in and out by balloons. There was no direct way of cabling, of sending a letter. And the balloons were often brought down by the Germans and the mail confiscated. But surely, if her father had been at all successful, he would have made more than one effort to get in touch with her.

Matters between Francis Levison and herself, had gone from bad to worse. Their relationship was strained almost to the breaking point. Francis drank whatever, whenever, and wherever he could. Just as he was doing this afternoon. And then when Isabel returned to the tiny flat

there would be a quarrel, harsh, bitter, reproachful words.

This afternoon, while Isabel desultorily rolled
her bandages in the dressing station and watched
for any incoming mail, Levison sat in the apartment with two of his friends, returned soldiers.
They had secured a bottle of cognac and were
now discussing the one subject which occupied
all of Paris, the siege.

"Never did I think that the Germans would
come so close to Paris," one of the men whom
Levison addressed as Henri was saying. "Do
you remember, two months ago, when we were
called to the colors? No one thought that such
a thing could happen."

"No." The tall, lithe, dark-haired man called
Carlo shook his head. "We all thought the war
would end quickly enough . . . but not this
way. Why we should have been defeated all
around . . ."

"It was gross neglect, carelessness," Levison
put in. "Remember the day war was declared?
We all went to Antoine's."

"Yes, I remember," Carlo put in. "And now
Antoine's is closed. Ah, for one morsel of his
filet of sole Marguery!"

"Don't speak of it!" Henri poured himself
a drink and shuddered. "The rations are getting
worse and worse. During the Revolution the
French were reduced to eating the sewer
rats . . ."

"Hold your tongue!" Levison exploded sav-
agely. "I can't stand it!"

"All right," Henri shrugged. "But the Germans are starving us out."

"Yes, and King William takes his ease at the Palace of Versailles, while we starve to death," Levison said grudgingly. "Why can't an end be put to the thing? The Germans have got back Alsace and Lorraine. What are they waiting for now?"

"There's been too much enmity between France and Germany for too many years for an end to be made so quickly, my friend," Carlo answered. "Remember how many times France has taken from Germany what she wanted. Under the Great Napoleon Prussia was almost annihilated because she dared to assert her rights; while Germany was divided up and given to members of the Little Corporal's family. No, there's long-lasting hatred there."

"Did you know that France had lost three hundred thousand men in this war?" Henri asked casually.

"To say nothing of billions of francs," Levison nodded. "And now Germany is demanding a five billion gold francs indemnity. You know, I bought up some securities just before war was declared, thinking that France would be successful. I don't suppose they're worth the paper they're written on, at present."

"I shouldn't feel so discouraged about the securities," Henri put in hopefully. "Germany has demanded, but the collection of the amount will be quite a different matter."

"A German army will remain on French territory until the collection is made," Carlo explained. "And France will have to support the German army. France will pay. Indeed, I've already heard that the Norwegian mathematician, Doctor Ole Jacob Broch . . . he's the professor of mathematics and French at the University of Christiania, and certainly one of the greatest mathematicians of to-day . . . will be called to Paris to count out these millions of francs indemnity."

On and on they talked, until the light of afternoon faded and dusk settled upon the room . . . talked until the cognac was finished and the soldiers departed to collect their scanty rations doled out by the government.

At last Isabel rose from her work and piled her bandages in preparation for the next day. From a cupboard in the cold room she brought out a cape that looked as though it had seen better days and more cheerful sights. She pulled it around her and arranged her hat, scarcely bothering to push back the wisps of hair that had fallen about her face. Listlessly she went downstairs, determined to speak once more to the postmaster.

The elderly little Frenchman behind the mail window nodded to her as she entered. This poor English lady! Every day, twice a day, she came to ask for the post. And never did he have anything for her. It was very sad, he thought. But then, there was so much that was sad in Paris now. He wished that he could have a letter for her. Her face was always so white. She must be in very great trouble. His voice was gentle when he spoke.

"I am very sorry, Madame," he said in French. "There is nothing yet."

"Are you quite certain, Monsieur?" Isabel persisted, staring wistfully at the little pile of envelopes on the counter.

"I'll look again." One by one the postmaster went over the few letters which had not been called for. Finally he shook his head.

"Do you think there is any possibility of receiving a cable from England?" Isabel asked.

"That is very hard to say, Madame." The little Frenchman didn't want to hurt the English lady. "We are fortunate enough to receive a cable once in a while. Yes, I'm certain that a cable would reach Paris. But a letter might have more chance of getting through."

"Thank you, Monsieur." Sighing, Isabel turned away. If only her father would write something, anything. But this horrible strain of waiting . . . she couldn't go on much longer.

For a few moments she stood in the sheltering doorway, dreading to step out into the cold; dreading that short walk which would take her back to the flat, to an evening with Francis. Something must happen soon, she thought desperately. Some word must come. Surely her father had made every effort on her behalf. And if he had told Robert how she felt, Robert wouldn't forbid her seeing the child. He couldn't be so cruel.

But if no message did come, then what should

she do? Should she attempt to return to England herself and see the baby? Perhaps she might be able to persuade Joyce to bring him to her if she were in England. Joyce stood in fear of Cornelia, but Joyce had been faithful; had done what she could. Joyce would do that much for her, she knew. But to return to England right now was almost impossible, because of the war.

The war! What did this war mean to her, she wondered apathetically. She hated to see others suffering, resented the bloodshed, but as for herself, it scarcely seemed to touch her. It mattered so little after all, what one wore, what one ate. Francis seemed to have a horror of it. He grumbled about the cold, swore at the coarse food, but he made no effort to leave Paris. She didn't understand that.

Several times she had suggested that he might use his diplomatic connections to get them out of the besieged city. But he had flown into a rage; had accused her of wanting to be rid of him; of thinking only of herself and her child. And then, when his anger had passed, he had grown sullen and refused to answer any of her questions.

"Ah, Madame Levison!" A hand touched her arm and she found herself facing Dr. Le Blanc, one of the physicians who came to the dressing station, a tall, pink-cheeked, black-bearded man. "You have forgotten your rations." He held out a package.

"Oh, thank you. I did forget them," Isabel tried to smile. The doctor was always so kind, even though his dark eyes daily grew more tired, more careworn from his long vigils. "I'm sorry you were troubled. . . ."

"No, no, it is nothing, Madame. I didn't know that you had gone from upstairs until just a moment ago. I am happy to be of service to you." He bowed.

There was a little pause. Then: "You must be very tired," the doctor said gently. "I'm afraid you are working too hard."

Isabel could feel the tears start to her eyes. The doctor's sympathetic words touched an answering chord. She was tired, desperately tired, but it was weariness of the mind rather than of the body; the utter absence of any desire, any wish, save one, that made her spirit faint. She was like a candle, burning itself out, wishing only to flicker long enough to carry out her purpose, to see her child.

If there were someone to whom she might talk! If only she had someone to confide in. But there was not one person in all Paris to whom she could go. She had no friends. And as for Francis . . . she couldn't tell him her troubles. He knew most of them entirely too well, anyhow. The thing he didn't know, she thought, was that she had sent her father to see Carlyle, and if he knew that he would thoroughly resent it.

For one mad moment she was tormented by a desire to burst into tears and sob out her story to this doctor. But one just didn't do that sort of thing. One didn't confide such personal affairs to a complete stranger. She took a deep

breath and pulled herself together, fighting back
the weakness.

"No, I'm not working too hard." She shook
her head. "I . . . I'm just a little tired to-night.
But there's so much to be done and so many
wounded men."

"I know," the doctor agreed. "It's a great
strain, however. I'd advise you to get a little
more rest. Don't come back so early to-morrow
morning. Sleep a little longer."

"Thank you, Doctor. Perhaps I shall. Good
night."

"Good night, Madame."

Isabel started down the street, the bundle of
rations under her arm. The cold wind stung her
face and whipped her skirts about her ankles.
The drizzling rain of the afternoon had turned
to sleet, and now the icy drops pricked her skin
like a thousand needles. She bent her head to
shield herself as best she could.

In front of one building she saw a bread line
that reached to the street corner and bent around
it. Women with children clinging to their skirts;
ragged little gamins, their red, chapped hands
dug deep in their pockets; old men huddled
against the wall, shivering, their coat collars
pulled up about their ears; all waiting for their
piece of black bread, a bite of cheese, or perhaps
a bowl of thin cabbage soup.

Isabel tried to keep from staring at these gaunt,
hungry creatures, so miserable, so pathetic, the
victims of a great machine called War . . . a machine whose mechanism they did not compre-

hend, even though they themselves had set it in motion. A Frankenstein monster they had created, which now turned to rend them. But she couldn't keep her eyes from them. She could understand what had happened to them. Much the same thing had happened to her.

She pushed on, battling against the wind and sleet that tried to sweep her off her feet. She must formulate some plan of action in case no letter or cable came from her father. If she could get to England! If there were only some way of leaving Paris. She had no money, but there were always her mother's diamond pendant and earrings, the only jewelry she had brought with her from East Lynne.

Somehow, through all their adversities, she had managed to keep those; wore them always in a little chamois bag hung about her neck and hidden in the bosom of her dress. All her other jewels had gone. There hadn't been very many, and Paris prices had soared to exorbitant heights; the pawnbrokers loaned less and less accordingly.

But the diamonds . . . they would pay her passage to England. At best, they were all she had to depend upon now.

CHAPTER XVII

"Good King Wen—ces—laus looked out . . .
   On the Feast of Ste—phen . . .
   When the snow lay round a—bout . . .
   Deep, and crisp, and e—ven . . ."

THE jubilant voices of carol singers rang out
lustily upon the crisp, evening air of Merrie Olde
England. Through the crooked, twisted streets
of London Town wandered groups of waits, bearing their tidings of Christmas cheer. The salt-
sprayed, ice-massed quay of Dover heard the messages of gladness and good will on earth and
peace to men. Red Devonshire, snug in thatched
cottages, brewed mulled wine and pulled at long-
stemmed pipes. Smoky, murky Lancashire was
bright for the nonce with holly and evergreens.
The two knights in armor who for hundreds
of years have hourly done battle before the
ancient clock in the tower of Wells Cathedral,
once more braved the icy blasts and stepped from
their secluded niches on either side of the clock
face. A pike beat against a bell, announcing to
the surrounding countryside of Somerset that ten
o'clock had come. The spot on the road out from
Glastonbury where King Alfred burned the cakes
lay buried beneath an unbroken, white blanket.
The narrow windows of the ancient Norman

Church at Wool, whose walls were new in the year of 600, sent forth warming beams of light to those who traveled the highways of Dorset.

Snow lay thick and heavy over East Lynne. It banked in great, white drifts against the sides of the manor house; piled high in niches where the huge chimneys jutted out from the flat walls. It made little mounds along the ledges of the casement windows; covered the iron balcony like creamy icing on a cake. Frosty fingers wove delicate patterns of intricate lacework over the windowpanes, obscuring the outside world.

Within the house enormous holly wreaths tied meticulously with a stiff bow of red satin ribbon gladdened each window and door. Garlands of smilax were evently looped above mantelpieces and over archways. Great branches of holly and mistletoe were carefully arranged in vases on the tables. The pungent, spicy odor of cedar, spruce, and pine made aromatic the vast old rooms and corridors.

In the wide, open hall there was a hum of activity, the stir and bustle of preparations under way. A bright fire burned in the fireplace, shooting up licking tongues of flame around the fat logs. The low-hanging, prism-decked candelabra in the center of the room blazed with lighted candles. In the corner, where the stairway turned, stood a tall Christmas tree, the tip of its needled branches pointing upward like slender fingers.

Beneath the tree a white sheet was draped to simulate snow, and to catch the falling needles. A stepladder stood near by, ready to do service when the topmost limbs should be adorned with the sparkling ropes of tinsel, the strings of pink and white popcorn, the glittering, fragile balls, the tinsel-rimmed pictures of little angels and the Christ Child, the multicolored, tiny candles in their tiny holders, and the big silver and tinsel and gold star that crowned the very tip-top branch.

Halfway up on the ladder stood the butler, Dodson, draping in well calculated loops the strand of gold tinsel he unreeled. Stooping over a box and lifting out the tissue wrapped ornaments was the present Mrs. Robert Carlyle. With careful fingers Barbara brought forth the shining little figures and globes and placed them on the stand beside her, from which stand Robert Carlyle was passing them up to Dodson.

In the center of the hall, standing so that she could survey the tree and the little group around it, was Cornelia. Her arms were folded, enwrapped in the corners of her shawl, but now and again she freed one hand to point out some desired change, the arranged spot for each particular ornament.

"No, Dodson," she was advising, "that loop should be just a little higher. Try the next branch."

"Yes, Miss Cornelia." Obediently Dodson rearranged the loop.

"Oh, what a funny little pig!" Laughing, Barbara unwrapped a gleaming toy, a very bright pink in hue.

"That goes at the back of the tree. Put it with

these other things." Cornelia withdrew her right
hand from her shawl and pointed to a pile of
ornaments on the stand. "I don't think pigs are
quite nice on a Christmas tree. But we've always
had it. It came with some of the ornaments I
once ordered. And all those chipped ones do
very well where they're not seen so plainly."

"That," she continued, as Barbara drew forth
a bright yellow ornament in the form of a canary,
"goes on the front of the tree, with these." She
pointed to another pile. "So that they face the
door."

"You know just where each piece belongs, don't
you?" said Barbara with something of admiration in her tone.

"I should," Cornelia retorted. "I've decorated enough trees. A great many of these ornaments we've had since Robert was a little boy.
I always put them away each year. It seems such
an extraordinary amount of fuss and bother for
such a short time, doesn't it? Only a week, and
then everything has to be taken down. But then,
I suppose it's necessary." She sighed. "I always had a tree for Robert."

"It does mean a great deal of extra work,"
Barbara agreed. "It's weeks before everything's
back in place."

"And no matter how much care you take, it always seems as though these pine needles are lit-
tering up the house," Cornelia went on. "I do
declare! I believe they're already beginning to
drop from the tree." She inspected the sheet

beneath the tree. "Robert, are you quite certain this trée was freshly cut?"

"Of course, Corney," Robert answered. "Carter hauled it in only two days ago."

"I think it's the warm room," Barbara suggested. "Heat always makes them drop just at first."

And so until the last bright star, after many detailed suggestions from Cornelia, after much skillful manipulation on the part of Dodson, was in place. The stepladder was removed by the butler; the maid hurried in with dustpan and brush and swept away the evidence of unpacking. The tissue paper was carefully put back into the boxes, and the boxes sent off to the storeroom. Then Cornelia's practiced eye surveyed the room. She nodded in approval.

"Yes, that's just the way it has always been decorated. No more . . . no less." She went to thè tree and brushed a particle of stray tinsel away. "I do hope," she turned to Barbara, "your father's finished making the punch. A man in a kitchen!" She shook her head in quick, jerky movements. "You know what that means!"

"Oh, listen!" Barbara exclaimed. "I think I hear the carol singers. They're coming along the road now."

> "God rest ye, merrie gentlemen . . .
> Let nothing you dismay . . .
> For Jesus Christ, our Saviour . . .
> Was born this Christmas day . . ."

The deep voices of men blended in the beautiful old carol came softly across the stretches of snow. Nearer and nearer it sounded as the singers tramped along the roadway until they reached the main entrance of East Lynne. There they stopped, stamping the snow from their feet. The mellow lights within made the diamond windowpanes sparkle, set them aglow with warmth and brightness. The holly wreaths shone green and glossy where the frost had not reached.

"Hark the herald angels sing . . .
Glory to . . . the newborn King. . . ."

Now the voices took up the strains of another carol, singing lustily. The breath, as it came from opened mouths, froze and then vanished smokily. Flat white flakes caught on the fuzz of woolen mufflers and lived there a moment, before dying into a dewy, glistening particle of water. Soon the door would open and the hospitality of East Lynne would be spread about them in return for their songs.

As Cornelia entered the dining room, Sir Richard Hare appeared coming from the regions of the pantry, a great silver wassail bowl balanced in his hands. Behind him was Dodson, watching the bowl as though he feared it might drop at any moment. Sir Richard's red face was glowing and his step was jaunty. He placed the bowl on the massive sideboard, settling it carefully, and then turned to Cornelia.

" 'Pon my soul!" he chuckled, highly pleased with himself. "No one on this tight little island can brew a Christmas punch with half the genius of your humble servant." He made a deep bow. "And on this occasion, I outdid meself in honor of m' daughter and m' new son-in-law. Ah, here they are!"

As he spoke Barbara and Carlyle came into the room, arm in arm, smiling happily.

"And now!" Sir Richard picked up a silver cup and a silver ladle of the same design as the bowl. "I shall drink to a long and happily married life to both of 'em."

"Thank you, Father. . . . Thank you, sir!" Barbara and Carlyle responded to the toast while Sir Richard filled the cup.

Cornelia's mouth compressed a trifle. She went over to the sideboard and looked down at the silver bowl. She sniffed.

"You've made enough for a regiment!" she exclaimed tartly, staring at Sir Richard.

Sir Richard laughed boisterously. "Madame, I am a regiment, meself!" He filled a second glass with punch and handed the first to Cornelia. "Will you do me the honor?"

Cornelia took a glass, smelled at the punch suspiciously, and then put it delicately to her lips. Sir Richard waited in anticipation of approval. Cornelia made a little grimace. Then she replaced the glass on the sideboard.

"Too much lemon peel," she objected acidly and unhesitatingly.

"Lemon peel?" Sir Richard repeated incred-

ulously. This was the first time in his life his
Christmas punch had ever been criticized.

"Take that out, Dodson," Cornelia turned to
the butler, motioning toward the bowl. "I'll
make the punch myself."

"Cornelia," Robert interrupted. "The carol
singers are outside. You won't have time to
make another bowl."

"I shall make another bowl, Robert." With
a little swish of her skirts Cornelia disappeared
into the pantry.

"Too bad she didn't live when they were burning witches," Sir Richard muttered under his
breath.

"What did you say, Father?" Barbara asked.

"Nothing . . . nothing. Only you'd better invite the carolers inside before the punch is cold."

"Yes, I'll get them." Robert returned to the
hall and threw open the door. A big oblong of
yellow light fell across the snowy threshold.

"Merry Christmas!" he called.

"Merry Christmas . . . Merry Christmas!"
came the answering shout.

At his invitation the half dozen choristers filed
into the hall, brushing the snow from their hats,
rubbing their chilled fingers, and pulling off their
heavy gloves, shaking hands with Carlyle. Out
into the dining room they trouped to greet Barbara and her father. With Dodson's help Sir
Richard began filling up the glasses and passing
them about.

"A Merry Christmas to all of us!" came the
general toast, and glasses were uptilted.

In the midst of the confusion and noise of clinking glasses, laughter, and conversation, Carlyle caught Barbara's arm and drew her toward the hall.

"Let's go into the drawing-room," he whispered.

Together they opened the doors and entered the festive, garlanded room. The big logs in the fireplace were glowing red, sending out cheerful warmth. Candles flickered in the sconces, throwing wavering, dancing shadows against the walls. Carlyle turned to his wife, taking her hands in his.

"This is our first Christmas together, my dear," he said softly.

"Yes," Barbara answered, just as softly. "And I shall never forget it."

"Well, then," Carlyle began to reach into his coat pocket, "close your eyes and make a wish."

Obediently Barbara closed her eyes while Robert drew forth a gleaming emerald pendant and dropped it into her hand.

"Oh!" Barbara's eyes flew open and she held up the chain with the dazzling jewel. "Oh, my darling! How exquisite! Oh, it's perfectly beautiful!" She raised her face up to Robert, standing on tiptoe, and kissed him. Then she held out the pendant and bowed her head.

Carlyle took the chain and clasped it about his wife's neck. "There! A Merry Christmas, dearest. You look lovely."

Barbara's fingers closed over the cold stone, warming it, fondling it. "You're so good to me,

my dear," she said. Little tears of ecstasy
glistened on her brown eyelashes. "And I'm so
happy."

"I want you to be happy, Barbara," Carlyle
said simply.

There was a long pause. Barbara still fingered
the pendant at her throat. From the dining room
came the sounds of jubilant voices. The room
was warm, the fire bright, and her husband stood
beside her. It seemed terrible, Barbara was
thinking, that anyone should be unhappy to-
night; that she should be so surrounded by com-
forts when other persons were in misery. At
last she raised her eyes to Carlyle and spoke.

"Robert," she began, "I've been thinking all
day to-day about Lord Mount Severn. You remember he was here several weeks ago? You
. . . you haven't seen him since, have you? You
didn't change your mind about what you told him
then?"

Carlyle frowned. "I don't know why you
should interest yourself in this matter, Barbara.
Or in Lord Mount Severn. My decision is the
same now as it was then."

"Yes, but Robert, dear, this morning I received
a letter from him. Of course, I hardly know
Lord Mount Severn."

"You received a letter from Mount Severn?"
Carlyle demanded, astonished. "He has no right
to correspond with you."

"I know, my dear," Barbara explained hastily.
"The letter was deeply apologetic, of course.

He said that he was taking a great liberty in writing to me . . .''

"Indeed he was!" The frown on Carlyle's forehead deepened and his mouth took on a firm, harsh line. "But what did he say. Was it . . . was it about *her?*" He brought out the last word as though it burned his tongue.

"Yes," Barbara nodded. "No, Robert, dear, please listen." She raised her hand in a silencing gesture as her husband was about to speak. "I want to tell you. Lord Mount Severn urged me to speak to you again. He said that I, being a woman, might understand. And I think I do. Isn't there some way . . .''

"Barbara!" Carlyle's voice cut across his wife's words. "You know how I feel about this matter. I was very plain in my explanations to Mount Severn. I am amazed that he should make any second appeal, and especially to you."

Barbara stared at the fire feeling, slightly uncomfortable, and yet trying to do what she thought right. She herself felt, as did Carlyle, that Isabel, the unmentionable name in the household of East Lynne, had forfeited all claims on the child by her conduct. But, at the same time, if what Lord Mount Severn said was true, then Isabel must be suffering, and Barbara's heart was touched.

"But Robert," she began again. "The . . . that letter implied that there might be serious consequences if . . .''

"And so there might be!" Carlyle interrupted.

"There might be very serious consequences indeed if William ever learned of his mother's past. Mount Severn knows how I feel. It was impertinent of him to appeal to you. I told him the chapter was closed, once and for all. William is never to learn any more of his mother than I can possibly help. And now, my dear, I think we may consider the matter at an end. I would rather that you didn't discuss it."

"Of course," Barbara assented hurriedly. "I'm sorry, dear. I'll never mention it again."

"Thank you." Carlyle kissed his wife and they started back toward the dining room.

While upstairs, in the nursery, Joyce was patiently trying to induce a wriggling figure to lie still and go to sleep. But it was Christmas Eve, and there were so many things to keep one's eyes open. There was a Santa Claus who might be coming down the chimney right now, a big pack of toys on his back; and the tall green tree would be glittering with beautiful, bright things and shiny stuff.

"Joyce," William put out an appealing hand. "I'd like awfully much to see the tree now. Couldn't I? If I'd go right to sleep?"

"Oh, Santa Claus wouldn't like that," Joyce reproved. "You be a good boy an' go to sleep, an' when you wake up in the mornin' you'll see all the fine presents he's left." Smiling, she bent over and kissed the child. Then her face saddened a little, and she kissed him again.

"Why do you always give me two kisses?" William asked drowsily.

"Oh, one is from me," Joyce explained softly.
"An' one is from someone who loves you best of
all. Good night, darlin'."

Softly she tiptoed from the bed, turning down
the oil lamp until the room was lost in darkness.
The poor little lad, she was thinking. With his
own mother so far away and goodness knows
what was happening to her away off there in that
foreign land. There was war there, too, so they
said, and maybe her ladyship was ill. It wouldn't
harm the master none to allow the child to see
his own mother.

The master was too hard on her ladyship, that
he was. And her always so good and kind, never
doing a wrong, never harming a soul. If it
wasn't for Miss Cornelia keeping after him all
the time, the master might forgive her ladyship.
Not that there was anything to forgive! But if
her ladyship came to England she, Joyce, would
see to it that the child was taken to his mother.
The poor lady! And it being Christmas Eve
and all.

CHAPTER XVIII

To Isabel the weary days dragged by, one following the other in ceaseless routine. She still worked on in the dressing station, waiting . . . waiting . . . waiting for the message that never came. She still thought and hoped and planned for a means whereby she might escape to England. She caught herself clutching the chamois bag about her neck, terrified lest it should disappear. And if that disappeared her last possible chance of escape went with it.

Sleet and rain and driving snow fell without stopping. For four long months the entire city of Paris had been prey to the miseries of partial starvation. Any animal whatsoever, no matter how revolting, became food for the besieged people. Corn husks, even, made grateful eating. And with the consumption of the loathsome food, the lack of decent provender and fuel, the pestilence settled over the town. Dead bodies lay in the streets, or were piled in alleyways, or flung into the sewers.

And with tormenting regularity, like the drip . . . drip . . . dripping of water, the German guns belched death and destruction, reminding the Parisians that they were there, waiting, encamped about the city.

For hundreds of years France had maintained

a policy of self-protection by creating internal
disturbances among her neighbors, thus keeping
them weak. But at last the tables were turned.
The very war which had been instigated by
France had served to bring the German states
together in a common cause and had made them
forgetful of their petty differences. So in the
palace of Versailles, only a few short miles from
Paris, the Count Bismarck read the proclamation
which marked the coronation of King William as
the first Emperor of a united Germany.

Yet Paris still starved . . . and froze . . . and
writhed in the agony of death, a hideous sacrifice
to Mars. How much longer would it go on? How
much longer could it go on? The triumphal as-
surance of success, the confident assumption of
victory which had marked the beginning of the
war, was now submerged in a kind of hopeless
apathy, a crazed desire for the barest existence.
People lived only from hour to hour, from minute
to minute, snatching whatever trifle of food or
warmth they might find.

Night after night, the tiny packet of rations
clasped under her arm, Isabel straggled back to
the one solitary room that now gave her and
Francis shelter. Even the cheap, small, shabby
flat had proved too expensive. Their money was
at an end . . . everything was at an end, and a
bitter end, too. It was only a matter of days
until there would be nothing left to them but the
streets, the parks, or perhaps . . . the river.
The Seine took to its bosom many bodies that
winter.

To-night, Isabel struggled against the storm, hugging the walls of houses closely for what little protection they afforded. Sometimes she wondered why she bothered to struggle at all, and then, her teeth set tight, her hands clenched, she knew that she would keep on struggling until she had accomplished her one purpose, until she had seen her child, until she had gone home . . . home to East Lynne again.

At last she turned into a narrow alleyway that led to a dingy, unkempt court. Here and there a single burning candle showed from behind a stained and dirty, curtainless window. She groped her way up a flight of narrow, rickety stairs, the bare treads echoing hollowly to her heavy, dragging footsteps. Up and up, until she reached the top of the last flight. She stood before a door and listened; then knocked and listened again. Finally she opened the purse that hung from her waist, took out a key and opened the portal.

Once inside the drafty room she dropped her bundle on the table and lighted a candle. The flickering, wavering illumination, kindly as it was, showed the paper peeling from the walls, the battered, broken furniture. Only the necessities of the barest living were left. Her fingers cold, almost to numbness, fumbled with her hat and finally set it on the table. She sank into a chair and tried to warm her hands over the candle's scanty flame.

With the soft glow of light spreading about her, Isabel's pale, drawn face looked almost ethereal. Blue and pinched from hunger and cold, her skin had taken on a kind of transparent beauty that had in it an unreal loveliness, like a night-blooming cereus glowing with a luminous whiteness in the dark. The purple rings about her eyes only accentuated the great, dark pupils. The golden hair, drawn back now in a simple knot, still fell away in wide waves from her temples, and little damp tendrils clung to her cheeks.

The sound of footsteps on the stairs, the door handle turning, and Levison stood on the threshold. Isabel looked up as he closed the door behind him and came into the room. There was no word of greeting between them, no smile, no sign of any sort.

He had been drinking heavily, Isabel knew. But then, that was nothing unusual nowadays. The Francis Levison who had once been a beau in London society, who had always looked as though he had just come from the hands of a most fastidious valet, now looked as though he might have stepped from the gutter. His damp clothes were wrinkled and spotted with stains. His cravat was knotted untidily and had slipped a little to one side.

Levison's face, like Isabel's, was thinner. And the thinness served mainly to reveal the lines that a hard and fast course of dissipation had left upon him. His eyes were haggard and bloodshot. There was a thick stubble of beard on his jaws. His hands shook when he touched anything. His temper was inflammable.

Vaguely Isabel wondered why it was that they were still together. All the little pretenses of nicety, of decency, had fled. At times they were like two savage animals, snarling and snapping at each other. Francis, far more than Isabel, hated and resented their poverty, this starvation, the privations of war. That was what infuriated him, made him so ready to burst into an uncontrollable tirade on the slightest provocation.

Isabel still couldn't understand why he made no effort to leave Paris. For with all his angry reproaches he had never told her of his dismissal from the diplomatic service. They had left Vienna so suddenly that she had had no opportunity of hearing the news from any of their friends. And here, in Paris, they never saw their old associates, the people who would have known the circumstances and discussed them.

"Well?" Finally Levison dragged a chair to the table, scraping it against the floor, and banged it down. "What's for to-night?" He tore away the wrapping from the package Isabel had laid on the table. "Corn husks! Black as pitch!" he grumbled. "Is that all we have?"

Isabel nodded, paying very little attention to the man. "That's as much as anyone has," she answered drearily.

"Why don't they stop it!" He rose to his feet suddenly, his voice harsh and strident. "Why don't they stop it! The madness of these people who think they can go on living in this besieged city! Nothing but starvation . . . eating dead rats, and cats . . . and ground bones! People

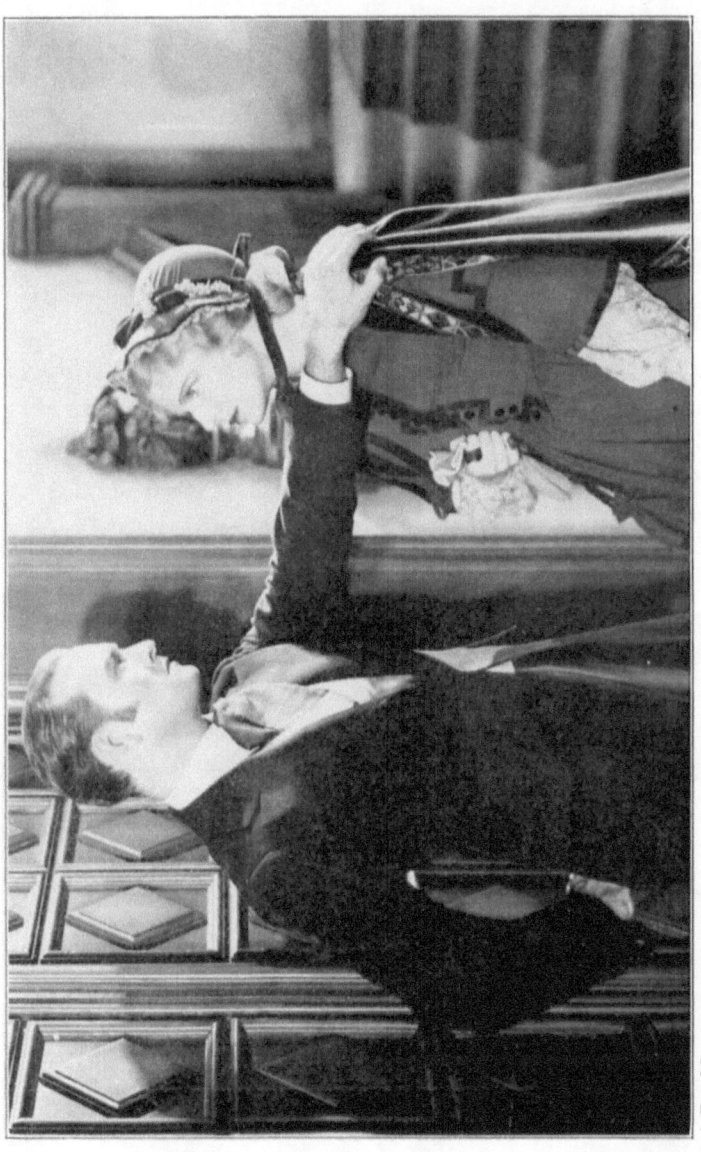

A Fox Movietone Production.   *East Lynne.*
CARLYLE WARNS ISABEL THAT IF SHE LEAVES EAST LYNNE SHE WILL REMAIN AWAY
FOREVER.

dying like flies! Disease and pestilence . . . and
dead bodies! Why don't they surrender?"

Isabel made no answer. She didn't know why
Paris didn't surrender. It was so patently evident that there was no relief, no escape in sight.
Every day there were more deaths. If this kept
up there'd be no living soul left in the city.

"Why don't they surrender?" Levison repeated, pacing the floor. "I tell you, if they
don't . . . I heard it at the café . . . it's all over
town! If Paris doesn't surrender to-day it will
be bombarded! And not lightly, either, as they've
been doing. This'll be severe. They've got to
surrender, or we'll all be caught like rats in our
holes!"

"Stop it! Stop it!" Isabel commanded harshly.
"Can't we do something? It's no good talking
about it and doing nothing. We must get out.
There must be something you can do!"

The reference to his ability, or inability, to
cope with the emergency brought Levison to a
halt. He was sick and tired of having Isabel constantly nagging at him to do something, to get
them out of Paris. If he had any power, didn't
she suppose that he'd have used it long before
this? Did she think that he wanted to stay on in
this horrible mess? Well, he could tell her that
he didn't; he could tell her that if it hadn't been
for her he wouldn't have to stay here.

There were times, many times in the past few
weeks, when he had been tempted to shout the
whole story from the housetops; to make Isabel
understand that upon her shoulders rested the

blame for his shortcomings. But in setting forth
that explanation he would be humiliated in her
eyes. He had made an attempt, and he had failed.
At first his self-pride had not counted nearly as
much as his desire to inflict no hurt upon Isabel.
Now as the weight of circumstances beat him
down, his very weakness fed that self-pride.

He had ruined himself for this woman, he
thought angrily. His career, everything that was
his life, he had sacrificed for her. What was
there before him? Disgrace . . . being cast out
by his friends, cut by his acquaintances. There
was no return to England for him, even if he
could scrape together the money to go. It was for
her sake that he had come to this. And now she
sat there, telling him to do what she, herself, had
made it impossible for him to do.

"Something I can do?" His laugh was grimly
sarcastic; his lips twisted in mockery. "I might
take my pistol and see you safely through the
enemy lines. And after that heroic gesture . . ."

"Oh, don't joke with me!" Desperately Isabel
spoke, clipping her words short. "I can't stand
it. I can't! I must get out!"

"Must you?" Levison shrugged. "With all
means of communication cut off, the railroads destroyed?"

"I know . . . I know," Isabel repeated patiently. "But I must go. All these weeks I've
been waiting for news from England . . . waiting for a letter, a cable . . . hoping that my
father . . ." She broke off, shaking her head.
"Oh, but you wouldn't understand."

Why should she try to explain this to Francis, she reflected. The mention of East Lynne or her child only infuriated him. And what was the good of starting a quarrel? It was hard enough without that. The result would be sharp, angry words, insinuations which she would resent. They were both worn out, both on the ragged edge, with nerves frayed and jangling. It was no wonder they couldn't get along.

"I wouldn't understand?" Again Francis laughed that mocking, empty laugh. "I understand better than you think. Don't you suppose I've known that you're waiting for a cable from your father? Don't you suppose I know why you sent for him?"

"I never mentioned the matter to you," Isabel reminded him. "How should you know?"

"Do you think I'm blind?" Levison snapped. "You sent for him because you wanted to go back to England."

Isabel waited in a frenzy of suspense for Levison to continue. But he stopped, watching her with a sort of inebriated intensity. He didn't really know, then, what her messages to her father had been. He was only surmising why she had sent for Lord Mount Severn. If she told him nothing more, a painful scene might be avoided. Actually, she didn't care whether he knew that she had asked her father to see Carlyle for her. She just couldn't face a scene.

"Well, m'dear," Levison steadied his hand on the back of the chair near the table. "I'm afraid you'll have to make up your mind to stay here.

There's not a chance of getting out. Sorry, but
. . . here we are.'' He sounded as though he
were deliberately trying to hurt this woman op-
posite him.

"But I don't understand why you can't . . .''
Isabel began.

"We won't discuss what I can or can't do,''
Levison returned, his tone one of dangerous calm.
"So you might just as well forget about it. No,
you'll have to live up to those pretty speeches
you made in Vienna about sticking to the end, and
so on.''

"I would have stuck to the end,'' Isabel protested, her eyes reproachful. "I've never com-
plained, have I? I never found fault. Not even
when you didn't ask me to marry you . . . after
you knew that the divorce had been granted.''
Her voice wavered, broke, as she tried to hide
her emotion.

"Oh, that doesn't matter now,'' she hurried on,
striving to regain her composure. "But you
shan't say I haven't been fair.''

"Why shouldn't you be fair?'' Levison flamed.
"You've had no cause to be anything else. I've
done everything I could for you. I never knew
what failure was until I met you. Do you think
I'd be here now if it weren't for you?''

"I don't understand,'' Isabel faltered.

"You don't understand,'' Levison mimicked
nastily. "You don't understand that if it hadn't
been for you I shouldn't have been kicked out of
the diplomatic service? Yes, that's what happened in Vienna. That's why I left. I was

forced to leave. I didn't tell you before. What
was the use? I had to have money . . . money
for you to waste. Well, I got it . . . from the
French Government. I told you that I'd been
gambling with my future. I lost!

"They told me I'd not be welcome in England
. . . after that, I had some friends in the diplomatic circles here. I thought I might be able to
make some money through them . . . money to
supply your demands. But there wasn't a chance!
The war broke out too soon. I had nowhere to
turn. No way to get money for you . . . you and
your extravagances . . . your luxuries . . . your
gay entertainments! Did you think I could pro-
vide them on my income?''

Isabel stared in bewilderment, hearing yet
scarcely comprehending the meaning of Levison's
words. She tried to reconstruct the story, to
grasp its import. Something that Francis had
done had caused his discharge from the Service.
He had needed money . . . for her! She could
hardly believe that. But he had said so. He had
got money from the French Government, he said.
Money for her extravagances . . . her luxuries!

Her head felt dull and heavy; her temples were
throbbing painfully. She knew that she was
gasping, staring wide-eyed, and she couldn't stop
it. Francis had turned dishonest, to get money
. . . money for her. He had ruined his future
. . . for her. Sacrificed his career . . . for her.
It was horrible . . . horrible! That was why he
couldn't get them out of Paris. That was why
he grew angry when she mentioned the Diplomatic

Service. So she had wrought havoc in his life.

A pitiful little moan escaped her lips. It seemed to her then that a Fate with cruel fingers had marked out her pathway. If only she had known! She would have done anything to have spared Francis this reproach. But she had never realized what was happening. Francis never told her anything concerning his affairs. Why hadn't he told her? Why hadn't he explained matters before it was too late?

"Why didn't you tell me?" she asked, putting her thoughts into words.

"I don't know," Levison answered dully, conscious now that he had said more than he had intended to say, and half ashamed that he had said it; then angry because he was ashamed.

"But I might have changed my way of living," Isabel persisted. "You never asked me to live simply."

"No? Well, why should we discuss it now?" he flared, his tone defiant. "I didn't say anything before because I was too foolish. I was afraid I might lose you. And now, since my financial condition's changed your one thought is of getting away!"

Isabel drew back as though she had been struck. Then she jumped to her feet, her eyes blazing.

"That's not true!" she cried. "It's not true! When I sent for my father I asked him to go to Robert for me. I wanted to see my baby . . . just once. That was all I wanted. Is that criminal? I can't stand being kept away from him like this!"

"Yes, so you've informed me time and time and again!" Levison shouted. "You never thought about me; you were never concerned about what happened to me. You never thought of anything but that child. Oh, I've seen it all the time; I've known it. You couldn't hide that from me."

"I never tried to hide it from you!" Isabel defended herself hotly. "I realized that it made you unhappy when I talked of the baby, so I stopped talking about him. But that didn't stop my thinking about him. I would have stopped if I could. I've tried to convince myself that he was dead! But I couldn't do that, either. And now . . . now I can't stand it any longer! I'm going to see him. . . . I can't stand it! I'm . . . Oh-h-h-h!" Her words trailed off into a piercing scream.

Above the sound of their raised voices came the heavy booming of the guns. Shrill cries broke through the wailing winter wind. The swift pad-pad of running feet reached their ears.

"My God! The bombardment!" Levison's voice was high and strained. He rushed to the little, deep-set window and looked out. "Why don't they surrender!" he shouted, panic-stricken. "Do they want to see innocent people killed? Innocent lives destroyed?"

"Innocent lives destroyed!" Without realizing it Isabel was repeating the words, whispering them to herself. Her white face was a tragic mask in the candlelight. "Innocent lives destroyed! My life . . . without seeing him . . . just once. I can! I must!"

A rumble, like thunder in a summer storm, coming closer and closer. A heavy burst of gunfire rending the air. Again the dull rumble . . . closer and closer! An explosion! The whine of shells!

"Isabel! Where are you going?" Turning, Levison caught sight of the girl as she flung open the door.

"I'm going to get through!" she shrieked. "Some way I'm going to get through!" She was gone.

Levison ran out into the hallway. An explosion rocked the building, making it tremble like a live thing. Below, on the stairway, he could see the girl clutch at the railing.

"Isabel!" he shouted. "Don't go out! Isabel, come back! Isabel!" Down the steps he went after her, taking the stairs three at a time. "Come back! Are you mad? Isabel! You can't get through!"

He was out on the street, running. Ahead of him he could just make out the slight figure. Another explosion. A wall beside him trembled violently. The stones shook loose. The flash of an exploding shell lighted up the way. A shower of bricks and stones and loose mortar fell all about him. Another explosion! And still another! Until the city resounded from *porte* to *porte*.

He had almost reached her. He was stretching out his hand to snatch at the flying cape. The pavement rose suddenly in mid-air. Came a thundering storm of flying missiles. A house collapsed, shaken from its foundations.

Only the steady tread of marching feet broke the vast stillness that at last settled over the city. The steady tread of the marching feet of the countless hosts of Germany resounding beneath the Arc de Triomphe . . . the steady tread, marching down the Champs Élysées . . . the steady tread . . . marching . . . marching. . . . The siege of Paris was over,

CHAPTER XIX

Isabel's head rested still and quiet on the white pillow of a convent cot. Her head, a mound of bandages as white as the pillow itself; her face swathed in bandages which revealed only her nose and chin. She could hear snatches of conversation; knew that the doctors and a Sister of Mercy, whose voices she had come to recognize, were there at her bedside. One of them was Dr. Le Blanc. There were two others who she thought must be Prussians because of their thick accent when they spoke in French.

Now deft fingers were loosening the long strips of cloth, unwinding them gently, until she knew that her head was freed from bandages. But the covering still remained over her eyes. At last one of the doctors began to release that covering. She knew it was one of the doctors, and not the sister. She could tell the difference in the touch. She kept her eyelids closed, but now she could feel a dim light striking her face. Slowly she opened her eyes.

She was in a narrow little room, on a narrow little cot. The shutters on the one window had been partially closed so that the bright light of day might be dimmed. The sister was gathering together the strips of bandages and piling them on a tray to be taken out. There was one doctor with closely cropped, graying hair, a tall man dangling a pince-nez in his broad, spatulate fingers. There was another, a short, rotund blond with dark blue eyes.

And there was Dr. Le Blanc, the French doctor who had spoken so kindly to her whenever he had come to the dressing station where she had worked. Dr. Le Blanc, whose voice had soothed her when she raved in her delirium, whose practiced hands had quieted her when she tossed in pain and agony. She managed a wan, thin smile, looking up at the physician.

The tall man cleared his throat, drumming his pince-nez lightly against his fingers.

"My colleagues and I," he began, addressing Isabel, "have decided that it is better that you should know the truth about your injury. The optical nerve has failed to respond to treatment."

Slowly Isabel turned to look at the speaker. "You mean," she said huskily, "that eventually I will be . . ." She hesitated and then whispered the word, "blind."

"I am afraid so." The doctor shook his head.

"Blind!" Again Isabel whispered the word. "How—how soon will that be?"

"That is difficult to say, Madame," the doctor answered. "Complete rest and quiet in a semi-darkened room is, of course, necessary. That is the only advice we can offer at present."

Rest and quiet in a semi-darkened room! And little by little that room growing darker and darker until the blackness of an eternal night settled over it. Watching, waiting, knowing that the night would come to blot out forever shapes and forms. Never again to see the soft, yellow greens of springtime, the long lovely twilight creeping over the country, the brightness of flowers. Groping . . . groping through life; reaching out fingers to touch things; never again to see them. Never again to see . . .

Isabel took a deep breath. "Thank you, Doctor," she said quietly, "but I'm afraid what you advise is impossible. If . . ." her voice faltered for an instant, and then she went on bravely. "If I am never to see again, there is something I must do. Someone . . . someone I must see, before . . . before it is too late."

"Where, Madame?" the doctor questioned.

"In England. I must go to England."

The doctor raised his eyebrows, pursed his lips, and shook his head firmly. "If you undertake such a journey," he said sharply, "I cannot be responsible for what may happen."

"You are very kind, Doctor," Isabel smiled faintly at the physician. "But I am not afraid."

"Very well, Madame." The doctor's heels clicked, he made a little bow and started toward the door, beckoning for the others to follow.

As he went out, Dr. Le Blanc stopped beside the bed, "I shall return in a few moments, Madame, to talk with you." He disappeared after the others.

So she was to walk through the world, groping. The thought returned to Isabel with renewed importance. Groping, reaching out. But always,

always, she had been groping; always reaching
out for happiness, for love; always they had
eluded her. Everybody went through life, groping for something. Yet some people seemed to
be able to find the things for which they searched;
attained them with such ease.

Now, life for her was almost finished. Only
one more thing for her to do. And after that
. . . nothing. With a short sigh that was partially one of relief she faced the enigmatical
future. Only one more thing to do. Idly her hand
strayed to the bosom of her coarse, regulation
nightgown. Her fingers clutched at her breast
in a convulsive spasm. The chamois bag! It
was gone!

Trembling, she began a search of the cot, feeling beneath her pillow. She turned toward the
bedside table, scrutinizing each object. A water
carafe, a glass, medicine, a spoon . . . that was
all. Her diamonds! The only possession she had
which would take her to England. And they were
gone. How long had she been here? What had
happened? She tried to collect her scattered
senses; tried to recall all that had taken place.

Gradually some recollections came back to her.
She remembered that evening with Francis. What
was it he had told her? Yes . . . yes! That he
had ruined himself on her account. That was it.
He, too, had been groping through life. Where
was Francis? What had happened to him? She
had said that she was going to get through . . .
get to England. The bombardment had begun.

She ran out into the street. She could hear Francis calling to her . . . calling . . . calling! And then?

She must have been hit by the falling stones. Everything was a blank after that. But her diamonds? Suppose someone had found them on her before she was brought to the convent! The streets were always full of starving people, gamins, beggars, ready to snatch the very rations from one's hand. Suppose they had found her, taken the pendant and earrings. She must know. She must!

As she tried to pull herself up to a sitting position, the door opened and Dr. Le Blanc entered.

"You mustn't try to sit up yet," he cautioned the girl, going quickly to her cot and pushing her shoulder back onto the pillow. "You're not strong enough."

"Doctor, what happened? I want to know. When I came here, did they find a little chamois bag around my neck? It was very valuable!" In her anxiety, Isabel seized the physician's arm, clutching impetuously at him.

"There, there, my dear lady," he said soothingly. "The little bag is here in the keeping of the sisters, quite safe. You mustn't worry about it. It will be returned to you when you leave here. Your diamonds are all right."

"Oh!" Isabel breathed a long sigh of relief. "Thank you." She lay back, relaxing her tense body, closing her tired eyes.

"How did I get here?" she asked finally.

"You were found in the street by some of the

sisters, Madame," the doctor told her. "Evidently you were in the bombardment and were struck by a heavy piece of timber. It had pinned you to the ground, and you were unconscious for days. Paris surrendered, and the siege is ended. The Germans have taken over the city. We were all called upon to help with the wounded. I came here one day and identified you."

"You've been very good to me, Monsieur," Isabel said gratefully. "Many times I've heard your voice, but I was so ill."

"I am glad that I could be of service," the doctor smiled. Then his face became grave. He hesitated before he spoke. Then: "And your husband, Madame," he said gently, "Monsieur Levison. I also identified him. But I am sorry . . ." Again he hesitated.

"He . . . he's dead?"

"Yes, Madame."

There was a silence. Isabel stared at the gray wall in front of her. Francis was dead! Yet she felt no emotion. She didn't cry out; she didn't even have a desire to weep. It was as though she herself were dead. And somehow, as she lay there, she knew that nothing would ever again make her want to cry out; nothing would ever arouse her. She would fulfill her one purpose, that was all.

"If I can be of any assistance," the doctor was saying. "I know that you have been deeply troubled. Please believe me, Madame, I have no wish to pry into your affairs. But in your delirium you talked a great deal."

"Did I talk about England?" Isabel nodded.

The doctor nodded.

"And about . . . about my baby?"

"Yes, Madame," the doctor answered, and his voice was very gentle. 'That is why I should like to help you, if I may."

Isabel looked at the physician standing there beside her bed. He had always been kind to her. She must have some assistance in getting out of Paris. She knew nothing of how to obtain money on her jewels. And that was what she had to do. Francis had always attended to everything. But now, Francis was dead. Rather absently she wondered how she could say that, even to herself, so unemotionally. Yet she could.

"Then you understand why I must go to England?" she asked the doctor.

The man nodded. "I understand."

"What do you think about . . . about my eyes? How long will I have my sight?"

The physician waited a moment before answering. Then: "I am afraid that what the Prussian doctors said was true, Madame. They're splendid men, and they know. If you could have absolute rest, no worry, there might be just the slightest possibility that we could prolong your sight. You are very weak; you've gone through a tremendous struggle, a strain from which it will take a year, two years, to recover. If you exert yourself, if you should pass through any great emotional crisis, you would undoubtedly go blind immediately."

"How soon may I leave the convent?"

"In a week, if you like. If you could find some place where you might rest . . ."

"No, Monsieur." Isabel shook her head. "You understand why it is that I must return to England immediately. I must see my baby before . . . before . . ."

"Yes, yes!" The doctor patted the hand that pulled at the coverlet. "I can make arrangements for your passage, if you wish it. That might facilitate matters a little. If you take every possible care of yourself . . ." He broke off, wanting to be hopeful, yet knowing that there was all too little hope.

He had heard enough of this English lady's story to make him sympathetic. She seemed so helpless, and she was utterly alone. If she wanted to go back to see her child before blindness overtook her, she should have at least that comfort. The fatigue of the journey and the emotional shock she would sustain in seeing her baby would undoubtedly destroy her sight. But that would be destroyed anyhow . . . perhaps even in a few weeks. And for the remainder of her sightless life she would have that remembrance, he thought.

"Oh, Doctor, if you only would!" Isabel exclaimed. "I'm afraid I know very little about matters of business. I hate to trouble you so much, but I have no one . . . no one to help me," she said simply. "I am in need of money. Could you . . . could you take my diamonds and . . . and . . . well, get me money enough to take me to England?"

The doctor thought for a moment. He would

have liked to offer to buy the passage himself.
It seemed terrible to think of this woman pawning
the last of her jewels. But she was very proud,
he knew. And he was afraid that his offer might
offend her. If he took charge of the diamonds,
at least he would see that she got as much as possible for them.

"I shall be very glad to attend to everything
for you, Madame," he said, bowing formally.

While Isabel prepared for the journey, dispatched a letter to Joyce, and waited impatiently
for the doctor to conclude the arrangements, all
unknown to her another sick bed was being
watched over anxiously.

In the nursery at East Lynne William lay in
his crib, his breath coming in short, harsh gasps.
Beside him sat the elderly, bearded doctor who
had brought him into the world, noting his every
slightest movement. He had diagnosed the case
as pneumonia. Now, if he were not mistaken, the
crisis had arrived. The child was naturally strong
and healthy, but the case was extremely severe.
He glanced at the other watchful, worried faces
in the room.

At the head of the crib was Cornelia, her brows
puckered in a frown. Carlyle was beside her,
white-faced, his eyes red from lack of sleep and
constant vigils. Barbara was beside him, and her
face, too, showed signs of the strain they all were
undergoing. Joyce waited behind the doctor, and
the corner of her white apron dabbed at the tears
that would try to roll down her pink cheeks.

The poor little thing, she was murmuring. The poor little master, so sick and all. And his poor mother coming all this way to see him, and her not knowing he was sick. It would kill her, that it would, if anything happened to Master William. Her that should rightfully be at his bedside this very minute. She could feel Lady Isabel's letter rustle inside of her dress where she had carefully hidden it.

But even as they watched, the child's breathing became labored. A half hour passed. Ceaseless, subdued commotion. Basins of hot water and hot towels were hurried back and forth into the room. The child emitted a wheezing, rattling cough. The doctor bent closer, waiting, listening. The breath caught, choked, loosened, and then began to come more easily. Another half hour. The doctor leaned back in his chair, and he, too, was breathing more easily. The crisis was past.

At last the physician stood up, relaxing his tall form, straightening his shoulders. Again he bent over the child. William was asleep. He nodded to the boy's father.

"He'll be all right, now," he spoke encouragingly. "If he awakens during the night," the physician turned to Joyce, "continue the treatments as I have explained them to you. Above all, avoid drafts or any sudden changes in temperature. I shall return in the morning."

"Yes, sir," Joyce bobbed.

At a gesture from the physician, Carlyle, Cornelia and Barbara filed out of the room. Cornelia disappeared along the corridor, while Carlyle and his wife saw the doctor downstairs.

"He came through the crisis splendidly," the doctor turned to Carlyle as they stood in the hall. "His condition now is excellent."

"I can't tell you what a relief this is," the father exclaimed, taking a deep breath.

"Is there anything further that we can do, Doctor?" Barbara questioned anxiously.

"Yes, there is." And the doctor smiled paternally as Dodson held his coat for him. "I would advise both of you to get a good night's rest yourselves. The child will be quite comfortable, now, and Joyce is a fine nurse."

"Thank you, sir." Carlyle went to the door with the man. "We appreciate all that you've done. I shall see you to-morrow morning, then. Good night."

As the doctor stepped into the carriage he did not notice the figure that slipped along a garden path leading to the balcony and the long windows of the drawing-room. He picked up the reins and started the horses briskly down the drive as the figure sheltered itself in the thick shadows of the bushes. Isabel waited, her heart throbbing so loudly that she felt certain the visitor must have heard it. But the carriage passed on.

The entire trip had been a sort of vague nightmare to Isabel. She moved and acted like a person in a dream. She thought of nothing save the child, thought of his round, baby face, the hands that would cling to hers. Out of Paris, across to

the coast of France, overnight on the boat, then
part way across England . . . and her eyes saw
nothing but the image of her child.

She had come as far as the boundaries of the
estate in a carriage. But before she reached the
bridge she dismissed the driver, paid him off and
sent him away. She could not run the risk of the
sound of wheels being heard by anyone in the
household. Now, in the chilling, bleak fogginess
of the night, her cape proved only a slight protection. But she didn't feel the cold; she didn't
feel anything.

She could hear the little trickling sound of running water. That was the ravine. She paused on
the bridge, thinking of the dark, craggy depths
below. Here, on this same spot, Robert had first
pointed out her home. Even now, in her mind's
eye, she could see the rising gray walls, the
stretches of green lawn, the avenue of trees, the
rose beds. She was coming home . . . home to
East Lynne.

There was the park, where she and William had
played "bears." There were the great, spreading trees under whose shade she had sat during
many a long, summer afternoon. There were the
rockeries, bare and brown now, but to her they
were alive with dancing spots of bright color.
Then she heard the carriage, and slipped off into
a sidewalk, crouching into the shadows until it
had passed. She was coming home!

From the drawing-room windows came a shaft
of light, as though someone had forgotten to pull

the draperies. That was unusual. She crept
closer, barely able to distinguish the figures in the
room. As she grew accustomed to the light, however, she could see Robert . . . Robert, standing
there by the mantelpiece, as she always remembered him. And there in his arms was Barbara
Hare.

And as she watched, without a flare of jealousy, without a sensation of hurt, she knew that
she had loved this man as she had never loved
anyone else; as she never would love anyone else.
But now she had neither love nor longing. She
felt only a strange glow of happiness, a rejoicing
in his happiness that warmed her through and
through.

"I'm so sorry, dear," Barbara was saying.
"It's been most trying for you. I feel as anxious
about William as if he were my own child."

Isabel couldn't hear the words, but she could
see their lips moving; see Robert tenderly kiss
the woman in his arms. And she was glad.

"The greatest comfort I have is your love and
devotion," Robert smiled. "You've been wonderful. But I think the doctor was right. You
need a good night's rest. It's almost twelve
o'clock now."

Together they went into the hall.

"You may lock up for the night, Dodson."

"Very good, sir."

"Good night . . . Good night, Dodson . . .
Good night, sir. . . ."

Isabel heard the clink of the bolts as they were
slipped into place; heard the key turn in the lock.

One by one she saw the candles being extinguished; the oil lamps turned down, blown out; until the whole house lay shrouded in darkness. Then, gathering her cape about her, the Lady Isabel made her way along the path that led to the rear of the dwelling, to the servants' entrance.

CHAPTER XX

The tall old clock in the hall chimed out twelve mellow strokes. As the musical tones died away, leaving the house to the stillness of the night, the door of the nursery opened gently. Joyce thrust her head out of the opening and looked up and down the corridor. The oil lamp at the end was burning low. The other doors, up and down the passageway, were closed. The woman stood still for a few minutes, then stepped quietly outside, closing the door behind her.

Down the hall she went, moving slowly toward the stairs in the back, her footfalls making no sound. About midnight, her ladyship had said in her letter, and she would be waiting at the servants' entrance. Her that had used to be the mistress of East Lynne, waiting at the servants' entrance. A crying shame! Joyce declared to herself, shaking her head.

Noiselessly Joyce went through the pantry, feeling her way along the narrow hallway that led to an outer door. She fumbled for the key in the lock, turned it, and slid back the bolt and chain that made for added protection against intruders. Cautiously she opened the door. The night was as black as ink. She couldn't see a thing. Then a soft rustle greeted her ears, and a hand was reaching to touch her.

"Is it you, milady?" Joyce whispered.

"Yes, Joyce, it's I. Oh, Joyce . . . Joyce!"
A little tremor of relief, of gladness, filled Isabel's
voice. "How is he? How is my baby?"

"Sh! milady," Joyce counseled. "Come inside,
first." She found the girl's hand and led her into
the hallway, closing the door and carefully re-
placing lock and bolt. "Now don't make a sound!
Master William has been ill, but he's better now.
Sh!" she stopped Isabel's cry with her warning.

"Joyce, you must tell me! What's the matter?
What's happened to my baby?" Isabel's voice
was frantic.

"There, now, milady. Don't you be getting
alarmed. The doctor's been an' gone an' he says
Master William's goin' to be all right. It was
pneumonia, but the crisis is over. But your ladyship mustn't disturb him, the doctor says, an'
he'll sleep all night."

"Oh, I'll not disturb him, Joyce," Isabel promised. "Just let me stay through the night with
him, and I'll go away at dawn."

"Yes, milady. If your ladyship will hold onto
my hand an' be careful of the stairs." Joyce took
Isabel's hand and went ahead, guiding her
through the pantry and up the back stairway.

They waited for a moment before stepping out
into the corridor while Joyce looked to see if anyone was about. Then, motioning for Isabel to follow, she trotted on to the nursery and opened the
door. Isabel looked at the dim light burning in
the corridor. Yes, the same lamp . . . the one
that had always burned there. And there was

Cornelia's room. And . . . there was a little catch in her throat . . . her very own rooms, where once she had lived. It was . . . it was just like coming home again.

She stumbled a little as she tried to step over the threshold into the nursery, and Joyce caught her arm.

"Take my hand, Joyce," Isabel faltered. "I . . . I don't see as well as I used to."

Joyce, a little startled, stared briefly at her mistress, and then quickly dropped her eyes. Something had happened to her ladyship! But she made no comment; merely took the girl's hand and led her over to the crib, beside which a night lamp burned.

"There he is, milady, sleepin' peaceful an' quiet. I'd light the candles for you, knowin' how you always liked the light, but I'm afraid of wakin' him, an' the doctor said . . ."

"No, no, Joyce! Don't light the candles. I can see him." Isabel dropped to her knees beside the crib and stared hungrily at the round, childish face on the pillow, flushed a little now with fever, but so familiar, so beloved.

She stretched out her hands hesitantly, wanted to feel her fingers caressing the soft, baby skin; wanting to press the warm, pulsating body close to her breast; to hold it always. Slowly she drew back. He might awaken. And the doctor had said he mustn't be disturbed. It was torture to be so close to him, her baby, her own baby, and yet not to brush back the yellow curls that lay

damp and glistening on the rounded, white forehead.

"Joyce," Isabel motioned to the woman.
"Bring me a chair, please, so that I can sit here
beside him."

"Yes, milady." Quietly Joyce pulled forward
the heavy armchair and arranged it beside the
crib. "Let me help you." Deftly she removed
Isabel's cape and hat. "Why, your clothes are
wet through. I'll get a cup of tea for you. You
must have somethin' hot."

"No, don't bother, Joyce. I'm quite all right.
I don't want anything. I'll just sit here beside
you. We mustn't wake him."

Joyce nodded. "I've been sleepin' here at
nights with him, milady." Joyce pointed to a
couch along one side of the room. "When you're
tired, you can lay down there."

"I won't be tired." Tired! Isabel thought.
Tired, after all these long months of waiting!
She could sit here forever, and never grow tired.

"Yes, milady." Joyce tried to smile, tried to
pretend that she felt that everything was just as
it had always been. But she couldn't, at least,
not to herself. Isabel's white face, thin and
pinched, haunted her. The great, deep staring
eyes that had once flashed with life and sometimes
happiness, were now twin wells of misery; dark
wells of troubled waters. She looked as though
she ought to be in bed herself, that she did, Joyce
thought.

"You go to sleep, Joyce." Isabel settled herself in the chair, her hand resting on the white counterpane of the crib. "I'll look after Master William, and if there's anything he wants, I'll wake you."

"Thank you, milady," Joyce bobbed and went to the couch. She propped up the pillows so that she should be in a sitting position, able to keep an eye on the baby, and settled herself for the nightly vigil.

How natural it seemed to be sitting here, Isabel reflected dreamily. This was her home. And her baby was asleep in the crib beside her. All the old, familiar pictures were about the walls; the same long lace curtains at the windows, the heavy drapes, just as she had seen them, just as she had remembered them. And dear, kind Joyce, never asking a question, never making a comment, as faithful as ever.

And William! The little face she had dreamed of night after night was here, where she could touch it. Those fingers that had so often curled round her own, were half shut in the moist, pink palms of the chubby hands. Her baby! He had been ill, and she had known nothing of it. But now she was with him again; always she'd be able to see his face as it lay there on the pillow.

She leaned closer to the crib . . . closer, as though she would imprint every tiny feature, every tone of coloring, on her mind. Her eyes blurred with tears but she wiped them away. She was happy . . . so happy to be here. Again she stretched out her hand. She must remember the smooth softness of the velvety skin! And he was so sound asleep. It wouldn't waken him. Her hand brushed a little closer than she had intended. Sometimes her eyes deceived her as to distances. William stirred, whimpered a little.

Quickly, but with the lightest, most delicate touch, she placed her hand over the baby fist. Joyce raised sleep-laden eyelids. William moved his head and turned restlessly. Isabel leaned closer, trying to soothe him. Slowly his eyes began to open. He mustn't be disturbed; he mustn't be awakened, Isabel remembered Joyce's words. She bent over him, peering for one lingering moment into his blue eyes. Then she began to hum softly the song that she had sung to him evening after evening . . . the song Robert had loved.

"When other lips . . . and other hearts
  Their tales of love shall tell . . ."

The child stirred again. But his eyes began to close. His head rolled to a comfortable position. Gently stroking the soft, clinging curls, Isabel crooned the melody.

"Of days that have as happy been
  And you'll remember me . . .
  And you'll remember . . . you'll remember
    me."

The child slept. Joyce dozed fitfully. Isabel sat, her hands folded in her lap, watching . . . watching. She remembered how those round,

blue eyes had been wont to stare up at her, sometimes quizzical, sometimes laughing, sometimes
hurt, but always trusting. She remembered how
those red, parted lips had crinkled in gurgles of
joy when "mummy" came to play here in this
room. She remembered how those sturdy, fat
legs would give way when they tried to run too
fast to meet her.

And what would the baby remember of her?
Nothing . . . nothing! But it was better that
way. Better that she should never come back into
his life, after all that had happened. Robert
thought so; everybody thought so; it must be so.
There would be this one night, and forever her
heart would carry the memory of all that had
been. That was enough.

Her mind wandered back once more to the first
evening when she had met Robert. Life had been
such a gay, beautiful toy, then, to be played with
and enjoyed. She had tried to play, but the toy
had broken in her hands. She thought of St.
Paul's Cathedral, and the way the sun coming
through the stained-glass windows had made the
marble floor alive with rainbow colors. She had
walked up the nave on Robert's arm, the Lady
Isabel Carlyle.

A vision rose before her of the long drive to
East Lynne. She could smell the sweet scent of
the clover wafted from the meadows, the pungent
odors of fresh earth and growing things. She
could see the chestnut blooms drifting from the
leafy trees to form a white carpet over the green-
sward. She could hear the pounding of the

horses' hoofs on the soft dirt road. And beside
her, her hand in his, was Robert. They were
coming home.

Oh, to come home again in Robert's arms! To
know love and safety and all that was good in the
world. But that was past. And yet, that strange
feeling came to her again, that somehow she
would never want to cry out, never desire anything more. It was like this evening, when she
had seen Robert hold Barbara to him and kiss
her, and had felt no resentment, no jealousy.
Only a warm, glowing sensation because he had
found happiness.

She bent a little closer to look at the baby's
face. The light was growing so dim. Perhaps it
would go out soon and she must remember . . .
remember every line, every contour. It must be
etched on her brain. But the light was so dim
. . . so very dim. The face was blurred so that
she could scarcely see it. She stretched out her
hand, then drew it back again. She mustn't wake
the child. Her fingers were groping . . . groping . . .

Very quietly Joyce arose from the couch and
pulled back the draperies. The cold, gray light
of early morning filtered through the lace curtains, giving the objects in the room a shadowy,
mysterious look. She went over to the chair
where Isabel sat, her hands still folded on her lap,
her eyes half closed, leaning back wearily. Very
gently she put her hand on her mistress' arm.

"I'm sorry, milady," she whispered, "but you
must be goin'. It's daylight."

Isabel opened her great, deep eyes. "Is it, Joyce?" she asked softly.

For a moment Joyce stood there, stunned. Now she knew it! Something was terribly wrong. She should have known it last night . . . it was her ladyship's eyes, that it was, that was so queer. She was going blind! She was blind now! Joyce choked back a cry of amazement. That must be it. Swiftly she passed her hand across the girl's line of vision. There was no blinking, no motion of the eyeballs.

"Oh, milady!" The startled exclamation broke through Joyce's guarded lips. "Oh! You . . . you're . . ." She couldn't say it!

"Yes, Joyce," Isabel nodded slowly. "It came in the night as I looked at him. It's all right. His face was the last thing I shall ever see. And that's the way I wanted to have it. It will always be there before me, in my heart and in my mind. That's why I came last night."

There was a peaceful look on Isabel's face . . . far more peaceful than ever it had been before. The strain, the tenseness had gone. It was as though she had been lifted by an unseen force to rare, great heights. She could feel that peacefulness stealing over her, the peacefulness of a vast void where nothing stirred, nothing moved.

"Please, Joyce," she murmured, holding out her hand. "Just once more . . . let me touch him . . ."

The tears rising to her eyes, Joyce took the thin, white hand and gently guided it to the baby's soft cheek. The fingers ran lightly over the child's forehead, and then dropped. Isabel rose from her chair, feeling for the back to steady herself.

"My hat . . . and cape," she requested.

Joyce, scarcely realizing what she was doing, brought the wraps and began to put them on her mistress. As she dressed her, she heard footsteps in the corridor. Putting Isabel's hand on the chair back so that she should not fall, she hurried to the door and opened it a trifle.

"Good morning, Joyce." It was Carlyle, already dressed, and still tired and sleepless. "How is he?" He pushed open the door to look in at the sleeping child. But it was the figure standing beside the chair that arrested his attention. For a moment he was speechless. Consternation and anger overspread his face. He stepped into the room.

"How dare you come here!" His voice was very low, but firm. He turned to Joyce. "Are you responsible for this?" he demanded.

"Please don't blame her," Isabel interrupted, realizing now what had happened. "I wanted to see my baby. I have seen him. I shall never annoy you again." With a steady step she started across the room.

Joyce rushed to her mistress, taking her arm and leading her past Carlyle into the corridor.

"Joyce!" Carlyle followed them, closing the door of the nursery behind him. "Come here!"

"I'll be all right," Isabel whispered. "Go."

Hesitating, Joyce finally went to her master, standing before him, her mouth set in purposeful determination.

"You are discharged!" Carlyle informed the woman in no uncertain tones.

"Beggin' your pardon, sir," Joyce retorted, "but I'm leavin'. I don't understand how anyone could be as cruel an' heartless as you are."

As Carlyle stared in astonishment at the usually mild, plump little woman, Joyce was looking over her shoulder to see that Isabel found her way down the stairs. But Isabel knew every turning, every bit of furniture so well, that she scarcely faltered on her way through the hall. Her fingers felt for the latch; she opened the door, and was gone.

"If you'll excuse me for sayin' it, sir," Joyce was hurrying on anxiously, "it's you that's responsible for what's happened to her. She never did do what you accused her o' doin'. She loved you too much. If she hadn't loved you, do you suppose she could of put up with the life she had to live in this house? Oh, no, sir, that she couldn't. I know her ladyship better than you."

"What do you mean?" Carlyle demanded.

"I mean with what she had to put up with from Miss Cornelia. That's what I mean. I have never been able to speak before, but I know of the many lies told against her, an' her never sayin' a word of complainin', because she didn't want to make you unhappy. This house was a hell for her, sir, an' I don't mind sayin' it!"

Joyce took another breath and went on. "But she never did nothin' wrong, that she didn't. An' if you live a thousand years you'll never have anyone love you like she loved you. An' you sendin' her away, now that she's alone an' blind!"

"Blind!" Carlyle caught the woman's shoulder and shook it roughly. "Blind?"

"Blind, I said, sir," Joyce repeated defiantly. "But she's not goin' alone! I'm gettin' my things an' goin' with her, that I am." She pushed the man aside and ran down the corridor to the back stairway.

Blind! Isabel blind! Carlyle frowned. Was it possible? He could scarcely believe it, and yet Joyce's words rang true. But if she were blind . . . and he had sent her away. What if he had been wrong? What if all that Joyce had said had been right? And she was going away . . . blind! No . . . no . . . impossible! He turned and fled down the stairs, across the hall and out of the door.

Away off down the road he could see Isabel running . . . running! Her feet stumbled, but she kept on. Suppose he had been wrong? At least he could have allowed her to see the child. Had he been unfair? Joyce's accusations rang in his brain. They were the same accusations Isabel had made. He must reach her . . . reach her before something happened to her. He must tell her . . . tell her . . .

Isabel was at the bridge. She paused a mo-

ment, as though trying to remember which way
to turn. She could hear the water falling over
the stones into the ravine below. She knew which
way she intended to turn. That was why she felt
so peaceful. For the first time in her life she
knew which way she intended to turn.

"Isabel! Isabel! Isabel!" She could hear
Robert calling to her. She must go on.

She fled across the bridge, around the stony
pathway. Her foot caught between two rocks.
She jerked herself free. She stumbled again.
She was falling, falling, like the water, falling
over the stones into the ravine below.

With a cry of horror Carlyle ran across the
bridge, ran down the flight of stone steps that
had been built out of the rocks of the ravine. His
feet slipped on the icy stairway. He caught himself and went on. He dropped to his knees beside
the girl and lifted her in his arms. For one long
moment he held her close. Her eyes widened;
seemed to be staring up into his face.

"Isabel!" he whispered, his voice hoarse and
trembling. "I . . . I understand. Forgive me!"

Her lips parted in a trembling, wistful smile.
Her eyelids fluttered briefly, and then were still.
Slowly her body relaxed in his arms. The smile
died on her face.

How long he knelt there, holding that cold form
in his arms, Carlyle didn't know. At last, dazed
and shaken, he lifted the body and carried it up
the rocky stairway. With slow, faltering steps he
made his way along the drive. On, and on, up to

the main entrance of East Lynne. The door was open, as he had left it. He lifted the still, silent figure a little higher in his arms and stepped over the threshold.

Isabel had come home.

THE END

There's More to Follow!

More stories of the sort you like; more, probably, by the author of this one; more than 500 titles all told by writers of world-wide reputation, in the Authors' Alphabetical List which you will find on the *reverse side* of the wrapper of this book. Look it over before you lay it aside. There are books here you are sure to want—some, possibly, that you have *always* wanted.

It is a *selected* list; every book in it has achieved a certain measure of *success*.

The Grosset & Dunlap list is not only the greatest Index of Good Fiction available, it represents in addition a generally accepted Standard of Value. It will pay you to

Look on the Other Side of the Wrapper!

In case the wrapper is lost write to the publishers for a complete catalog

www.ingramcontent.com/pod-product-compliance
Lightning Source LLC
Chambersburg PA
CBHW031002260626
47169CB00002B/665